THE GHOST
WHO WAS SAYS I DO

HAUNTING DANIELLE

The Ghost of Marlow House
The Ghost Who Loved Diamonds
The Ghost Who Wasn't
The Ghost Who Wanted Revenge
The Ghost of Halloween Past
The Ghost Who Came for Christmas
The Ghost of Valentine Past
The Ghost from the Sea
The Ghost and the Mystery Writer
The Ghost and the Muse
The Ghost Who Stayed Home
The Ghost and the Leprechaun
The Ghost Who Lied
The Ghost and the Bride
The Ghost and Little Marie
The Ghost and the Doppelganger
The Ghost of Second Chances
The Ghost Who Dream Hopped
The Ghost of Christmas Secrets
The Ghost Who Was Say I Do
The Ghost and the Baby

HAUNTING DANIELLE - BOOK 20

THE GHOST
WHO WAS SAYS I DO

USA TODAY BESTSELLING AUTHOR
BOBBI HOLMES

The Ghost Who Was Says I Do
(Haunting Danielle, Book 20)
A Novel
By Bobbi Holmes
Cover Design: Elizabeth Mackey

Copyright © 2019 Bobbi Holmes
Robeth Publishing, LLC
All Rights Reserved.
robeth.net

This novel is a work of fiction.
Any resemblance to places or actual persons,
living or dead, is entirely coincidental.

ISBN: 9781796297690

*Dedicated to science fiction author and friend Stephen Arseneault, for giving me the title for Walt's book, **Moon Runners**.*

ONE

Coffee spewed from Claudia Dane's mouth, and she began to cough. Grabbing a napkin from the kitchen table without taking her eyes off the television program, she used it to mop up the coffee from her chin and down the front of her robe. Letting out another sputtering cough, she shook her head at the morning show. "I don't freaking believe this!"

"Are you okay?" her sister, Rachel, asked as she entered the kitchen a few minutes later. "Sounded like you were choking to death in here."

Claudia and Rachel had been sharing the apartment for the past seven months, after Claudia had been forced to sell her condo or face criminal charges. While they were identical twins, it wasn't difficult to tell them apart. Claudia had been bleaching her brown hair since she was a teen and wore it straight, falling midway down her back, its fullness and length aided by hair extensions. In contrast, her twin, Rachel, kept her brown hair short and spiky. Neither woman needed corrective lenses, yet Claudia's naturally hazel eyes were violet by virtue of the opaque tint contacts she wore.

Both women had tattoos; Rachel's wrapped around her neck and down one shoulder, a dark collection, including Day of the Dead skulls and serpents. Claudia's brightly colored tattoos, floral in design, covered just her right arm and left shoulder.

Coffee cup in hand, Claudia motioned to the television while picking up the remote from the table with her free hand and turning off the set. "You won't believe who they were talking about on the morning show."

Pouring herself a cup of coffee, Rachel asked, "Who?"

"Walt Marlow."

"The author of *Moon Runners?*" Rachel added almond milk to her coffee. "It must have been good, had you all choked up." Rachel laughed at her own joke.

Not amused, Claudia glared at her sister and said, "Walter Clint Marlow."

Rachel walked to the table and sat down across from her sister. "So you saying it wasn't the author?"

"Clint Marlow," Claudia snapped.

Squinting her eyes, Rachel scrunched up her nose. "You lost me, Claud."

"Don't call me that. You know I hate it."

Rachel shrugged. "Whatever. But I have no clue what you're talking about."

"You know who Clint Marlow is."

"Like I could forget?"

"He's also the author you know as Walt Marlow. The author of *Moon Runners*. Clint is actually his middle name."

Rachel sat up straighter in the chair. "Are you saying your Clint wrote that book?"

"He is not my Clint! And there is no way in hell he wrote *Moon Runners*. He's pulling some scam; I know it."

Rachel slumped back in her chair and sipped her coffee. "I don't get it. I thought you told me he was in some car accident in Oregon. Doesn't he have amnesia or something?"

"That's what they say."

"And he's written a book? A bestseller? Aren't they supposed to make a movie from it?"

"That's what they were talking about on the morning show a minute ago," Claudia said.

Rachel arched her brows, impressed. Before taking a sip of coffee, she said, "I've been wanting to read it. Now I have to."

"I knew Clint's real name was Walter, but I had no freaking idea he was *that* Walt Marlow."

"I'm sure there's more than one Walt Marlow out there. It's probably not him." Rachel shrugged.

"They showed an interview clip with Clint—or Walt, as they called him. It's him alright, and by what he had on, he's obviously dressing for the part."

"What part?"

"As an author." Claudia closed her eyes a moment, replaying in her mind the video she had just watched on the television. Clint's hair was longer than she remembered, but the face was the same. In one brief segment it showed him standing by a vintage black Packard Coupe, wearing a fedora hat, suit, and long dress overcoat. The Clint she knew never dressed like that. If she didn't know better, she would have sworn it was a clip from *Moon Runners*, set in the 1920s. Of course, it hadn't been filmed yet, and Clint was no actor. He was no author either. Opening her eyes, Claudia looked over at her sister.

Rachel set her cup on the table. "So are you saying he didn't write the book—or did he?"

"Everyone thinks he wrote it. But there is no way he did. Not in a million freaking years."

Rachel frowned. "Why do you say that?"

"For one thing, he has dyslexia."

"That doesn't mean anything. I read once that F. Scott Fitzgerald had dyslexia."

Claudia rolled her eyes. "Please, spare me. Clint is by no stretch of the imagination an F. Scott Fitzgerald. But I know for a fact he never opened a book. He hated to read, and no way did he write one."

"Just because he hated to read doesn't mean he couldn't."

"Didn't I just say he has dyslexia?"

"How do you know?"

"He told me. When Clint and I first met, it was when we both went to work for John. We were in orientation when the broker called on him to read something to the group. It was so embarrassing. He could barely get through it. Later he admitted to me he had struggled for years with dyslexia. I told him he should've just told the broker he forgot his reading glasses, and that way he would have avoided reading in public and spared himself the humiliation."

"Still doesn't mean he didn't write *Moon Runners*. He wouldn't be the first author who had dyslexia."

"No way. For one thing, *Moon Runners* required tons of research.

They were talking about it on the morning show. How does a nonreader do that?"

"I don't know. But they do have books on tape. And maybe he hired someone to help him with the research."

"The Clint I know would never in a million years write a book. It took him forever to write a letter."

"People do change."

"Not Clint." Claudia stood up.

Rachel looked to her sister. "Where are you going?"

"I'm going to Google that jerk. I want to see what he's up to."

"I understand your curiosity. Heck, I'm curious too. But don't let this consume you. Seriously. Considering everything, you just need to forget about him."

"I'm over him, Rachel. He can't hurt me anymore." Claudia turned from the table and headed toward the doorway leading to the hallway. Just before stepping out of the kitchen, she said, "But I sure as hell can hurt him."

THIRTY MINUTES later Rachel found her sister sitting cross-legged on the living room sofa, staring down at the laptop's monitor. No longer wearing her robe, Claudia sported navy blue leggings and a baggy, multicolored pullover blouse, her blond hair clipped in a messy knot on top of her head, and a laptop computer perched on her thighs.

"Did you find out anything interesting?" Rachel asked as she sat down on a chair across from the sofa.

Claudia looked up. "The jerk's getting married next month."

"Married? I thought his girlfriend was killed in the accident."

"You mean fiancée?"

"You're confusing me."

"The accident he was in last spring, the woman killed was his fiancée," Claudia explained.

"I thought you just said he's getting married next month?"

"Obviously to another woman."

Rachel let out a sigh and leaned back in the chair. "I suppose that shouldn't surprise either one of us. From what I remember about Clint, he didn't like to be alone. Didn't take him long after Mexico to—"

"I don't want to talk about Mexico," Claudia snapped.

"Sorry. Umm…are you sure it's current information? Maybe it was written before his accident."

Claudia shook her head. "No. I found the article on an entertainment website. According to the date, it was just posted yesterday. I have to assume Clint's agent—or publisher—is promoting a media blitz because of the movie deal, considering he was also featured on today's morning show."

"So what does it say?"

"Touched briefly on his accident. I can't believe it's been almost a year. The article said he moved into the B and B he and his fiancée were staying in before the accident. It's owned by some wealthy widow."

Rachel began to laugh. "Don't tell me, Clint hit on the rich widow?"

"Yes, but not in the way you think."

"What do you mean?"

Claudia looked over at her sister. "The way you said that sounded like you meant rich *old* widow."

"Are you saying it's not some vulnerable older woman seduced by Clint's dubious charms?" Rachel asked.

"Not if the photograph of her is accurate. She looks like she's in her late twenties."

Rachel arched her brows. "Oh…young and rich. Is she attractive?"

"Yes. From what I read, she helped take care of him after the accident, and they started dating a little over a month ago. They're planning to get married on Valentine's Day. He said it was a whirlwind courtship."

Rachel scowled. "He said that?"

Claudia nodded. "No kidding. Can you imagine Clint saying *whirlwind courtship*?"

"No. But wow, that is quick. Only dating for a month?"

"Technically, a month and a half, according to the article. But remember, he has been living with her since the accident."

"Does he still have amnesia?"

Claudia closed the laptop computer and set it on the coffee table while moving her feet to the floor. "That's what he claims."

"You don't think he really has it?"

Claudia shrugged. "I don't know. I'm still trying to process this."

"So how rich is this widow?" Rachel asked.

"Pretty rich. But Clint's not exactly poor himself these days. He's done really well with his book, and now with that movie deal…"

"Does this mean you now believe he wrote it?"

Claudia shook her head. "I know he didn't. I know Clint better than anyone, and I have the scars to prove it." She stood up.

"Where are you going?"

"Stay here. I want to get something," Claudia said.

Rachel waited quietly as her sister left the living room and then returned a few minutes later.

Claudia handed Rachel a folded piece of paper and then took her place on the sofa again and propped her feet up on the coffee table, waiting for her sister to look at what she had just handed her.

Opening the folded paper, Rachel stared at it a moment and then looked up at Claudia. Licking her lips, she carefully refolded the paper and stared at her twin. "What are you going to do?"

"You mean, what are we going to do?" Claudia smirked.

Rachel shook her head. "Uh-uh…I don't want anything to do with Clint Marlow."

"You don't have to do anything—just go with me, keep me company. It would look odd if I went alone."

"Where are you going?"

"We're going to take a little trip up to Oregon."

Rachel shook her head again. "No, we aren't."

Claudia nodded. "Yes, we are. Come on, don't you want to spend the week in a little B and B on the Oregon coast? You told me you had some sick days you need to use up."

"Why would you want to do that?" Rachel leaned over and tossed the folded document on the coffee table.

"Because Clint is rich now. And he's planning to marry an even richer woman. And I know how important money is to Clint. He would do anything to keep his new golden goose—I mean fiancée—happy." Removing her feet from the coffee table, Claudia leaned over and picked up the document and unfolded it again. Settling back in the sofa, she reread it and then said, "And with this I can get Clint to share some of that wealth with me. He owes me. About time he settled up."

"But he has amnesia," Rachel reminded her.

"Exactly." Claudia grinned.

"What if he doesn't?" Rachel asked.

"You mean, if he is faking and doesn't have amnesia?"

Rachel nodded.

"Either way, this little document will get him to pay up. If he's faking, I don't think he wants his rich bride to know he's been lying to her. And if he does have amnesia…he'll pay me."

TWO

If Kelly Bartley hadn't been rubbernecking the moving van parked next door to Marlow House, she would have noticed her brother's garage door was open before pulling into his driveway on Monday morning. She didn't expect to see her sister-in-law, Lily's car. Lily should be at work. But there it was, sitting in the garage, parked next to Ian's vehicle. Kelly was about to back out of the driveway and make a hasty retreat when her brother walked out the front door and waved. It wasn't that she didn't want to see her sister-in-law, but she was hoping for a visit with her brother—just her brother—without having to share him with Lily.

Smiling weakly, Kelly parked her car in the driveway and turned off the ignition. Just as she got out of the car, Ian jogged by her, heading to the mailbox.

"I'll be right back," he called out to her.

She stood by her car and watched her brother retrieve his mail and then jog back in her direction. It was in that moment she realized he hadn't come outside because he saw her pull up. He had come outside to get his mail, and she just happened to be there.

"What are you doing today?" Ian asked when he reached her, mail in hand.

"I thought I'd stop by and bum some coffee from you." She nodded toward the garage. "Is Lily home?"

THE GHOST WHO WAS SAYS I DO

"Yeah. She's sick. I think food poisoning. We had some sketchy seafood last night."

"You feel okay?" she asked.

"I think it was the tartar sauce more than the fish. I didn't have any tartar sauce. Come on in. I just made some fresh coffee."

Kelly followed her brother into the house and was greeted by his golden retriever, Sadie. After sufficiently petting the dog, she joined her brother in the kitchen, where he was already pouring her a cup of coffee.

"We should probably whisper," Ian said in a low voice, handing Kelly a hot cup.

Kelly glanced toward the direction of the master bedroom. "Is she sleeping?"

"I hope so. She spent most of the morning on the bathroom floor, hugging the toilet and puking."

Kelly wrinkled her nose. "Lovely imagery."

"That's why I'm a writer and make the big bucks." Ian picked up the stack of mail he had set on the counter before pouring the coffee, and started shuffling through the envelopes.

Kelly rolled her eyes at his comment and then sipped her coffee.

"She finally stopped throwing up and crawled back into bed about an hour ago. Last time I checked, she was sleeping."

"Maybe it's the flu," Kelly suggested.

"Considering all the germs she's exposed to at school, that's always possible."

Kelly sneezed. She sneezed again. And then again.

"You don't sound so great yourself. Coming down with a cold?" Ian asked.

Kelly shook her head. "No. Just stupid allergies. Hey, what's with the moving van across the street?"

"Didn't I tell you? We have new neighbors."

"I didn't even know the house was for sale."

Ian shrugged. "We didn't either. The people who owned the house were never here, and a for sale sign never went up. The only reason I know it sold, Adam told us."

"Do you know if they're going to live here full-time or be absentee owners like the last ones?" Kelly asked.

"No clue. I haven't met them yet. So, what are you up to today?"

Kelly took a seat at the kitchen counter with her cup of coffee while watching her brother absently sort through his mail. "I finished my blog early, and I had some time to kill before I meet Joe for lunch over at Lucy's Diner. Thought maybe you and I could catch up. We never see each other much these days."

Ian started to rip open one of the envelopes and said, "Don't be silly. We all went out to dinner a couple of nights ago."

"I meant just you and me."

"That's because you're always with that Joe dude you live with," he teased.

"I was also wondering if you might have some time to help me with an article I've been working on."

"Sure..." Ian muttered, his attention on the letter he had just pulled from an envelope instead of what Kelly was asking.

"This should have gone to Walt." Ian shoved the letter back into the envelope.

"What?" Kelly asked.

"My agent. He needs to get a new assistant. This is the second time this has happened, mailed something here that should go to Walt."

"Oh..." Kelly sipped her coffee.

Ian let out a sigh and then looked up at his sister and smiled. "What were you asking me?"

"If you could help me with that article."

"The one you told me about the other day?" he asked.

"Yes. I'd really appreciate it."

"Sure. I have some free time Wednesday morning."

Kelly smiled. "Great!" She glanced down at the mail for Walt. "You want me to drop that across the street when I leave?"

"Would you?"

"Sure." Kelly took another drink of coffee.

"I'd appreciate that. I hate to leave Lily alone if she wakes up and needs something."

"I wouldn't mind stopping over there. I haven't seen Danielle since Lily told me about their engagement the other night."

"I'm sure it surprised some folks."

"It surprised me. They haven't even been dating two months."

"But he has lived under her roof for almost a year," Ian reminded her.

"Yeah. And I remember when he first started staying with her, she couldn't stand him."

Ian shrugged. "She really didn't know him back then."

"You don't know him now."

Ian frowned at his sister. "What do you mean? Of course I know him."

"He doesn't even know himself. What happens when his memory suddenly returns and with it the feelings he had for his now dead fiancée? You don't think that's going to be a little awkward?"

"I don't think his memory is going to come back," Ian said quietly.

"You don't know that."

"If it does, then they'll deal with it. But it really isn't our business. And I'm just happy for my friends. After all, I found the woman I love. You found Joe. I think it's nice Danielle and Walt found each other."

"I think it's creepy." Kelly cringed.

IF SOMEONE HAD ASKED Walt Marlow about plaid flannel shirts and denim jeans, he would have told them lumberjacks wear flannel shirts and farmers wear denim jeans. He was neither a farmer nor a lumberjack, and until this last Christmas, he had never owned denims or flannel. But his friend Lily seemed to think he needed to expand his wardrobe.

He sat quietly in the parlor, waiting for Danielle to get off the phone, wearing his Christmas present from Lily and Ian. It was his first flannel shirt—and first pair of denim jeans. While he wasn't thrilled with the jeans—they were stiffer than the slacks he normally wore—he had to admit the flannel shirt was rather comfortable on a damp chilly day. And January in Frederickport was normally cold and wet. While the jeans were stiffer, they did keep him warmer than what he normally wore. However, the verdict was still out on if he would add more flannel or denim to his wardrobe.

"Sorry, we don't have a room with two queens," Walt heard Danielle tell the caller on the phone. "But we do have a room with two twin beds. Yes, it's available this coming week."

Danielle grabbed a pen. "Claudia Dane? Is that D-a-n-e? Okay. And Rachel Dane? Got it."

The doorbell rang and Danielle glanced up to Walt. He flashed her a smile and then stood up to go see who was there. A few moments later he opened the front door and found Ian's sister, Kelly, standing on his front porch.

"Hi, Walt," she greeted him. "Ian wanted me to drop this by." She handed him the opened envelope.

Walt opened the door wider. "Would you like to come in?"

"Is Danielle here? I'd like to say hi."

Walt stood to the side, making room for Kelly to enter. He nodded down the hallway. "She's in the parlor. You can go on in. She's on the phone taking a reservation, but she should be off in a minute."

Walt shut the door after Kelly stepped into the house and then glanced down at the envelope. "What's this?"

"I guess it's from your agent. They sent it to Ian's address by mistake," Kelly explained. "Ian said to tell you he's sorry he opened it."

"No problem. I guess having two clients on Beach Drive in Frederickport is challenging for our agent's assistant." He sounded more amused than annoyed.

Walt walked Kelly into the parlor just as Danielle was getting off the telephone.

"Hi, Kelly, what's up?" Danielle greeted her.

Kelly nodded to Walt. "Ian wanted me to drop a letter off to Walt. Something their agent sent to his address by mistake."

"Again?" Danielle asked.

"I offered to bring it over. I wanted to stop by anyway and say congratulations. I haven't talked to you since I heard the announcement."

Danielle looked from Kelly to Walt and smiled. She looked back to Kelly and said, "Thanks."

"How's Lily feeling?" Walt asked.

"You know she's sick?" Kelly asked.

"I talked to Ian earlier this morning," Danielle explained. "He told me she had a bad case of food poisoning."

"She was sleeping when I was over there."

"I'll leave you two to visit," Walt said, holding up the opened envelope. "I'm going to go see what this is about."

Kelly gave Walt a parting goodbye before he left the room, and then she took a seat on the sofa while Danielle moved from the desk to one of the chairs facing her.

"Lily told me you're getting married on Valentine's Day."

Folding her hands on her lap, Kelly glanced around the room and gave a little sniff. She wrinkled her nose and then turned her attention back to Danielle.

"Yes. We're having a small ceremony here, something like Lily's wedding. I was going to ask the chief to do the ceremony—but I decided I would like him to walk me down the aisle instead. So we need to find someone to officiate."

"Really? Does a woman need a man to give her away? I'm surprised you don't want to just walk down the aisle by yourself."

Danielle leaned back in the chair and studied Kelly a moment before responding. With a smile she said, "I don't really think of it as the chief giving me away, exactly. And I'm curious, if you and Joe get married, aren't you going to have your father walk you down the aisle?"

"I'd have Dad walk me down the aisle. He would be hurt if I didn't ask him. But if I didn't have a father anymore, I don't think I would have anyone else do it."

Danielle arched her brows. "Not even Ian?"

Kelly shrugged. "I don't know. To be honest, I've never really given it much thought."

"You're lucky."

Kelly frowned. "Lucky how?"

"You have a father—and a brother. When I married Lucas, my father was already gone," Danielle said quietly. "And you have a brother. A really great one. If I had an older brother—and if I was close to him like you are with Ian, I'd want him to walk me down the aisle if there wasn't a father to do it."

Kelly shifted awkwardly on the sofa and shrugged. "Yeah...well, Ian and I were always close. Of course, things have changed a lot. He's married...and..."

"That's life. Things change. But now you don't just have a brother, you have a sister."

Kelly smiled weakly and nodded. She glanced around the room and sniffed again. With a frown she looked at Danielle and said, "So strange."

"What?" Danielle asked.

"That smell...it's really gone...umm...not that I'm saying your house smelled bad or anything...just that...umm..."

"Ahh..." Danielle smiled. "You mean how it used to smell like someone had been smoking a cigar?"

Kelly nodded. "Yeah. It's not like I smelled it all throughout the house. Sometimes I would catch a whiff of it in here—or maybe the living room or library. It's like it moved around. But I haven't noticed it in months. Did you do something to get rid of it?"

Danielle smiled and glanced briefly up at the ceiling, wondering if Walt was upstairs in their attic room. She looked back to Kelly and said in a soft voice, "When a house is boarded up for as long as this one was, I don't think it's uncommon to have some lingering smells—remnants of those who once lived here. This place had been closed up for almost a hundred years when I moved in. It just took a while for the rooms to air out—for life to come back to the house and to get rid of all the old ghosts."

THREE

If anyone in Lucy's Diner could see Marie Nichols, they would assume she was a perky gray-haired elderly woman, severely underdressed, with her pink and green floral sundress, white sneakers, and floppy straw hat. Considering the frigid and wet coastal weather outside, a heavy sweater, slacks, boots and a wool cap and jacket would be more appropriate apparel for any person, regardless of age. Of course, Marie wasn't a person exactly. She was a ghost.

Sitting next to her in the booth was her grandson, Adam, and across from them was Melony Carmichael. Neither could see or hear Marie, which suited the spirit. If they knew she was there, Marie didn't imagine they would be as candid in their conversation. Marie didn't consider herself an eavesdropper—*exactly*. It was more that she was looking out for Adam and trying to find ways to guide him on the right path. At this moment, she believed the right path would be an escalation of his relationship with Melony. Before Marie moved on to the next level, she was determined to see her beloved eldest grandchild married and starting a family.

"I still can't believe this is true," Adam said for the second time as he absently fiddled with the handle on his coffee cup.

"It is rather quick, considering they only started dating after Thanksgiving," Melony conceded. "Although, I'm not totally surprised. Ever since he got out of the hospital, it seemed they were always together." Melony picked up her cup of hot chocolate and took a sip, leaving a bit of whipped cream residue on her upper lip.

"Maybe you should consider a double wedding," Marie said to deaf ears.

"Nice 'stache," Adam teased.

Melony swiped her upper lip with her tongue, removing any evidence of whipped cream. "A tasty one too." She grinned.

Before Adam could respond, a female voice said, "Afternoon, Melony, Adam."

They looked up and found Kelly Bartley standing next to their booth, smiling down at them.

Adam glanced around briefly, looking to see who Kelly was with. "Hi, Kelly. You alone? You're welcome to join us."

"Yes, please do," Melony agreed.

"Thanks, but just for a minute. I'm waiting for Joe. He just called, and he's running a little late."

To Marie's annoyance, her grandson scooted over into her spot, making room for Kelly.

Grumbling, Marie instantly moved from the seat next to Adam to the empty spot next to Melony.

Kelly sat down. "Did you hear about Walt and Danielle?"

"You mean about them being engaged?" Melony asked.

Kelly nodded. "Yes."

"We were just talking about it," Adam said. "I can't believe it."

"You need to stop saying that," Marie admonished. "It's getting tedious. You need to accept Danielle and Walt are getting married, and be happy for them."

As if she had heard Marie, Melony said, "Stop, Adam. I think they make a great couple. Be happy for them."

Now sitting next to Adam, Kelly wiggled out of her jacket and set it and her purse on the seat between the two of them. "I have to agree with Adam. I find the entire thing—well, odd."

"I don't know why you guys think it's so strange." Melony leaned back in the seat and looked from Kelly to Adam.

"Maybe it's just that I always found him—well, sort of creepy. But please don't tell Danielle that," Kelly explained.

Melony frowned at Kelly. "Creepy, how?"

"He looks so much like Walt Marlow. I mean the first one. And I know Danielle has always had a thing for the original Walt Marlow."

"A thing for him?" Melony laughed. "That's a little overstated, don't you think?"

"If you only knew," Marie muttered.

"Kelly sort of has a point," Adam said.

Melony flashed Adam a frown.

"No, I'm serious. I remember once, when I first met Danielle, she didn't like me talking about how Marlow was killed—it was like she didn't want to offend his spirit. Back then, most of us thought he had committed suicide."

"And wasn't she the one so determined to prove he was murdered?" Kelly asked.

"I can't blame her. I would have been curious too, had it been me," Melony said.

Setting her elbows on the tabletop, Kelly leaned forward and said, "And you know what else is sort of strange?"

"What?" Adam asked.

"Do you remember how it sometimes smelled like someone was smoking a cigar over at Marlow House?"

"What about it?" Adam asked.

"That smell is gone. I haven't noticed it in months over there. Have you guys?" Kelly asked.

Melony wrinkled her nose, considering the question. "Now that you mention it, I don't think I have. But what does this have to do with Walt Marlow—I mean the Walt Marlow who lives there now?"

"Because I can't remember the last time I smelled it, but I'm pretty sure it was before Clint Marlow's accident."

Melony shrugged. "That house was boarded up forever. Maybe it finally aired out sufficiently."

Kelly let out a sigh. "Yeah, that's pretty much what Danielle said."

"I wonder what Lily thinks about the engagement," Adam asked.

"Lily's the one who told me about the engagement," Kelly told him. "She sounded excited and happy for Danielle. So does Ian. I was over there this morning, talked to my brother some more about it. Lily was there, but I didn't talk to her. She was in bed sick."

"Sick? Oh no, what's wrong?" Melony asked.

"Ian said food poisoning. She was throwing up all morning."

Adam arched his brows. "Is he sure it's food poisoning? Maybe she's pregnant."

Kelly frowned. "Pregnant? No way. They're going to Europe this summer."

"So?" Adam said.

"A baby? Wouldn't that be wonderful?" Marie beamed.

"I think what Kelly is saying, it's highly unlikely they're planning to go to Europe while Lily is in her final stages of pregnancy," Melony said.

"Accidents do happen," Adam suggested.

"Oh, Adam." Melony laughed. "Stop trying to start rumors."

Adam shrugged. "It could be true."

"I know for a fact Lily is on the pill," Kelly told him.

Before they could continue their speculation, Joe walked into the diner with Brian Henderson.

"Oh, Joe is here." Kelly started to stand up.

"He's welcome to join us," Melony offered.

"Thanks. But he has Brian with him," Kelly said as she picked up her purse and jacket.

"WE REALLY SHOULD NOT BE GOSSIPING about Danielle," Melony told Adam when they were alone again.

"I wasn't gossiping."

"Yes, you were," Marie said with a nod. Of course, neither one could hear her.

"Yeah, we were," Melony argued.

Adam shrugged. "Okay. Maybe we were. But at least I know I'm not the only one who finds the entire thing odd. In fact, there are lots of things that are odd about Marlow House."

"You mean because the cigar smell has finally faded?" Melony teased.

"I never told you about the croquet balls," Adam said in a low voice. "Or the television set."

Melony frowned. "What croquet balls?"

"Oh, this is going to be interesting." Marie snickered.

"Remember when I told you about the time Bill and I broke into Marlow House, right after Danielle moved in. Looking for the Missing Thorndike?"

"Yes. You were lucky she didn't throw your butts in jail."

"I used to think she had security cameras in the house, and that's how she knew it was us. But I don't think so anymore."

"One of the neighbors could have seen you," Melony suggested.

"But the strangest thing were those damn croquet balls. Well, that and the television set in her room that kept turning back on."

"I remember you said something about you and Bill tripping over an old croquet set in the attic."

Adam let out a sigh and slumped down in his seat.

"I'm curious to hear this myself," Marie murmured.

"We didn't trip over them. They flew at us."

"What do you mean they flew at you?" Melony asked.

"I used to think it was some sort of remote control device she used. But since then, I've searched online and can't find anything like it."

"What do you mean they flew at you?" Melony asked.

"The balls—actually the entire set. At first I thought Bill had thrown a croquet ball at me. But then they just started flying at us."

Melony stared at Adam, her eyes wide. "Flying at you? How?"

"Like someone was throwing them at us. Only thing, no one was there."

Melony silently studied Adam for a few more moments, and then she broke into laughter.

Frowning at Melony, Adam asked, "What's so funny?"

Trying to suppress her giggles, Melony sputtered, "You didn't tell me you and Bill had been drinking before your bungled jewel heist."

"We hadn't been drinking!" Adam snapped.

Arching her brows, Melony stopped laughing and stared at Adam, challenging him to rethink his answer.

Finally, he said, "Okay, we had a couple of beers before we went over there. But we weren't drunk!"

"Adam Nichols! It's my understanding you went over there fairly early that day. What were you doing drinking before lunch?" Marie scolded.

"What were you smoking?" Melony asked.

"We weren't smoking anything! Well, Bill was. He's always smoking. But unless the cigarette manufacturers started adding something besides nicotine to their product, regular tobacco doesn't give you hallucinations."

Melony laughed again. "Come on, Adam, get serious. A croquet set doesn't just hurl itself across the room."

"It does if Walt throws it," Marie corrected.

"That's how I remember it!" Adam snapped.

Melony started laughing again. "You crack me up sometimes. Adam, remember that time we TP'd the coach's house and you swore you saw the ghost of his late wife shaking her fist at you from their bedroom window?"

"It looked like his late wife," Adam grumbled.

"More like his girlfriend at the time." Melony giggled.

"In either case, I saw something!" Adam insisted.

Melony rolled her eyes. "Yeah…right."

"And then there was the television set," Adam said.

"What about the television set?" Melony asked.

"When we broke in, the television set in Danielle's room kept turning on. She told us earlier it had some sort of short. So we unplugged it, but it turned on again!"

Melony stopped giggling and looked at Adam through skeptical eyes. "Really? Did it plug itself in again too?"

Adam frowned for a moment. "Bill said it did. But that's just crazy."

"Uhh yeah, you think? Just how much did you two have to drink?"

"I obviously don't think the TV actually plugged itself back in," Adam conceded.

"I hope not," Melony scoffed.

"I wouldn't be so sure." Marie snickered.

"Thinking back on that day, I thought I had unplugged it, but I didn't unplug it all the way," Adam said. "At the time I accused Bill of plugging it back in, which he adamantly denied."

Melony chuckled. "I can so see Bill plugging it back in and swearing he didn't just to mess with you."

"Maybe. But I know it was unplugged when it went on again."

"You're saying the television was unplugged, and it was still on?" Melony asked.

"It was. Look it up, computer monitors are dangerous to work on because you can get electrocuted even if they're unplugged. TVs these days are similar to monitors."

"I've never had a computer monitor that turned on without being plugged in to an electrical outlet."

Adam shrugged. "I only know what I saw. And you can ask Danielle. That television had some defect. If a computer monitor can hold electricity, why can't it use it to run the monitor—or in my case, the television?"

"I still say you were drunk," Melony teased.

Their conversation was interrupted when the server brought their food. A moment later, they were again alone at the booth—with Marie.

"Maybe Marlow House is haunted," Melony teased.

Adam shrugged. "Considering what I've seen over there, I wouldn't be surprised. And it took a lot of fast talking for me to get Bill to agree to remodel the attic room for Danielle."

"You mean because of the flying croquet balls?" Melony asked with a mischievous grin.

Adam picked up his hamburger and stared at it. "I have to admit, now that I say it out loud, it all sounds pretty silly."

Melony reached across the table and patted his hand. "Adam, as wrong as you and Bill were to break into Marlow House looking for that necklace, you really aren't a thief. I imagine you were pretty jumpy back then, afraid someone was going to catch you, and it would not only hurt your reputation and your business, but really disappoint your grandmother. It's funny what your mind can make you believe."

Adam nodded. "You're probably right." He took a bite of the burger.

FOUR

"Adam thinks the entire thing is weird too," Kelly told Joe and Brian after the server brought their food to the table.

"I heard Walt asked Chris to be his best man," Joe told her.

"Where did you hear that? I thought for sure he would ask Ian. After all, if it wasn't for my brother, he would never have gotten that book published."

"The chief told me," Joe said.

"I think that's kind of mean of him to ask Chris," Kelly said.

"Why mean?" Brian asked.

"Seriously? If you were crazy about a woman—and we all know how Chris felt about Danielle—and then she ups and marries some new guy, and the guy asks you to be the best man? How would you like that?" Kelly asked.

With a snort Brian said, "Sort of like *MASH*."

"*MASH*, the TV show?" Kelly frowned.

"Sure. Remember when Hot Lips gets married, her fiancé, Donald Penobscott, asks Frank Burns to be the best man?"

Kelly shrugged. "I don't remember that. But Frank was a married man, so not the same thing."

"The chief said Chris doesn't have a problem with it," Joe said.

"I think Chris has enough going on in his life right now," Brian suggested. "I don't think he has time to worry about an old girlfriend."

"You mean his uncles?" Kelly asked.

"Yes. From what I understand, their trial is going on. Last I heard, one brother flipped on the other, trying to get a better deal," Brian said.

"What about the charges here?" Kelly asked.

"It looks like they have two murder charges to get through in California first," Joe explained. "But I haven't been following the case."

"Two?" Kelly frowned.

"According to the chief, they have more evidence Chris's uncles murdered their gardener. He's the one who owned the storage unit where they found the woman's body," Brian told her.

"Poor Chris," Kelly murmured. "He loses Danielle, and his uncles turn out to be killers."

"I'm sure all his billions are a comfort," Joe said with a snort.

"I saw Danielle this morning. Congratulated her on the engagement," Kelly told them.

"Even though you think it's weird?" Brian teased.

Kelly shrugged. "She is my sister-in-law's best friend."

"Your brother seems rather fond of Walt too," Joe noted.

Kelly looked up from her plate to Joe. "Remember when we were talking about how that distinct cigar smell is gone from Marlow House?"

"Not sure if it's gone. It's not like I go over there that much," Joe said.

"It's gone. I talked to Danielle about it. And she said the oddest thing. I can't remember her words exactly. But something about how the house had finally come back to life and had gotten rid of all the ghosts."

Brian frowned at Kelly. "Gotten rid of the ghosts?"

"Something like that. I just mentioned to Danielle that it had been ages since I noticed the smell. She didn't contradict me. She didn't say the smell was still there, but I hadn't noticed. She talked about how the house had been closed up for years, and how it had taken a long time to sufficiently air out. And then she said that stuff about getting rid of ghosts—which I found odd."

"Some people do think that place is haunted," Joe teased.

"I know. I always found it weird that Lily never mentioned any of those stories. If I lived in a house people thought was haunted—

and if odd things were happening there—I sure would talk about it," Kelly said.

Joe flashed Kelly a smile and said, "No. You would write about it on your blog."

Kelly picked up a French fry and shrugged. "True." She popped the fry in her mouth.

Brian glanced at his cellphone sitting on the table and thought about the pictures it held—one picture in particular. It was of a letter he had come across at Ian and Lily's Christmas Eve party the previous month—a letter Walt had written Ian. Brian had deleted the image on Christmas morning, after feeling guilty for taking it. It was a silly notion, comparing the writing samples of Walt to some letter written by an anonymous person months before Walt—or Clint as he was known then—had arrived in Frederickport. A person whose handwriting was eerily similar to the original Walt Marlow.

While Brian had deleted the image, he wondered if it was still in his phone's trash folder. He knew his phone kept images for a specific number of days before they were purged automatically. He just didn't know how many days that was.

Joe and Kelly continued to discuss Marlow House while Brian stared at his phone. Paying little attention to the conversation, Brian picked up his cellphone and tapped the icon for photos and then opened the trash folder. He glanced up to Joe and Kelly, neither of whom was paying any attention to him, but chattering away. Glancing back down to the phone, he skimmed through the trash file—and then he saw it. The image had not yet vanished from his phone. On impulse, Brian moved the file out of the trash folder.

"WHAT ARE YOU LOOKING AT?" Joe asked Brian as they headed back to the station after lunch. Joe drove the police car while Brian sat in the passenger seat, his cellphone in his hand. "You keep staring at that."

Brian shrugged and turned his phone off, slipping it in his pocket. "Nothing."

"I have to agree with Kelly. I tend to think Danielle has let her sentimental feelings for a man who died almost a hundred years ago cloud her judgment."

"Do you believe in reincarnation?" Brian asked.

"Reincarnation? You aren't suggesting Clint is the reincarnation of his distant cousin?" Joe scoffed.

Brian let out a sigh. "The older I get, the more I realize there's a lot I don't understand. Millions of people believe in reincarnation."

Joe glanced briefly at Brian. "Do you?"

Brian shrugged and leaned back in the seat, staring out the windshield. "Not really. But I think you and Kelly are overlooking the fact Marlow seems to have genuine feelings for Danielle. I keep thinking of how he looked at Chris's uncles when he walked in the interrogation room with her. If looks could kill."

"I must have missed that. I was too busy watching Chris's uncles topple out of their chairs. Realizing Chris and Danielle were still alive and that they were probably going to be charged for attempted murder, obviously shook them up."

"That is one explanation," Brian muttered.

"I suppose living under the same roof for almost a year, it's not surprising they became close." Joe sighed.

Brian smiled and looked over to Joe. "So you're finally ready to accept Marlow and Danielle as a couple?"

"Don't say it like that. It's not that I was ever jealous. I'm with Kelly." With both his hands firmly on the steering wheel, Joe drove the car down the street.

"Of course not," Brian said under his breath.

"But Danielle is a friend, and just because we didn't work out, it doesn't mean I don't worry about her. After all, I still feel pretty crappy about how I handled everything back when her cousin was killed."

"You made up for it when you came forward as a witness after Stoddard was murdered. Hell, I don't feel guilty for any of it, and I was more than ready to lock Danielle up back then. We were just doing our jobs, and she looked guilty as hell."

"Maybe she did. But she has been through a lot."

"Yeah right. She has more money than she knows what to do with—is marrying a guy who seems crazy about her. Boatman is doing fine. Anyway, she's a bit like a cat, always lands on her feet."

"I thought you liked Danielle?" Joe asked.

Brian shrugged. "Who said I didn't like cats?"

WHEN THEY RETURNED to the police station, Brian left Joe in the front office as he made his way to the evidence room. He needed to delete the picture of Marlow's letter from his phone—completely—before someone accidentally saw it. How would he ever explain why he had a picture of a private letter from Walt to Ian on his cellphone?

On Christmas morning he had decided not to compare Walt Marlow's handwriting with the anonymous letter stored in the evidence room. After all, the entire thing was silly. He was letting his imagination run away with him. Looking back, he realized he could have permanently deleted the image from the phone on Christmas instead of just sending it to his trash file to be automatically purged days later. But he hadn't done that. He hadn't managed to bring himself to totally trash the evidence, and now he was going to compare the letters and then move on. After all, he was confident that once he actually compared the two letters, the handwriting samples would be nothing alike. Just because Clint Marlow—or Walt, as he now wanted to be called—signed his name just like his cousin of the same name didn't mean they would have the same handwriting. Of course, the letter he was about to retrieve was not written by the original Walt Marlow. *That would be impossible.* But he remembered the handwriting was eerily similar to a letter Marlow had written almost a hundred years before.

Brian unlocked the evidence storage room, walked in, and turned on the overhead light. It had been a year ago last June that someone had broken into Danielle's safe. Nothing had been stolen, but it looked as if her guests, the Sterlings, had been the perpetrators. Some anonymous person had foiled their burglary attempt and had locked Mrs. Sterling in the bathroom and bound Mr. Sterling in Danielle's bedroom, leaving him incapacitated with the Missing Thorndike safe and sound.

Whoever it was had left a letter on the bathroom door explaining what had happened. The identity of the author was never discovered, and briefly Brian wondered if Chris had foiled the robbery and, because he didn't want attention, had left an anonymous note instead of coming forward. Yet Chris had been in Portland that day, so it hadn't been him.

The Sterlings had claimed it had all been a publicity hoax perpetrated by Danielle. Without being able to identify the author of the letter, it was impossible to prove what had really happened

THE GHOST WHO WAS SAYS I DO

that day. To confuse matters, the handwriting matched an old letter they had found in Danielle's room—one written by the original Walt Marlow, who had been dead for almost a hundred years. Some speculated that whoever had left the note intentionally copied Walt's handwriting.

It took Brian just a few minutes to locate the case file. He removed it from the cabinet and shuffled through its papers. Until this moment, he had forgotten there had actually been two notes written that day. One was left on the bathroom door, the other with the Missing Thorndike. He found a copy of each note and removed them from the folder.

Setting them on a desk, he turned on the lamp, brightly illuminating the pages. He then removed his cellphone from his pocket and opened the image file of the picture he had taken on Christmas Eve.

Enlarging the image, Brian leaned close to the paper letters, comparing the cursive handwriting. Swallowing nervously, he felt his chest tighten. The handwriting on the letters left at Marlow House that day matched the letter Walt had written Ian.

Brian closed his eyes for a moment and then remembered what Lily had said when the FBI had questioned her about the notes and their likeness to the old letter.

Special Agent Wilson had asked Lily, "Are you trying to tell me Walt Marlow wrote those notes this morning?"

Lily had said, "No. What I'm saying, either someone with remarkably similar handwriting to Walt Marlow wrote those notes, or else Walt Marlow's ghost wrote them. You decide."

Licking his suddenly parched lips, Brian stared at the image on his cellphone. Without a second thought, he deleted it, this time permanently, before returning the notes to the evidence file.

FIVE

The last of Marlow House's guests for the past week had checked out early that morning, shortly after breakfast. Joanne Johnson, the housekeeper, had already come and gone, finishing up the last of the breakfast dishes and changing out the bedsheets and bath towels. She planned to return the next day to give the house a thorough vacuuming and cleaning and then would return early on Thursday to do it over again before the next round of guests arrived.

In the kitchen Danielle's black cat, Max, slept peacefully, curled up on one of the dining room chairs by the table. His white-tipped ears twitched occasionally while he slept.

Nearby, Danielle stood at the counter, dicing up celery and onions. On the stove a whole chicken simmered in an iron pot filled with water. Over her jeans and navy blue sweater, she wore the quilted apron Lily had given her for Christmas. Her dark brown hair, which fell just above her shoulders, was pushed back behind her ears as she focused on her task.

Outside the kitchen window, gray clouds stretched across the sky, concealing any hints of blue or white. While it felt damp beyond the walls of Marlow House, no rain fell. Inside, the heater turned the air toasty, removing January's chill.

"What are you making? It smells wonderful in here!" Marie asked when she appeared the next moment.

Having grown accustomed to the sudden appearance of spirits like Marie Nichols and Eva Thorndike—and Walt before them—Danielle barely flinched and went on with her dicing. She flashed Marie a smile and said, "I'm making Lily some homemade soup. Ian told me she stayed home sick today."

"I heard she has food poisoning," Marie said.

"I see word gets around quick in the spirit world." Danielle scooped up the diced vegetables and dropped them in a small stainless steel bowl.

"I didn't hear it from another spirit. But Adam thinks she might be pregnant," Marie told her as she took a seat at the table.

Danielle stopped what she was doing and turned to face Marie. "Pregnant? Where did he come up with that?"

"I had lunch with Adam and Melony this afternoon," Marie explained. "Although technically, I didn't have any lunch—and they didn't know I was there."

Danielle set the knife on the cutting board and folded her arms across her chest. "And Adam said she was pregnant?"

"Kelly stopped by their table and visited a while," Marie went on.

"Kelly said she was pregnant?" Danielle frowned.

Marie shook her head. "No. Kelly just mentioned Lily was home sick this morning with food poisoning, and Adam said maybe she was pregnant. It would be lovely if she was having a baby. Eva tells me babies can see spirits. I saw Eva when I was in the cradle. Perhaps Lily's baby will see me? Do you think she could be pregnant?"

Grabbing some more vegetables to dice, Danielle said, "I know Lily's on the birth control pill, and she and Ian are planning to go to Europe this summer when school is out. I don't really see her getting pregnant right now. If she was in the early stages of pregnancy, she would be like seven months pregnant for their Europe trip." Danielle shook her head at the thought. "I think Adam just likes to stir up rumors."

Marie chuckled. "You know, dear, that is pretty much what Melony said. However, even in this day and age, not all babies are planned."

"Who's having a baby?" Walt asked when he entered the kitchen the next moment.

"That's how rumors are started." Danielle chuckled.

"I was just telling Danielle that Adam suggested that perhaps Lily doesn't have food poisoning, but is pregnant," Marie told him.

"And Adam would know that, how?" Walt asked before placing a quick kiss on Danielle's cheek.

Danielle grinned up at Walt and said, "Just diner gossip."

"You two were also the topic of conversation," Marie told them.

"I bet we were." Danielle snickered. "I imagine everyone in Frederickport is talking about our engagement, the way news travels in this town."

"Not long after Kelly arrived, Joe and Brian showed up. They didn't sit with Melony and Adam. But I popped over to their table briefly, and they were talking about your engagement announcement. And I must give sweet Melony credit. She scolded Adam for gossiping about you two with Kelly."

Now dicing several carrots, Danielle's grin widened. "I like Mel. I'm glad she's my cousin, even if it's only by marriage." Danielle's great-aunt Brianna, who had left Danielle Marlow House and her estate, had been married to the brother of Danielle's grandfather. Brianna had been born out of wedlock, and since moving to Frederickport, Danielle had discovered her great-aunt's father had been Melony's great-grandfather, which made them sort of distant cousins.

Scooping up all the diced carrots, Danielle put them into the stainless steel bowl with the other vegetables. She grabbed a second bowl, a pair of tongs, and headed to the stove to remove the chicken from the pot and add the vegetables to the broth. Yet, just when she was a few feet from the stove, the broth began to boil over. Danielle let out a little yelp, scrambling to find someplace to set the bowls so she could grab a pair of hot pads and remove the pot from the burner. But before she could set the bowls down, the pot of boiling broth lifted like magic up from the stove, hovering in midair.

Unfortunately, the heavy iron pot, filled with boiling broth, seemed too cumbersome for whatever invisible hand held it, and it began to rock back and forth, splashing hot liquid in every direction, barely missing Danielle, who jumped backwards away from the stove just in time.

Startled from his nap by the outburst, Max lifted his head and looked to the commotion. Seeing the pot floating chaotically in midair, the cat leapt off the chair and raced out of the house into the side yard, sending the metal pet door swinging back and forth.

"Walt!" Danielle shouted. "Be careful! You almost burned me!"

The pot quickly righted itself and settled back on the stove.

"I'm so sorry," Marie said in a contrite voice.

Danielle looked to Marie and frowned. "Why are you sorry?" She glanced from Marie to Walt, who flashed her a half smile.

"I thought I could do it. But I'm obviously not very good at it and need more practice," Marie said weakly.

"Are you saying you lifted the pot off the stove?" Danielle asked.

Marie nodded guiltily. "I was just trying to help. I'm so sorry. I could have burned you if Walt hadn't taken charge."

Danielle looked to Walt. "You knew she moved it?"

"Well, I knew I didn't move it, and the last time I checked, cooking pans don't float around the kitchen on their own."

"Thank you, Walt," Marie said sheepishly. "I shouldn't have tried that with a pan filled with boiling water. I don't know what I was thinking."

Danielle set the stainless steel bowls she had been holding on the counter and turned to Marie. "How long have you been able to move things?"

Marie shrugged. "Not long. You didn't notice I moved the chair?"

"Chair?" Danielle frowned.

"When I came in the kitchen earlier, all the chairs were tucked under the table—aside from the one Max was using. You were busy and I didn't want to ask you to pull one out for me. And I really do hate sitting around cut in half by the tabletop. Recently I've managed to push pieces of paper around a bit. So when I came in here and tried to move the chair on my own—and it worked—well, I suppose I got a little cocky and figured I could lift the pan up off the burner. Obviously, I was wrong."

Danielle looked to Walt. "I'm sorry I snapped at you. I...I thought you had moved it."

"He did, dear—but only after I about dumped it on you." Marie sighed.

"No problem," Walt said, dropping a kiss on Danielle's nose. "I'm just glad you didn't get burned."

"Aside from the mishap, it's rather exciting you've managed to harness your energy," Danielle said as she wiped up what broth had spilled. "All you need is more practice."

"Have you been able to do anything else?" Walt asked.

"I seem to be rather good at this." The next moment the kitchen light turned off and then on again. "I'm also rather adept at turning off computers."

"Not sure why you would want to do that," Danielle said.

"You would be surprised," Marie muttered under her breath.

"Can I help you?" Walt asked as he watched Danielle return to her cooking.

"Thanks, but I got it. And the pot boiling over in the first place was my fault anyway. I should have been paying more attention."

"You're just trying to make me feel better," Marie chided.

Danielle flashed her a smile and finished wiping up the spilled broth.

"You say we were the subject of conversation today?" Walt asked Marie as he took a seat at the table.

"Interestingly, Brian and Joe seem to accept the engagement without much speculation. As does Melony, who said you are a cute couple."

"Oh, we are." Danielle giggled.

"Kelly and Adam seem to have an issue with it."

"I don't know what Kelly's problem is," Danielle said as she removed the chicken from the pot and set it in a bowl.

"Kelly finds the resemblance between the Walts—unsettling," Marie explained. "I think for my grandson he just feels protective. I do believe he looks at you like a sister."

Danielle grinned. "I have to say, Adam and my relationship has taken an unexpected turn." Standing by the counter, Danielle dumped the diced vegetables into the broth, and then began removing the chicken from the bones, returning the meat back to the pan with the simmering vegetables and broth.

"I will confess, there was a time I thought you might make a nice couple," Marie said.

Danielle resisted the urge to cringe.

SIX

"What's this?" Lily asked after she answered her front door late Monday afternoon. Danielle stood on the Bartleys' front porch, clutching a covered pot wrapped in a kitchen towel.

"Homemade soup. I didn't expect to find you out of bed. Where's Ian?" Danielle asked as she walked into the house.

"He took Sadie for a walk." Lily followed Danielle to the kitchen. "That smells so good!"

"How are you feeling?" Danielle set the steaming pot on the stove. "You look good."

"I feel better now." Lily hungrily eyed the pot of soup.

"Can I fix you a bowl? It's still pretty hot."

"I can get it," Lily offered.

Danielle shooed Lily to the breakfast bar. "No. Sit down, and I'll get it for you."

"If you insist." Lily grinned and took a seat at the breakfast bar.

She watched as Danielle removed a bowl from an overhead cabinet and began filling it with chicken soup. Danielle opened a drawer and grabbed a soup spoon, and then she picked up a napkin from a basket on the counter.

"Your guests all gone?" Lily asked.

"Yes. They left this morning." Danielle carried the bowl, spoon and napkin to Lily.

"When's your next reservation? I remember it was always pretty slow this time of year."

Danielle set the steaming bowl in front of Lily with the napkin and spoon. "We have one reservation that was made about six months ago. They're arriving Friday. They're coming to see family who live in town."

"Anyone I know?" Lily picked up the napkin and put it on her lap.

"I don't think so. We didn't expect to have any other guests until the following week. But just this morning, two more reservations came in. Both are arriving Friday and staying until next Thursday. So I'll have three full rooms."

"Really?" Lily picked up her spoon and dipped it in the soup. "Who are they?"

Danielle took a seat at the counter next to Lily. "Two sisters made one reservation. I'm giving them the room with the twin beds. And then a couple."

Lily blew on her spoonful of soup a moment before tasting it.

"You know what's interesting?"

"What? Oh…mmmmm…this is delicious!"

"Thanks."

"So what's interesting?" Lily asked, taking another bite of soup.

"Both the guests who made reservations today are from Huntington Beach, California."

Lily looked up. "Maybe they're friends?" she suggested.

"I don't think so. Neither one of them said anything about meeting someone here."

"Huntington Beach, isn't that where Clint was from?" Lily asked.

Danielle shook her head. "No. But he didn't live far from there."

"Is that where Chris had his boat?"

"It wasn't his boat," Danielle reminded her.

"I know. But was that where it was?"

Danielle shook her head. "No. That was Dana Point."

"This is really good soup. You going to have some?"

"No, thanks. I'm not hungry."

"I'm famished."

"Ian said you threw up all morning. You feeling okay now?"

"I've been feeling crappy every morning for the last week. But this morning was the worst."

Danielle frowned. "I thought Ian said you had food poisoning."

Lily set her spoon down and looked at Danielle. "Yeah, well. That's what he thinks. I didn't tell him how I've been feeling all week."

"Have you been running a temperature?" Danielle asked.

Lily shook her head, picked up her spoon, and then looked at Danielle. "I have a favor to ask you."

"What?"

"Would you pick me up a pregnancy test? And please don't tell anyone. Not even Walt."

Danielle's eyes widened. "You think you're pregnant?"

"Shhh...not so loud!" Lily looked around nervously. "Ian might walk in at any moment."

"You think you're pregnant?" Danielle repeated, this time in a whisper.

"All I know is that I've woken up every morning this past week feeling nauseated."

"Was this the first time you threw up?"

"Yes."

"Does Ian know about the nausea?"

"No."

"Why not?"

Lily shrugged. "He was always sleeping when I'd get up feeling sick. By the time he woke up, I'd had some cereal and my stomach seemed to settle, so I didn't say anything to him. I didn't think I could really be pregnant, since I hadn't missed a period and we always use protection."

"When are you supposed to start?"

"Yesterday."

"I thought you were on the pill?"

"I was."

"Was?"

Lily set her spoon on the table again and let out a deep sigh. "I went off the pill. Ian and I decided to go off of all birth control after we get back from Europe, and try to start a family."

"You never mentioned it."

Lily shrugged. "I just figured, considering everything, it would probably take me forever to get pregnant. I didn't want anyone—even you—asking if I was pregnant yet."

"If you didn't want to start trying until after you got back from Europe, why did you go off the pill already?"

"I wanted to get the pill out of my system. All that crap in it can't be good for a baby. Mom told me that's what she did when she decided to get pregnant. So I went off the pill, we started using condoms, and I figured when we got back from our trip, we'd stop using the condoms."

"Does Ian have any idea?" Danielle asked.

Lily shook her head. "No. He's so looking forward to this trip. And it could just be a bug. But I need to take a test. And I don't want to worry him. I just thought, if you could pick up a pregnancy test for me, take it to your house, and I can come over and take it there."

"If you aren't pregnant, are you going to tell Ian you thought you might be?"

"Of course. But when I tell him, I'll start with 'I'm not pregnant but,' and we can both get a good laugh out of it. But why freak him out now?"

"And if you are pregnant?" Danielle asked in a whisper.

"Of course I'll tell him. And well…then I guess we'll postpone the trip until right after the baby is born, and you and Walt can babysit. Newborns don't scare you, do they?"

Danielle laughed. "Oh right. You'd leave your newborn with us and take off to Europe."

Lily grinned. "Well sure, sounds like a great plan, doesn't it?"

KELLY CURSED herself for not picking up the allergy medicine when she had left the diner earlier that day. She had chili cooking in the slow cooker, and at lunch she had invited Brian to join them for dinner. Joe and Brian would be at their house within the next thirty minutes. She considered calling Joe and asking him to pick the medicine up on the way home, but the last time she had asked him to pick up allergy medicine for her, he had gotten the wrong brand.

Reluctantly, Kelly turned the slow cooker to low and grabbed her car keys, heading to the pharmacy. The moment she pulled in the parking lot, she noticed Danielle's Ford Flex parked by the entrance.

When she entered the pharmacy, she didn't see Danielle.

Wanting to say hello, she started looking down all the aisles. It was in the last one she spied her. Heading her way, Danielle's back to her, she was about to say hello when Danielle reached for a pink and blue box on the shelf. To Kelly's surprise, it was a pregnancy test.

Without saying a word, Kelly turned quickly and headed back down the aisle and ducked around the corner. Once out of sight, her curiosity got the best of her, and she peeked down the aisle again. Danielle was carrying the box with the pregnancy kit to the checker by the pharmacy counter, but by the way she was holding it, concealing it with her purse, she obviously did not want anyone to see her purchase.

Kelly stood there a moment, wondering if she was wrong. *Perhaps it's a box that just looks like a pregnancy test*, she asked herself. Turning down another aisle, Kelly headed for the display with the allergy medicine. After picking up what she needed, she headed for the front checker. Still thinking of what she might have just seen, Kelly failed to pay attention to where she was going and found herself about to walk into the very woman she had been thinking about.

Rattled, Kelly forced a bright greeting. "Hello, Danielle. I thought that was your car in the parking lot."

"Umm...hi, Kelly," Danielle stammered, clutching the paper sack concealing her recent purchase.

"I'm just picking up some allergy meds." Kelly held up the bottle. She couldn't help herself from looking at the bag in Danielle's hand, yet she didn't expect her to tell her what was inside.

"Well, nice to see you. Twice in one day! Hope your allergies get better. Gotta go!" With that, Danielle dashed out of the pharmacy with her package.

Still holding her bottle of allergy medicine, Kelly looked from the door Danielle had just run out of to the free cashier. She stood there a moment, then turned around and headed to the back of the pharmacy again, where she had first seen Danielle.

Curious, she walked down the aisle, to the spot she had seen Danielle take the box. Kelly stared at the items on the shelf. *It was a pregnancy test.*

KELLY TOLD herself it was the journalist in her that made it difficult to simply pretend she hadn't seen Danielle buy what she had seen her buy. She was dying to call her brother, but he would probably tell Lily, and the last thing Kelly wanted to do was embarrass Danielle by letting her know she had seen her purchase. Plus, she didn't want Danielle to think she was gossiping about her. Kelly considered Danielle a friend, and if she was pregnant, it explained a lot.

"Kelly—hello?" Joe repeated for the second time. Kelly looked up from her bowl of chili and looked sheepishly to Joe and then to their dinner guest, Brian. The three sat around the dining room table eating.

"Oh, I'm sorry. Did you say something?" Kelly asked.

"Brian was just saying how good your chili is," Joe said.

Kelly blushed. "Oh, I'm sorry—I mean, thank you, Brian. I'm glad you're enjoying it." Kelly looked back down at her bowl and absently stirred her chili with a spoon.

"Is everything okay, Kelly?" Joe asked. "You've been so quiet all evening."

Unable to hold it in any longer, Kelly set her spoon on the table and looked from Joe to Brian. "Okay, but you both have to promise not to say anything. Do you promise?"

"Say anything about what?" Joe asked.

"I think I know why Danielle is getting married so quick—so suddenly."

"She's pregnant?" Brian joked.

Kelly looked to Brian, her eyes wide. "You knew?"

Brian frowned. "I knew what?"

"Danielle. She's pregnant. Well, not for sure, but she thinks she might be."

"What are you talking about?" Joe asked.

"Well, it explains everything. Why Danielle announced her engagement after dating Walt for just a few weeks," Kelly said.

Brian laughed. "Kelly, I was joking. Danielle isn't pregnant."

"She obviously doesn't know for sure, or she wouldn't have bought that pregnancy test."

"What pregnancy test?" Joe asked.

"When I was at the pharmacy earlier, I ran into Danielle, and she was buying a pregnancy test."

"What did she say?" Brian asked.

Kelly wrinkled her nose at Brian. "She didn't know I saw her.

And when we ran into each other at the pharmacy later, she held onto that sack with the test in it like her life depended on it. But I knew what was in the bag. I saw her take it off the shelf. I saw her take it to the checkout counter."

"Pregnant?" Joe frowned. "I can't believe that."

"It explains a lot. Like a sudden marriage to a man she barely knows," Kelly said.

"If she is pregnant, I don't think you can say he barely knows her," Brian reminded her.

"Brian!" Kelly gasped.

Brian rolled his eyes. "Oh, come on, think about it. If this was a shotgun wedding, why put it off a month? And if she is buying a test, she obviously didn't know she was pregnant when they announced the engagement."

"Or she was afraid she might be," Joe suggested.

SEVEN

Walt's gray wool slacks, freshly polished leather dress shoes, and long-sleeved blue shirt suited his personality better than the denim and flannel he had worn the previous day. An added bonus, the shirt's color complimented his eyes. He sat with Danielle in the living room, discussing their upcoming wedding.

Her dress was less formal, flannel pajama bottoms and a fleece shirt. It was almost noon, and without guests in the house, she hadn't gotten around to dressing for the day.

They sat side by side on the sofa, Danielle's stockinged feet propped on the coffee table, Walt's right arm draped around her shoulders, as his right hand absently fiddled with the tendrils falling around one of her ears.

"I guess you and Lily won't be shopping for wedding dresses this afternoon like you planned?" Walt asked as Danielle thumbed through the bridal magazine.

"Not today. Hopefully she'll feel better tomorrow." Danielle glanced up at Walt. "You don't think we're silly going through with this wedding?"

Walt grinned at Danielle. "What, you don't want to marry me anymore?"

She gave him a gentle nudge with her elbow. "We are practically an old married couple."

Walt chuckled and kissed the top of her head. "I don't think we're silly. I'd like to have our friends here when we go public with our marriage."

Danielle closed the magazine and leaned back against Walt. "I'm glad you feel that way. I will confess, I'm really looking forward to this."

"Me too." Walt kissed the top of her head again.

Motion from the front window caught their attention. It was Ian and Lily. The pair waved and then continued to the front door.

"We were going to the kitchen door, but Lily saw you sitting in here," Ian said when he walked into the room with his wife. They hadn't bothered ringing the bell, but had come in through the unlocked front door and made their way straight to the living room.

"I don't know about having neighbors who spy on you and know where you are in the house," Danielle teased.

Holding a stack of envelopes in one hand, Lily tossed them to Danielle before taking a seat. "We also poked through your mail. I didn't see anything interesting, so I decided to give it all to you. And you really should lock your front door."

Danielle laughed. "Thanks, Lily. But why bother? Half the neighborhood has the key." She set her unopened mail on the coffee table without looking at it.

"How are you feeling today?" Walt asked Lily.

"Better." Lily looked at Danielle and said, "I think I'll feel up to looking at wedding dresses with you tomorrow. We could leave early in the morning, drive into Portland."

"If you feel up to it, that would be great."

Lily stood up. "If you'll excuse me, I need to use the little girl's room." She exchanged a quick glance with Danielle and headed out of the living room to the downstairs bathroom. Earlier she had phoned Danielle, who told her where she would find the pregnancy test.

Once in the bathroom, Lily opened the cabinet door under the sink. In the back of the cabinet she spied a paper sack with the local pharmacy's logo. Removing it from the cabinet, she sat on the toilet seat, using it like a chair, and removed the package from the bag. A moment later, after opening the box, she began reading the directions for the pregnancy test.

"HAVE you decided who will officiate the wedding?" Ian asked. "Did you ask the chief about walking you down the aisle yet?"

"No and yes," Danielle told him. "I mean, Walt and I have talked about who we would like to officiate—but we haven't finalized it yet. And I did ask the chief, and he said he would walk me down the aisle. Evan is going to be a ring bearer."

"And we'd like Sadie to be the flower girl," Walt told him.

"Sadie?" Ian laughed. "You aren't serious?"

"Yes," Walt insisted. "I've already had a long talk with her."

"Of course you have," Ian said under his breath, trying not to laugh some more.

"We thought Sadie could walk down the stairs ahead of us, carrying a basket of flowers," Danielle told him.

"What about Max? Is he going to be in the wedding too?" Ian asked.

"Don't be silly, Ian. Max is a cat," Danielle said with a snort.

Ian frowned. "Why would that be silly? Walt communicates with Max in the same way he does with Sadie. If he can get Sadie to come down the stairs with a basket of flowers, why not Max?"

Walt chuckled. "Like Danielle said, Max is a cat. Just because I can communicate with him doesn't mean he'll cooperate with us during the ceremony. One never knows what the little demon might decide to do."

"Hey, he is not a demon," Danielle argued.

"They got Bella to distract Chris's uncles," Ian reminded them.

"True," Walt said. "But that was different."

"Different how?" Ian asked.

"Trust me, from a cat's perspective, playing hero is far more enticing than carrying someone's flowers," Walt said.

Lily returned from the bathroom. She stood in the doorway a moment and looked as if she had something to say.

"What's wrong?" Ian asked.

"Nothing," Lily said quickly and looked to the sofa. "I just wanted to talk to Dani—in private—umm…it's about the wedding."

"Wedding secrets?" Walt asked.

Lily shrugged. "Well, there have to be some secrets."

Danielle got up from the sofa and walked with Lily to the parlor. As soon as they walked in the room, Danielle closed the door. "Well, are you pregnant?"

"I don't know. I didn't take the test."

"You didn't take it? Why not?"

"Because it said it's best if you take the test first thing in the morning. I don't want to risk a false reading and do this all over again. So I'll have to wait until morning."

"Are you going to take it home with you?"

Lily glanced to the closed door. "Not right now. I'll have to get it later, when Ian isn't with me, and sneak it in the house and hide it in the bathroom. Or I could run over here in the morning and take it."

"Or you could just tell Ian what's going on and stop trying to sneak around," Danielle suggested.

Lily shook her head. "No. I don't want to worry him. This morning he was talking about all the places he wanted to take me—what he wanted to show me. He was so excited."

"It's possible you aren't pregnant."

"Or that I am. I'm two days late now. I'm never late."

"Stress can do that too," Danielle suggested.

WHEN DANIELLE and Lily returned to the living room, Walt said, "We have our officiant."

"You asked him?" Danielle asked.

"What officiant?" Lily asked.

"I'm going to be marrying Danielle and Walt," Ian said proudly.

Lily grinned. "Really?"

"They said I didn't have to get my online license to do it, since they're already legally married, but I'm going to anyway," Ian explained.

Danielle took her place on the sofa next to Walt and picked up the mail Lily had brought in, while Lily took a seat next to Ian. Danielle absently thumbed through the envelopes while listening to Lily question Ian about what he was going to wear for the wedding.

"Clint got a letter," Danielle said aloud, interrupting the wedding discussion. All eyes turned to her. She looked to Lily and said, "You really didn't look through our mail when you got it out of the mailbox."

Lily frowned. "Of course not. But how did you know?"

"Because I think if you had, you'd wonder who from Huntington Beach had written Clint a letter." Danielle handed the envelope to Walt.

Now holding the envelope, Walt looked at it. "Technically speaking, it's not really for me." He handed it back to Danielle.

"I don't want it." She handed it back to Walt. "You need to read it. It is for Clint."

"Well, someone read it!" Lily burst. "I am dying to know what it says. Sheesh, the next time I rummage through your mail, I am actually going to look at it!"

Rolling his eyes, Walt shook his head and then ripped open the envelope and pulled out the letter. He began to silently read. Danielle, Ian and Lily sat quietly.

"Who's it from?" Lily asked as Walt continued to read.

Danielle shrugged. "There isn't a return address, but the postmark is Huntington beach. And the address is handwritten."

"This isn't good," Walt murmured.

"What's wrong?" Danielle started to look over Walt's shoulder. Now finished reading the letter, Walt handed it to her to read.

"What is it?" Lily asked.

"Don't tell me, someone Clint owes money to?" Ian asked.

"I wish it was that easy," Walt said.

Danielle finished reading the letter and set it on her lap. She looked at Walt and said, "I think we should show this to the chief."

"I'm not sure what the chief could do. There's nothing to work on."

About to explode from curiosity, Lily hopped up from the chair and snatched the letter from Danielle's lap. She began to read it.

"They're threatening you!" Lily gasped. She quickly finished the letter and then handed it to Ian to read. "Whoever it is didn't sign it, which is not surprising."

"What should we do?" Danielle asked.

"I don't know what we can do," Walt said. "We're just going to have to wait until they contact me again, like they said they're going to do."

After finishing the letter, Ian said, "It might have been better if we all didn't touch this. There might be some fingerprints on it. If you at least knew who sent this—"

"Maybe we do!" Lily said.

"We do?" Danielle asked.

"Didn't you tell me you have two guests arriving Friday, from

Huntington Beach? That's where the postmark is from. Maybe it's one of them...or both," Lily suggested.

Danielle frowned and picked up the envelope and looked at it again. "Whoever wrote the letter did say they would be in contact with Clint."

"I wonder what Clint did," Ian asked.

"I don't know, but whoever wrote that letter is definitely pissed," Danielle said.

Ian stood up and walked toward Danielle and Walt. He tossed the letter on the coffee table. "I think Danielle is right. You should take this letter to the chief. He needs to know someone has threatened you."

Walt let out a sigh and closed his eyes. He leaned back in the sofa and muttered, "What did Clint do?"

"But it's also possible this is all a hoax," Ian suggested.

Walt opened his eyes and looked at Ian. "Hoax? Why do you say that?"

"With all the recent publicity for *Moon Runners*, you have a lot of eyes on you. Anyone following your story knows you are doing well financially, knows you are about to marry a wealthy woman, and that you have amnesia. I always thought that was a foolish thing to put out there—which I mentioned to you and to our agent, but the publisher disagreed and felt that added to your persona. While it does, it also opens you up to scam artists."

"Why do you say that?" Danielle asked.

"I understand what Ian is saying," Walt said. "And I agreed with him when he initially brought it up. But at the time, it was too late to go back. For one thing, anyone searching for information on me would come across the news articles after Clint's accident."

"I still don't understand why that would open you up to scam artists," Danielle said.

"Because, while Clint Marlow with amnesia may not remember his past deeds—or misdeeds—it does not mean he won't still be held legally accountable for them. Which would mean someone could fabricate a crime, believing the now wealthy Clint will pay to keep it hidden," Ian explained.

"And there is always the other option," Walt said quietly. "That Clint did something I will regret."

EIGHT

After Ian and Lily headed back across the street, Danielle went upstairs and got dressed. While she wasn't opposed to lounging around the house in her pajama bottoms and T-shirt, she figured she'd better get dressed if she wanted to go with Walt down to the police station to show the chief the letter from the anonymous author.

Wearing skinny jeans, a red pullover sweater and knee-high boots, Danielle made her way to the first floor. Midway down the staircase, she heard the doorbell ring. Picking up her step, she hurried down the stairs.

When she threw open the front door several moments later, she found an unsmiling middle-aged woman standing on her front porch, her arms folded angrily across her chest.

"Hello, may I help you?" Danielle tentatively asked, eyeing the thin woman up and down. The stranger stood several inches taller than Danielle. She wore a blue overcoat over a long dress, with a matching blue cloche hat over her gray hair. She peered at Danielle with humorless gray eyes.

"Are you Danielle Boatman?" the woman demanded.

"Umm...yes."

"I'm your new neighbor."

Danielle's face broke into a smile, and she opened the door a little wider. "Welcome to the neighborhood!" Danielle began, but her smile quickly faded as the woman refused to soften.

"Is that black cat yours?" the woman snapped.

"Umm, you mean Max? Black cat with white-tipped ears?"

"I don't know if it has white ears or not. I didn't get that close a look at it. It was in my backyard, and when I yelled at it, he ran over in your yard. I need to know if it's yours or not."

Danielle frowned. "Is there a problem?"

"Yes, there's a problem! I do not appreciate your cat making my flower garden into a litter box. I'm going to be living here full-time, and I will not put up with negligent pet owners. Do you understand me?" the woman practically yelled.

"Is there a problem here?" Walt asked, stepping to Danielle's side. He placed his arm protectively around Danielle's waist.

Scowling, the new neighbor looked Walt up and down. "And who are you?"

"I'm Walt Marlow, and you?" Walt asked.

"I've heard about you. You're just a boarder here. My business is with the owner of the property, and you can just butt out."

"The owner happens to be my fiancée," Walt snapped back. "And her business is my business. Now what is going on here?"

"Oh, lovely," the woman said with a snort. "Another reason you shouldn't be allowed to run an illegal commercial enterprise in a residential neighborhood. It's just an excuse for all sorts of immoral conduct to take place under your roof! Just keep your cat out of my yard. If I see it again, you won't."

Danielle glared at the woman. "Have you just threatened to hurt Max?"

"I'm simply expressing my intention to use whatever legal means are open to me to exterminate any pests on my property."

"I think you need to leave," Walt told her.

"Just keep the cat in your house." The woman turned and started to walk away but then paused and turned back to the door and said, "And you might want to consider a new business. One that is not run in a residential neighborhood."

When the woman turned her back to Walt and Danielle again, her cloche hat flew off her head, which was an amazing feat, considering there was no wind blowing. An imaginary gust of wind sent the hat spiraling toward the street, just out of the woman's reach as she raced to catch it, chasing the stubbornly elusive hat all the way down to the sidewalk, down the street, and back to her house.

Together Walt and Danielle stood on the front porch and watched their new neighbor chase her hat.

"Walt, did you do that?" Danielle asked with a sigh.

"Well, I couldn't hit her, could I? She is a woman; it would not have been very gentlemanly of me."

DANIELLE STOOD IN THE KITCHEN, waiting for Walt to finish his little chat with Max so they could head to the police station. The cat sat on the floor by Walt's feet, looking up to him.

"She threw a rock at you?" Walt asked.

Max silently stared at Walt, his black tail swishing back and forth.

"Just stay out of her yard. Remember how it used to be for you before you moved here? How some of those people treated you?"

Max continued to stare; his golden eyes blinked.

"Next time it might be something worse than a rock. Just stay out of her yard. And whatever you do, never eat anything over there or take food from her. Okay?"

Max meowed.

"WALT, if you weren't here, I keep wondering what I would do about poor Max. He would be miserable locked in the house. He's too old to become a house cat. But I would be constantly worrying about him if I left him outside, never knowing what that woman might do. I can't believe she's our new neighbor!" Danielle said as she drove the two of them to the police station.

"I just hope Max listens to me." Walt sighed.

"You mean he might not?"

Walt glanced over to Danielle and smiled. "Max is a cat, Danielle. I have made him fully aware of the danger. I've explained he is not allowed to go in her yard. But he is a cat."

"You keep saying that. He is a cat. What does that mean?"

Walt chuckled. "Even before my—gift—in communicating with animals, I recognized the difference between cats and dogs. Dogs want to please. Cats, not so much. If Max decides it's amusing to torment your new neighbor, a threat of reprisal on her part is not going to stop him. Why do you think they say cats have nine lives? You seemed to understand all this earlier when Ian asked why we wouldn't put Max in the wedding."

"I just figured this was different, sort of like how Eva and Marie got Bella to help distract Chris's uncles."

"One thing I have learned," Walt said, "is that cats can be extremely protective of their humans. They are often underestimated in that regard, and many people think only a dog will come to a human's defense."

Danielle glanced briefly to Walt and smiled and then turned her attention back down the road again. "I agree. I remember watching a video of a cat online who went after a dog who was attacking his owner. It was epic. That snappy little dog was going after the kid, and the cat just flew at the dog and chased him away."

"Max would do that for you," Walt said.

"Then why won't he just agree to stay out of the neighbor's yard?" Danielle asked.

"Because they are two different things. One is about your safety and the other is about his. Think about little Bella, who is so much smaller and physically weaker than Hunny. A pit bull Hunny's size could kill Bella in a second if she wanted to. But does that stop Bella from tormenting the poor dog?"

"True. I guess cats like to live on the edge."

Walt reached over and patted Danielle's knee. "There is one thing to consider. Max is older and more street smart than Bella. If you'll notice, he tends not to tease Hunny to the same degree as when Hunny was a pup. Max is more aware of the risk. So hopefully, he'll be more reluctant to test your neighbor."

WHEN DANIELLE PULLED into the parking lot at the police station, she spied Joe and Brian stepping out of the front entrance. As she and Walt walked toward the station a few moments later, they came face-to-face with the police officers, who were on their way to a patrol car.

"Hi, Joe, Brian," Danielle greeted them.

"Morning," Walt added.

Brian nodded. "Good morning."

Joe looked Danielle up and down briefly and then looked over to Walt for a second and back to Danielle. "How are you feeling?"

Danielle smiled at Joe. "Things are great."

"You getting enough rest?"

Danielle frowned. "Why, do I look tired or something?"

"No, you look fine," he said hastily. "It's just, umm, I know how busy you are, running the bed and breakfast, planning a wedding. Are you still waiting until Valentine's Day to get married?"

Danielle glanced to Walt, who returned with a shrug, and back to Joe. "What do you mean waiting?"

"Umm…I don't know. Thought you might just decide to elope. Weddings take a lot of time and money. The most important thing is the marriage, not the wedding."

"WHAT IN THE hell was that about?" Brian asked Joe as the two got into the patrol car a few minutes later.

"I just think if Danielle is pregnant, it's irresponsible of her to wait; she should get married now." Joe shut the car door.

Putting on his seatbelt, Brian looked over to Joe with a frown. "Irresponsible? What are you talking about?"

"Two consenting adults don't need to be married," Joe began.

Brian chuckled. "Like you and Kelly?"

Joe glared at Brian and shoved his key into the ignition. "I'm just saying that once you drag a child into a relationship, then your priorities change. The child should be your first concern."

"What are you saying, Joe?"

"They should get married now if Danielle is pregnant, and not wait for when it's convenient for them. Kids have it hard enough without the stigma that your parents had to get married."

"Joe, you were born after the 1950s, why are you living there?"

"I THINK JOE NEEDS A VACATION," Danielle told the chief when she and Walt walked into his office. She closed the door behind them.

MacDonald stood briefly and shook Walt's hand before settling back behind his desk. "Why do you say that?"

"I guess he doesn't think we should spend our money on a wedding," Danielle said as she took a seat.

"What?"

Danielle shook her head. "Never mind. He just says the strangest things sometimes."

Walt handed the chief the envelope with the letter. They had already called him on the phone, informing him of the situation.

"So this is it?" MacDonald asked, removing the folded page from the envelope. He began to read. Danielle and Walt sat silently, waiting for him to finish.

When he was done reading he stood up. "Do you mind if I keep this? I'll make you a copy."

"Are you going to check for fingerprints?" Danielle asked.

"The chances of getting good prints are slim, considering everyone who has already read it," the chief began.

Danielle sighed. "It happened so fast. The letter got passed around before we realized that probably was not the smart thing to do."

"I'm not saying we won't be able to get something. But right now, I can't justify spending resources on having this tested. But, if they do contact you again and something more comes of this, I would feel better having this," the chief explained.

"So we just do nothing?" Danielle asked.

"To me, this sounds like an extortion letter. I expect the person to contact you again with demands, not blow up your car. At least, not yet."

"Gee, that makes me feel better," Danielle grumbled.

NINE

It wasn't Ian's snoring that woke her. It was the fact she had to use the bathroom. Still groggy, Lily tossed the blankets to one side and sat up in the bed, careful not to wake her husband. She assumed it was the middle of the night considering the only light came from the glow of a nightlight in the hallway. It made its way through the open doorway. Plus, the curtains were dark, with no sign of sunlight slipping in. But once she placed her feet on the floor and glanced at the alarm clock on the nightstand, she groaned. It was 7:23 a.m.

Lily sat there a moment and closed her eyes. She really needed to pee, but she also wanted to take that pregnancy test, and she wanted it as accurate as possible. According to the instructions, that meant she needed to take the test during her first trip to the bathroom of the day—which would be now.

Why didn't I bring that pregnancy test home with me? She had intended to return to Marlow House when Ian was not around and bring the test home and hide it for the morning. But then the day got away from her, and she had decided she could just as easily take the test at Marlow House. That sounded fine last night, yet not so much right now.

With a reluctant sigh, Lily stood up and put on her slippers. She opened the drawer to her nightstand and pulled out a flashlight, making an unintended rattling sound.

"Where are you going?" Ian mumbled. He rolled over in the bed to face her.

"Just to the bathroom," she whispered. "Go back to sleep."

"You taking a flashlight with you?"

"Umm...I'm taking Sadie out."

Sadie, who had been snoozing in the nearby dog bed, lifted her head and looked at Lily, her ears perking up.

"She has to go out?" Ian asked, still not totally awake. "Want me to take her?"

"No. I got this. Go back to sleep," Lily whispered.

With a groan, Ian rolled over and resumed his snoring.

Lily headed for the door and almost tripped over Sadie, who was no longer in her dog bed, but at Lily's side, her tail wagging. Looking down at the golden retriever, Lily let out a sigh and muttered, "I guess you're coming with me."

PEARL HUCKABEE HAD BEEN awake for an hour already and was on her second cup of Earl Grey tea. The first cup had been hot, the second lukewarm. Placing a scone on the saucer with her teacup, she headed to the living room.

She hadn't turned on any house lights yet; instead she enjoyed the fireplace's glow. From her perspective, turning on unnecessary lighting was a waste of energy. With logs burning in the fireplace, she had both heat and sufficient light. It wasn't that she couldn't afford to pay the utility bill, but she believed it was wasteful to spend money unnecessarily.

Walking to the living room window, saucer with teacup and scone in hand, she opened the curtains. It was still dark outside, but the sun would be coming up shortly. Just about to turn from the window, she spied a light zigzagging across the street in her direction. Quickly ducking behind the curtain, she stayed there just a moment before peeking back out the window and peering into the darkness. Whoever was out there would not be able to see her anyway, she reminded herself.

Setting the saucer on a side table, she snatched up the scone and hurried to the front door and eased it open, ever so gently, so as not to be heard or seen. Taking a nibble of the scone, she looked outside. Whoever was out there stood by her neighbor's side gate.

Pearl patted her sweater's front pocket, making sure her cellphone was close at hand. She then grabbed the baseball bat she kept in her umbrella stand by the front door. Pearl didn't play baseball, but she did like to protect herself. She slipped outside and closed the door behind her and made her way down the front steps of her porch.

Slinking through the near darkness, hiding behind shrubbery, Pearl clutched the baseball bat in one hand and held the scone in the other. She listened.

"Sadie, calm down. You're going to have to stay in the backyard while I go in," Pearl heard a female voice say. She then heard a whining sound.

Whoever is breaking in has a dog with her! Pearl thought, moving closer to the wrought-iron fence separating her yard from Marlow House. Hiding behind a shrub, she looked through the fence. The rising sun broke some of the darkness, allowing her to see into her neighbor's side yard. She spied a dark figure fiddling with the side door while the shadow of a large dog stood nearby. The next moment the door opened and the intruder slipped inside the house, leaving the dog outside.

"Oh no!" Pearl gasped, pulling her cellphone from her pocket and shoving her half-eaten scone where her phone had been. Frantically she dialed 911.

On the other side of the wrought-iron fence, as Pearl was busy reporting the break-in, Sadie's ears perked up and she looked south and cocked her head. Forgetting her mistress's command to stay, Sadie took off running, easily slipping through the side gate, which had not been relatched after they went into the yard.

Sadie's sudden appearance startled Pearl, who dropped not just the cellphone, but the baseball bat, which rolled away. It was impossible to retrieve the bat, not without getting around the dog.

Crouching before Pearl, with its butt in the air, the golden retriever made a series of hopping motions, as if preparing to jump on the woman.

"Stay away!" Pearl shouted. On the cellphone, now on the ground nearby, the dispatcher could hear Pearl's cries and relayed the urgency to the patrol car already heading to the house.

Looking frantically from the dog to the nearby toolshed, Pearl remembered the scone. Taking it out of her pocket, she broke off a piece and tossed it to the dog, who quickly gobbled it up. Smiling in satisfaction, Pearl continued to tear off pieces, tossing them to the dog while leading it to the toolshed. Once there, Pearl hurriedly opened the door and tossed the remainder of the scone inside. Taking the bait, Sadie rushed into the shed, only to have the door slammed shut on her.

The next moment the police car pulled up in front of the house.

JUST AS BRIAN HENDERSON stepped out of the police car, a woman rushed in his direction. He had never seen her before, but he assumed she was the one who had made the 911 call, as she had identified herself as the neighbor to the south of Marlow House. Considering what the dispatcher had told him she had overheard, he assumed the threatening perpetrator had been scared off by the approaching police car.

"Thank heavens you're here, officer!" the woman said as she rushed to him.

"Are you Pearl Huckabee?" Brian asked.

"Yes!" She nodded.

"Which way did he go?" Brian looked around cautiously, his hand prepared to draw his gun.

"She's still in the house. At least, it sounded like a woman."

Brian frowned. "The dispatcher heard you shouting for someone to stay away from you."

The woman nodded frantically. "Yes. It was the dog."

"Dog?"

Pearl pointed up into her yard, to the small outbuilding. "I locked him in the toolshed."

"Dog? The intruder brought her dog with her?"

"It's a very big dog. I don't know what might have happened to me if I hadn't been able to lure him to the toolshed."

Brian glanced to Marlow House. "So tell me what you saw."

Pearl pointed across the street. "I looked out my window and saw a light coming across the street."

"A light?"

"I assume it was a flashlight."

"Then what happened?" Brian asked.

"She broke into the side gate."

"How do you know it was a woman?" Brian asked.

"I heard her. She told her dog she would have to stay outside or she might wake up the people who live there. Oh, I remember, she called the dog Sadie!"

"Umm...Sadie?" Brian tried not to laugh.

"The woman broke into the side door of the house! I could see through the fence. She's in there now! You need to hurry. She could be upstairs murdering them as we speak!"

"And this dog, you say it's in your shed?" Brian asked.

"Yes!"

"Why don't we let the dog out," Brian suggested.

"Are you going to shoot it?" Pearl sounded delighted at the idea.

"Umm...no. I don't think Ian would appreciate it."

"Ian?" Pearl frowned.

"He lives across the street. That's where Sadie lives," Brian explained.

"So the woman stole the dog and now broke into Marlow House!" Pearl gasped.

"Umm...I don't really think so."

They heard someone whistle. It was coming from Marlow House's side yard. Pearl rushed to the fence and looked through it. "She's outside, looking for the dog!"

Brian walked to the fence and looked through it. Since the sun had barely risen, he couldn't quite yet make out her features, but by her size and shape, he had no doubt about the identity of Pearl's intruder.

"Let the dog out," Brian told Pearl.

"Aren't you going to go arrest that woman?"

"Not today." When Pearl made no move to release the dog, Brian walked to the toolshed and opened the door. Sadie rushed out and started to bark at Brian and Pearl.

"You let him go!" Pearl shouted.

LILY'S first thought after stepping out of Marlow House's back door was that Sadie had ignored her command to stay and then had entered through the doggy door after Lily had gone to the bathroom. She groaned, thinking Sadie was probably already in the attic, waking up Danielle and Walt, but then she heard Sadie's bark. It was coming from the neighbor's yard.

Lily took off running toward the gate, wearing her fuzzy slippers and jacket over her pajamas. She came to an abrupt stop as she headed out of the yard and onto the sidewalk, greeted by Brian Henderson, Sadie, and a gray-haired woman she had never seen before.

"That's her!" the woman shouted, pointing an accusing finger at Lily.

"Morning, Lily," Brian said, trying his best to keep the laughter out of his voice. "Over having morning coffee with Walt and Danielle?"

"Umm...no. They're still asleep."

"I saw you break into their house!" the finger-pointing woman accused.

Sadie, who was now sitting by Lily's side, looked from Lily to Brian to the shouting woman.

"I doubt Lily broke in," Brian told the woman. "She was probably borrowing a cup of sugar."

"Yeah right, a cup of sugar," Lily said with a snort. "What are you doing here?"

"This is your new neighbor, Pearl Huckabee. She saw someone breaking into Marlow House."

Lily looked at Pearl. "You called the police on me?"

"Who is this woman?" Pearl demanded of Brian.

Lily flashed her accuser a smile. "I suppose I should be grateful you called the police if you thought you saw a break-in." Lily extended her right hand to the woman and said, "Hi. I'm Lily Bartley. I live across the street. And this is Sadie."

Pearl frowned at the canine creature. "Yes. I have met your dog." She looked at Brian and asked, "Isn't there a leash law in Frederickport?"

Lily dropped her hand back to her side as the woman ignored the friendly offer.

"Don't worry, we don't generally let Sadie run loose," Lily told her.

"Do you make a habit of breaking into your neighbor's house while they're sleeping?" Pearl asked Lily. She then looked at Brian and added, "And you don't have a problem with that?"

"I have a key, so I didn't exactly break in," Lily explained.

"I am curious, why are you over here so early?" Brian asked. "And still in your pajamas."

Lily flashed Brian a mischievous smile. "None of your business. But if you aren't going to arrest me, I'm going home and back to bed. See you later, Brian!" She ignored the unfriendly new neighbor and headed back across the street, Sadie trotting along by her side.

TEN

"That's it?" Pearl asked indignantly. "The woman clearly broke into my neighbor's house and you do nothing?"

Behind them the early morning sunrise cast a warm glow over Beach Drive. Brian watched Lily hurry across the street. She paused briefly when reaching the sidewalk, turned, and gave Brian a parting wave before disappearing into her house a few moments later.

With a shrug, Brian turned to face Pearl. "I'll admit, I am curious why she was over here so early, especially since she claims everyone at Marlow House is still sleeping. But it is Lily."

"What is that supposed to mean?" she snapped.

"I assume you're new in Frederickport, Ms. Huckabee?"

"It's Mrs. Huckabee! But what has that to do with anything?"

Brian smiled patiently. "And you are new to Beach Drive?"

"So? Are you saying on Beach Drive the neighbors just let themselves into each other's houses at all times of the day?"

"Pretty much." Brian couldn't stop chuckling this time.

Pearl frowned. "I don't understand. And are you laughing at me?"

Brian quickly curbed his mirth and gave a little cough. "No, I'm not laughing at you. I understand why you called the police, and you did the right thing, Mrs. Huckabee. I wish all our citizens were so diligent. But I assure you, after you get to know your neighbors, you'll find this incident amusing too."

"I seriously doubt that. And I don't particularly feel comfortable living across the street from someone who just barges into her neighbors' homes while they're sleeping."

"Mrs. Huckabee, I can assure you, Lily Bartley won't be breaking into your house. She is a close friend with Danielle Boatman, the owner of Marlow House. In fact, she lived at Marlow House when she first moved to town. As did another one of your neighbors, Chris Johnson, who lives there." Brian pointed down the street to Chris's house. "I wouldn't be especially surprised to find Chris going into Marlow House with his own key. Or even Heather for that matter." He pointed to the house on the other side of Pearl's. "In fact, Heather stayed at Marlow house for a while, too. So you see, this is a very close-knit neighborhood."

"I prefer my privacy. And while I do feel somewhat comforted knowing there was not an actual break-in, I am not thrilled knowing the people in this neighborhood let their pets run free. If I wanted to pick up dog poop, I would get my own dog."

"I don't think you need to worry about Sadie."

"Oh really? The dog was off a leash and in my yard unsupervised."

"If there is a future problem with Sadie, I'm sure a chat with Lily or Ian will resolve your issue."

"And if it doesn't?"

"Then you can call me, Mrs. Huckabee." Brian removed a business card from his pocket and handed it to her. "I promise you, if you have any problem with the neighbor's dog that they won't resolve, I'll take care of it."

LILY SET the flashlight and set of keys on the entry table after returning to her house. She hung her jacket back on the coatrack. Before returning to the bedroom, she stopped in the kitchen and grabbed some crackers from the pantry. She ate them on the way to her bedroom. When she got there, Sadie was already back in her dog bed, and Ian continued to snore soundly. Crackers now consumed, Lily crawled back into her bed, never expecting to be able to fall back asleep.

SUNLIGHT STREAMED INTO THE BEDROOM. Reluctantly Lily opened her eyes and blinked. She reached out and patted the spot next to her; it was empty. *What time is it?* she wondered. Rolling over to face the alarm clock, she was surprised to find it was after nine in the morning.

Combing her fingers through her messy red hair, she sat up and rubbed sleep out of her eyes. She sat there a moment and thought —*was it all a dream?* With a sigh she shook her head and mumbled, "No, it was no dream. I need to talk to Ian."

Lily hurried out of bed and went to find her husband, expecting he would be alone. But when she found him, he wasn't alone; he was sitting at the kitchen table with his sister, Kelly, papers strewn across the tabletop.

"Morning, sleepyhead," Ian greeted her cheerfully.

Lily stopped short in her tracks and looked grumpily to Kelly.

"Morning, Lily. Ian told me you played hooky today to go wedding dress shopping with Danielle," Kelly said brightly, ignoring the sullen look from her sister-in-law.

"What are you doing here?" Lily blurted.

Startled, Kelly's eyes widened. She blinked several times, momentarily speechless.

"Wake up a little grumpy, did you?" Ian teased.

Rubbing her eyes again, Lily shook her head. "Umm…I'm sorry, Kelly. I didn't mean it like that sounded. I just didn't expect anyone to be here."

Kelly looked Lily up and down, taking in her disheveled appearance. "Yeah, I sort of got that."

Running her fingers through her hair again, Lily looked at Ian and asked, "What are you guys doing?"

"Remember, I told you Kelly was coming over this morning so I could help her with a story she's working on."

"Oh…I forgot." Lily stumbled to the coffee pot. She was about to pour herself a cup and then paused. Abandoning her still-empty coffee cup on the counter, she opened the refrigerator and took out a carton of orange juice.

"What, no coffee?" Ian asked.

"I feel like juice," Lily grumbled.

"So Danielle is really going to go shopping for a wedding dress today?" Kelly asked.

With her glass of juice, Lily took a seat at the table. "That's the plan. After all, the wedding is next month. We should have started shopping months ago."

Kelly chuckled. "Before she even started dating her fiancé?"

Lily shrugged and took a sip of her juice.

"I just hope the dress she picks still fits her next month," Kelly murmured as she sorted through the papers before her.

Lily frowned at Kelly. "Why wouldn't it fit?"

"MORNING, DANI," Lily greeted Danielle thirty minutes later when she breezed into the back door of Marlow House, finding her friend alone in the kitchen. No longer wearing her pajamas, Lily was dressed in jeans and a button-up flannel shirt.

"Morning, Lily. Want some coffee?" Danielle asked as she poured herself a cup.

"No, thanks. Where's Walt?" Lily asked.

"He's up in the attic, writing. Do you need to talk to him?"

Lily took a seat at the table. "No, I wanted to talk to you alone. Anyone else here? Marie maybe?" She glanced around, wondering if the spirit was nearby and listening.

"No. What's up?" Danielle picked up her now full cup and said, "You sure you don't want some?"

"I can't have any coffee. I'm pregnant."

Danielle practically dropped her cup as she let out a squeal. "Oh my god, you're going to have a baby!"

Lily smiled up at Danielle. "Yeah. Looks that way."

Walking to the table, Danielle asked, "This is good news, right?"

Lily nodded and flashed Danielle a smile. "A little bittersweet. Ian and I wanted to start our family after our Europe trip. This, of course, means there will be no Europe trip. At least not now." She let out a sigh.

"I'm sorry about that." Danielle took a seat at the table.

Lily shrugged. "I'll be honest with you; I've been a little worried—doubtful if I could even get pregnant. And while I really wanted to go on this trip—I feel relieved."

"Relieved?" Danielle frowned. "I don't understand."

"If given the choice of having a baby with Ian or going to

Europe, well, I'd pick the baby any day."

"But why the relief?"

"Like I said, I always had this doubt lurking in the back of my mind that I wouldn't be able to get pregnant. I have a tipped uterus, and my mom had endometriosis. She was just lucky she got it after she had her babies."

"But you don't have endometriosis," Danielle reminded her.

"I know. But it runs on both sides of our family. And then there's Ian. He's not exactly a spring chicken."

Danielle almost spit out some coffee when she laughed at Lily's comment. "Not a spring chicken? What does that mean?"

"I don't imagine his little swimmers are as active as a twenty-year-old's."

"Obviously they did the trick; you are pregnant."

"True." Lily grinned. "But you can't tell anyone yet. Not even Walt. I need to tell Ian first."

"He doesn't know?"

Lily shook her head. "No. When I got up this morning, Kelly was at our house. I really want to tell him when we're alone."

Danielle frowned. "So when did you take the test? I thought you left it here?"

"I was over here early this morning." Lily then went on to tell Danielle about her morning.

"You didn't tell Brian why you were here?" Danielle asked after Lily finished her story.

"I told you I didn't."

"I can't believe he just let you go home without telling him."

Lily laughed. "What was he going to do, haul me down to the police station and force it out of me?"

"I could see him doing that." Danielle grinned.

"Yeah right." Lily rolled her eyes. "But that new neighbor, she wouldn't even shake my hand!"

"I told you what she said about Max!"

"I want Walt to have a talk with Sadie about her," Lily said. "I don't want Sadie going back in her yard. After what you told me and how she looked at Sadie, she seems like the kind of woman who would leave out poison food for animals."

Danielle groaned. "I don't even want to consider that. But yes, I'll have Walt talk to her."

"Are we still going to Portland today?"

"You feel up to it?" Danielle asked.

"I didn't barf this morning. In fact, I feel pretty good right now. And I did take the day off."

"Are you going to tell Ian before we go?"

Lily glanced briefly to the back door. "Yeah. If Kelly would just go home."

"We don't have to leave right away. Maybe in a couple of hours. That should give you time to tell him."

"I need to do it before Brian tells Joe about what happened here this morning. And then Joe tells Kelly, and Kelly tells Ian."

"Yeah, rather hard to keep a secret around here."

"Oh, and Kelly said something odd to me when she heard we were going wedding dress shopping."

Danielle frowned. "What was that?"

"She said something about—how she hoped the dress still fits you next month."

"What the heck is that supposed to mean?" Danielle glanced down at herself. "Does it look like I've been gaining weight?"

"Actually, I was thinking the opposite."

"Opposite?"

"You've lost some weight since Walt moved over to this side," Lily reminded her.

"That's only because Walt keeps pilfering my cinnamon rolls."

"Obviously Kelly must have noticed, and maybe she wondered if you plan to lose more weight by the wedding."

"I hadn't planned to lose this weight. Although, it is the best way to do it—without really thinking about it."

Lily stood up. "Well, I'd better get going. I need to figure out some way to get my sister-in-law out of the house so I can talk to Ian. I hope he won't be too disappointed about the trip."

Danielle smiled at Lily. "I have a feeling he's going to be too preoccupied with preparing for the new arrival to be thinking of the trip."

Lily let out a sigh. "I hope you're right, Dani. But even after I tell Ian, I really don't want to tell anyone else. Not until I see my doctor, and I'm sure everything is okay. Maybe even wait a few weeks…in case something happens."

"Nothing is going to happen. But I understand. Can I at least tell Walt?"

Lily nodded. "Yeah. But no one else. Okay?"

ELEVEN

When Lily returned home after telling Danielle about the results of the pregnancy test, she found Kelly still sitting at the kitchen table, but instead of talking to Ian, she was on her cellphone. Assuming her husband had gone into the living room to give his sister privacy for her call, Lily poured herself a glass of milk and then went looking for him.

"Is Kelly still on the phone?" Ian asked when Lily walked into the living room. Sadie, who had been napping by Ian's feet, perked up and looked to Lily, her tail wagging.

"Yes. How long is she going to be here?" Lily whispered.

"Do you have a problem with Kelly?" he asked as Lily took a seat next to him.

"No. But I wanted to talk to you about something, and I need to do it alone."

"What do you want to talk to me about?"

"I don't want to start this discussion until after your sister leaves," Lily said.

Kelly walked into the room and announced, "I'm off the phone!"

"We about covered everything," Ian told his sister. "I think you can take it from here; plus I need to get to work on my project."

Kelly stood in the living room, looking from her brother to Lily, who sat next to him on the couch, drinking a glass of milk. "Why didn't you tell me about the neighbor calling the police on Lily?"

"What are you talking about?" Ian asked.

Kelly looked at Lily. "You didn't tell him?"

Lily groaned.

Frowning, Ian looked from his sister to Lily, back to his sister. "Tell me what?"

"It was nothing," Lily said. "When I took Sadie out this morning, our new neighbor called the police on me. It was still dark out. I guess she thought I was a prowler."

"That's not what Brian told Joe," Kelly said, taking a seat on one of the chairs. "He said when he got here, your new neighbor had Sadie locked in her toolshed and you were in Marlow House."

"She what?" Ian snapped. "What do you mean she had Sadie locked in her toolshed?"

Lily frowned and cocked her head to one side. "I didn't know that," Lily muttered under her breath.

"Where were you when Sadie was being locked up?" Ian asked.

"According to what Brian told Joe, she was in Marlow House. And it was dark over there; everyone was still sleeping." Kelly looked at Lily. "I know you wouldn't tell Brian why you were there, but I'm dying to know. What were you doing?"

"I want to know why Sadie was locked up in a toolshed!" Ian demanded.

Masking her glare with a forced smile, Lily looked at her sister-in-law and said, "Brian is obviously making this a much bigger deal than it is. I took Sadie out this morning, and I remembered I left something in the kitchen at Marlow House, so I decided to pick it up. I didn't want to wake Walt and Danielle, so I left Sadie outside. I must have forgotten to latch the gate, because when I came back outside, she was with Brian. I didn't know anything about the neighbor locking Sadie in the shed."

"What did you leave at Marlow House?" Kelly asked.

Lily frowned. "Excuse me?"

"What did you leave in the kitchen at Marlow House? What did you pick up?"

Lily shook her head. "Why does it even matter?"

"It just seems it must have been important if you went into someone's house while they were sleeping. I'm just curious."

"It really isn't any of your business," Lily snapped.

Ian frowned at his wife. "Lily, I'm not sure why you're so testy this morning. Kelly asked a perfectly reasonable question."

Lily slammed her now empty glass on the coffee table and stood abruptly. "I have to go to the bathroom." She marched out of the room without another word. A moment later Ian and Kelly could hear the bathroom door slam shut.

"I'm sorry, Kelly," Ian said. "I honestly don't know what's gotten into Lily."

"She doesn't like me," Kelly said, standing up.

"That's not true. She likes you."

"She certainly doesn't act like it sometimes," Kelly snapped. "And I'm sorry, Ian, but I think she's keeping something from you. Why was she going into Marlow House when everyone is asleep? She can't even tell us why she really went in there. She obviously didn't tell you about Brian coming out this morning or how she had words with the new neighbor."

"What do you mean they had words?" Ian asked.

"Joe told me that Brian told him the new neighbor was really upset about Sadie being off the leash. She practically demanded Brian give Lily a ticket."

"Lily got a ticket?"

Kelly rolled her eyes. "No. But I guess the new neighbor was pretty upset Brian didn't do anything about Lily or Sadie. Brian ended up giving the woman one of his business cards and promised he would intervene if there were any more problems. Maybe I can understand Lily refusing to tell Brian why she was over there, but to refuse to tell you?"

"In fairness to Lily, she hasn't really had a chance to tell me. I was working with you in the kitchen when she got up this morning."

"But she could have told you then. What's the big secret?"

LILY HAD JUST FINISHED MAKING the bed when Ian walked into the room.

"Is she still here?" Lily asked as she tossed the throw pillows on the bed.

"She just left. What's going on that you couldn't tell me in front of my sister?"

Lily turned to face Ian and grabbed his hand. "Let's discuss this in the living room." She led him out of the bedroom and back to the sofa they had been using fifteen minutes earlier. Together they sat down.

"What's going on, Lily?"

Taking Ian's hand in hers, Lily looked him in the eyes. "Ian, I know you really wanted to go to Europe this summer."

Ian frowned. "You don't?"

"I do. But I really don't want to go if I'm seven months pregnant."

Speechless, Ian stared at Lily, her green eyes boring into him.

"You're saying—how is that possible?" he muttered.

"No one ever said condoms were a fail-safe form of birth control." The corners of Lily's mouth twitched into a smile.

"Are you sure?"

"If the pregnancy test I took this morning was accurate, then yes. That's why I was over at Dani's."

"That's why you were throwing up."

"Yep." Lily then went on to tell Ian about her suspicions, why she hadn't immediately told him, and what had happened that morning. When she was done, she said, "I told Dani she could tell Walt after I told you. But I would rather not tell anyone else until I see a doctor to confirm it. Plus, I would rather be a few months along before I make an announcement. I…well…if something happened, I really don't want to have to explain it to everyone."

"Nothing's going to happen," Ian said, throwing his arms around Lily and pulling her into a hug. "I love you."

Still wrapped in his embrace, she asked in a whisper, "You aren't disappointed about having to cancel our trip?"

"Nahh. It will still be there. And anyway, I've always wanted a motorhome."

Lily pulled out of Ian's embrace and looked at him quizzically. "A motorhome?"

"Sure. It would be a great way for us to travel with a baby. You've always said you wanted to see more of this country." He grinned.

Lily laughed and shook her head at Ian. "Here I'm thinking of how I want to fix up the nursery, and you're working out a new travel agenda."

Ian pulled Lily back into his arms and kissed her nose. "We should probably hold off on the motorhome for a little while. At least wait until after the baby's born and we've figured things out a little."

"Not sure that will ever happen—I mean figuring things out. At least, that's what my mom's always saying." Lily leaned into her husband.

"Can I tell Kelly? It might make her feel better. She thinks you don't like her."

"That's silly. I like Kelly. But sometimes—well, sometimes she can be a little intrusive. Like grilling me about this morning."

"She was just curious. And Lily, Kelly doesn't do that to everyone. She does it to me because I'm her brother, and I like to think she does it to you because she thinks of you as a sister."

Lily let out a sigh. "You're saying I need to make more of an effort with your sister?"

Ian kissed the top of Lily's head. "I get the feeling Kelly is a little jealous. But it isn't because she sees you as some sort of competition for her brother's attention."

"Oh really?" Lily didn't sound convinced. She stayed nestled in Ian's arms on the sofa, her feet now propped on the coffee table.

"I think it's Walt."

Lily frowned and looked at Ian. "Walt? Why would he have anything to do with my relationship with your sister?"

"Not Walt per se—but the secret behind Walt. And Marie and Eva and Chris and Heather—"

"You mean our shared secret?"

"Kelly isn't stupid. And I know she senses something is going on —that we all know something that she doesn't, but she can't put her finger on it."

"I guess I can understand that. But I do think part of it is that she resents the fact there are things in our relationship that are just between the two of us."

"That's why I would like to tell her about the baby, that she's going to be an aunt."

Lily turned to face Ian. "Can we just wait a little while? It's not just Kelly, but you know she will tell Joe, and then Joe will tell Brian. And I really do not want all of Frederickport to know just yet. It's not anything against Kelly. But if something were to happen…like I lost the baby—"

"Nothing is going to happen."

"You sound like Dani. But, Ian, I had a good friend who got

pregnant and found out pretty early. She was so excited, she told everyone. And then she had a miscarriage, and I swear, it was a thousand times harder for her because people kept asking how she was doing—how far along she was—it made it worse for her. I know there is no guarantee, but I'd like to be farther along and have a few doctor visits before I tell anyone else."

Ian studied Lily a moment and then nodded. "Okay. I understand. And you're right, there is no way Kelly wouldn't tell Joe."

Lily snuggled back in Ian's embrace, and the two sat in silence for a few minutes, considering all the upcoming changes in their life.

TWELVE

Marlow House's new garage stood where the carriage house had once been over a century earlier. During his first life, Walt had converted the carriage house to a garage. Unfortunately, it had burned down, leaving the back end of Marlow House property vacant until Danielle decided to rebuild. The new garage housed Walt's Packard and her Ford Flex.

On Wednesday afternoon Danielle drove her car from the garage to Lily's house. She parked by the sidewalk and waited for her friend. She didn't have long to wait. A few minutes after she pulled up, Lily came rushing out of her house, purse in hand, ready to go wedding dress shopping.

"You can tell Walt," Lily said as she climbed into the passenger side of the car. The engine was still running.

"So you told Ian?" Danielle asked.

"I sure did!" Lily grinned. She closed the car door and fastened her seatbelt.

"You look happy, so I take it he took the news well."

"He did. We were planning to start a family soon anyway, so it's not like we didn't want a baby. It will be something I can throw at the kid when he—or she—is a brat." Lily laughed.

"What do you mean throw at the kid?"

"Oh, you know—*and to think I missed a trip to Europe for you!*" Lily laughed again.

Danielle pulled the car away from the sidewalk and started down the road. "You wouldn't really do that."

Lily leaned back in the seat. "You never know…my parents loved to tell me and my siblings that the only reason they didn't get a divorce was that neither of them wanted us."

"That's terrible!" Danielle couldn't help but laugh.

"My mother thought it was hilarious. I finally had to tell her to stop saying that, it wasn't funny."

Danielle chuckled. "I love your mom. But that is a little twisted."

Lily smiled and gazed out the passenger-door window. "So, which store do we hit first?"

"We're going to Astoria."

Lily turned to face Danielle. "I thought we were going to Portland?"

"We were. But Melony told me about a shop in Astoria that sells vintage wedding dresses. I figure it's closer, and we're getting a later start."

"I'm sorry about that."

Danielle shook her head. "Don't be. Anyway, I'm anxious to see this shop. But I confess, I feel guilty making you miss school today. After all, you missed the last couple of days."

"That's okay. I have it covered."

"Have you thought about what you want to do with school?" Danielle asked.

"I'd like to finish out the year if I can handle it. Of course, many mornings like the last few, not sure."

"I've heard morning sickness goes away after a few weeks."

"My mom was sick for a long time when she was pregnant with my brother," Lily told her. "But the upside, I feel much better today. I think part of it is the crackers I've been eating first thing when I get up."

"What about next year?" Danielle asked.

"I'm not going back. I want to be a stay-at-home mom. I'm lucky—we can afford it. When our kids are ready for school, I might go back to teaching."

"Walt will approve," Danielle said with a laugh.

SINCE JOE WAS WORKING a later shift on Wednesday and

wouldn't be home until after seven in the evening, Kelly stopped by the police station to bring him something to eat. The two stood in the front office together, Joe now holding the lunch box Kelly had just handed him.

"I still can't believe how snotty Lily was to me this morning," Kelly told Joe.

"You did say she hadn't been feeling well," Joe reminded her.

"That was Monday, and she's fine now. She must be fine; she went wedding dress shopping with Danielle today. And it would have been nice if they had asked me to go too. It sounded kind of fun," Kelly whined.

"I imagine Danielle can sense you aren't exactly supportive of this engagement," Joe suggested.

Kelly frowned. "Neither are you."

"Because we both think the entire thing is odd."

"Since they're getting married anyway, it would be fun to go dress shopping."

"I suppose if you want to be included in the wedding more, you might want to show a bit more enthusiasm."

"You don't think that would be hypocritical of me?"

"Kelly, it's not like they asked for either of our blessings—or advice. And they are both adults. If they are going to do this, we might as well wish them the best."

"I suppose. It's not like she's marrying Jack the Ripper. I really could never support that."

Joe laughed. "I hope not."

"So how do I look like I'm more…I don't know…supportive of her wedding?"

Joe shrugged. "Not sure."

Kelly considered it a moment and then smiled. "I know what I can do!"

"What?"

"I'll stop at the library and check out some bridal books. I'll tell her I was over there picking up some books and happened to see them and thought of her. If I can win Danielle over, maybe I can get closer to Lily. After all, they are best friends."

"I've always thought you and Danielle were already friends," Joe said.

"Oh, come on, Joe, we've talked about it before. It's like they all have this secret club, and we're not included."

"I CAN'T BELIEVE you found one at the first shop you went to," Walt told Danielle. She had returned from Astoria minutes earlier with a ravenous appetite. Fortunately for her, Walt already had dinner in the oven, roasted Brussels sprouts and a chicken dish. The two were alone in the kitchen, setting the table as Danielle told Walt about her wedding dress.

"It's so beautiful—a one-of-a-kind vintage dress. The fabric is silky ecru, with intricate lacework. It just needs minor alterations. They don't do them there, but they recommended a local seamstress, so we dropped it off before heading home."

"Did you get a picture of it?" Walt asked.

"Of course I did." Danielle set a fork atop a folded napkin on the kitchen table.

Walt stopped what he was doing and faced Danielle. "Let me see it."

"Don't be silly; it's bad luck for the groom to see the wedding dress before the wedding."

"Need I remind you, you are already my wife?" He grinned.

Setting the last piece of silverware on the table, Danielle turned to Walt and gave him a hug. "True," she whispered into his right ear. "But I'm not taking any chances!" She gave him a quick kiss.

"You are superstitious," he teased.

"Yes. And I also believe in ghosts."

He laughed, released her, and then gave her backside a playful swat as she went to finish setting the table. He walked to the oven and opened it.

Danielle immediately stopped what she was doing and turned to Walt and wrinkled her nose. "Oh, that smell!"

"The Brussels sprouts," Walt explained apologetically. "I like roasted Brussels sprouts, but I forgot how badly they can make a room smell." He switched on the exhaust fan.

"Let me open the door, let some fresh air in," Danielle suggested. "I don't want that smell to go through the house."

"It's cold outside," Walt reminded her.

"A little cold is better than that smell."

A few minutes later Walt and Danielle sat at the kitchen table, eating their dinner with the back door propped open a few inches.

"I have something to tell you," Danielle began.

Walt looked up from his food. "Is it about the wedding?"

"Lily is pregnant." Danielle grinned.

"She is? That's wonderful!" Walt's smile quickly faded, and he asked, "Certainly they aren't going to Europe this summer now?"

"No. They'll have to cancel the trip. Plus, she doesn't want anyone to know she's pregnant yet, not until she sees the doctor."

"If she hasn't seen the doctor, then how does she know she's pregnant?"

"She took a home pregnancy test."

"What's that?" Walt frowned.

"It's a test women can buy at the store and take at home. If her urine turns the tester a certain color, it means she's pregnant."

Unknown to Walt and Danielle, Kelly had parked her car in front of their house a few minutes earlier. When she spied the kitchen lights on and the gate unlocked, she decided to cut through the side yard to the back door. With an armful of bridal books, Kelly approached the partially open back door just in time to hear Walt say, "And the pregnancy test was positive?"

Kelly froze in her tracks and listened.

"Yes. It looks that way," came Danielle's voice through the open door.

"Any chance it could be wrong?" Walt asked.

"I suppose. But I doubt it."

"Considering the travel plans, a pregnancy is rather inconvenient. Frankly I'm surprised."

"It came as a shock to me too."

"I thought women had these things taken care of," Walt noted.

"What is that supposed to mean?" Danielle asked.

Kelly turned and quickly made her way from the house and to her car without hearing another word of Walt and Danielle's conversation.

"You always tell me women these days can decide if they want to get pregnant or not. I'm just surprised Lily decided to get pregnant now, when they were planning a trip to Europe," Walt told Danielle.

"Fact is, even the birth control pill is not fail-safe. But in Lily's case, she went off it because they wanted to try for a baby when they got back from their trip. They switched to condoms, which obviously didn't work."

"While I should feel sorry for them, missing their trip, I must say the news of a baby is wonderful."

"Don't feel too sorry for them. According to Lily, both she and Ian are thrilled. And frankly, I love the idea of a baby!"

JOE GOT home from work and found Kelly sitting on the sofa, eating chocolate mint ice cream out of the carton, a pile of bridal books stacked on a nearby table. When he entered the room, he glanced at the books and then looked to Kelly.

"We do have bowls," he teased.

"There was just a little ice cream left anyway." She took another bite.

Joe sat on the sofa next to Kelly and nodded to the pile of books. "I see you went to the library. When are you taking them to Danielle?"

"I'm not." She scraped up the last bit of the ice cream and ate it.

"But I thought…?" He frowned.

Dropping the spoon in the now empty carton, she looked at Joe. "I already took them over there."

"She didn't want them?"

Kelly set the empty carton on the end table. "Danielle didn't know I was there. I went up to the back door, and it was partially open. She was in the kitchen with Walt. They were talking. And I was right. Danielle's pregnant."

"She told you?"

"Not exactly. They didn't know I was standing there. And I left so they wouldn't know I had overheard. It was both embarrassing and awful. You were right. Walt is a major jerk."

"How so?"

"He obviously is not happy about the pregnancy. I guess he wanted to do some traveling and didn't seem happy about having to change their plans. And then he said something that made me so darn mad that I knew I had to get out of there before I kicked him!"

"What did he say?"

"It was like he was blaming Danielle for getting pregnant. As if it was all her fault. He said something about how women took care of those sorts of things."

THIRTEEN

On Thursday morning Joanne arrived early at Marlow House. She had vacuuming and dusting to do in preparation for the bed and breakfast guests who would be arriving on Friday. Before starting with her chores, she and Danielle inventoried the pantry and refrigerator while Danielle made a shopping list.

Danielle and Walt intended to go to the grocery store and then stop at Old Salts Bakery while Joanne cleaned the house. But first, they planned to have breakfast at Pier Café. It wasn't raining, and the sky seemed unusually blue for January, so Walt offered to drive his Packard.

When they arrived at Pier Café, Joe and Brian were there having breakfast, seated at a booth. Walt and Danielle greeted the two officers and then went on to a table at the other end of the building. After Carla brought their coffee, the couple—so engrossed in discussing their wedding plans—failed to notice the hostile glares Joe flashed their way as he watched Danielle drink her coffee.

They also didn't notice Brian's curious glances as he listened to Joe recount the conversation he'd had the night before with Kelly, along with his disappointment in Danielle for not taking better care of herself for the baby's sake. According to Joe's sister, a pregnant woman should not be drinking coffee.

Up the street, across from Marlow House, Ian sat alone in his living room with Sadie, flames crackling in the nearby fireplace. Lily had gone back to work, insisting she felt much better. She hadn't thrown up that morning, yet she did confess to waking up feeling nauseous. Fortunately, the bowl of Cheerios she'd had for breakfast made her feel much better. If Ian had his way, Lily would quit work now and stay home and rest. However, he knew his wife—that was not going to happen. She loved her students and her job, and he told himself he should just be grateful she was on board with staying home after the baby came.

Feeling especially content, Ian let the house rules slide. Instead of Sadie napping on the floor by his feet, she curled up beside him on the sofa, her chin resting on his thigh. Absently petting his canine companion, Ian thought about how things were going rather well in spite of having to cancel their trip to Europe.

He had been privy to Walt's remarkable transformation, a story he would love writing about, but knew he never would. The Cubs had won the World Series this past October, something he had been waiting years to see. And now he was going to be a father and was sharing that adventure with the love of his life.

Still stroking the dog's back, Ian asked, "Well, girl, we're having a baby. What do you think about that?"

Sadie lifted her head and looked at him.

Ian smiled down at the dog, who clearly had no idea what the words meant. Giving Sadie's head a pat, he said, "Perhaps I will have Walt talk to you about it."

MARLOW HOUSE'S first pair of guests—the Russoms—arrived Friday morning. While check-in was normally in the afternoon, Danielle had told them they could check in earlier so they could drop off their luggage and then leave to visit their other family members, who were meeting at a relative's house in Frederickport. They had already come and gone, leaving their suitcases in the downstairs bedroom.

At lunchtime Chris and Heather showed up, bringing tacos and burritos from Beach Taco. They had left Bella and Hunny back at the Glandon Headquarters Office. After sharing the food with Walt and Danielle, the four sat in the living room while Danielle showed Heather a picture of her wedding dress on her cellphone. The two women shared the sofa while Walt and Chris sat on the chairs facing them.

"It's gorgeous!" Heather gushed. She glanced up to Walt and Chris and was startled at Walt's sour expression. "What's wrong? Don't you like the dress?"

"She won't let me see it," Walt complained.

"It's because it's bad luck," Danielle reminded him.

"But we're already married."

"Trust me, the dress is beautiful, Walt. But I agree with Danielle. You need to wait until your wedding to see it," Heather told him. "It doesn't matter if you're already married."

"Danielle would look beautiful in whatever she wore," Walt declared.

Danielle flashed him a grin and said, "Flattery—although much appreciated—will not get me to show you the dress before the wedding."

Chris stood up and walked to the sofa. "I'd like to see it."

"He can't see it if I can't!" Walt protested.

Chris laughed. "It doesn't work that way. You get to marry her; that means I can see the dress now."

Walt shrugged and leaned back in the chair. "Okay. I suppose that's a fair trade."

Rolling her eyes, Danielle handed Chris the phone.

"Very nice," Chris murmured as he stood by the sofa looking down at the picture on the cellphone.

"I met that new neighbor," Heather told Danielle as she took the cellphone back from Chris.

"The way you say that, doesn't sound like she made a much better impression on you than she did on me." Danielle turned off her phone and set it on the coffee table. "Or on Lily."

"When I was leaving for work this morning, I had Bella with me. The new neighbor came marching over, and I thought she was going to introduce herself."

"Let me guess, she said something nasty about Bella?" Danielle asked.

"She said if she saw Bella in her yard again, she would shoot her!" Heather said.

"Wow. That was even more direct than she was with me," Danielle noted.

"I don't think it's legal to go around shooting your neighbor's pets, even if they step on your property," Chris said. "Unless they're considered a threat."

"Which means you need to be especially careful with Hunny," Danielle warned. "In fact, you should have Walt talk to her."

Chris frowned. "Why? I don't let Hunny run loose."

"No, but sometimes you let her off the leash, and if she dashed in that woman's yard, well, you know how some people are about pit bulls," Danielle reminded him. "And if that woman is talking about shooting a harmless little cat like Bella, I'm fairly certain she would feel justified shooting poor Hunny."

"I'm not sure I would characterize Bella as a harmless little cat. Have you met her?" Chris teased.

In response, Heather crumpled up a napkin and hurled it at Chris. "She saved your life, brat."

Chris chuckled. "Exactly. She's a tough little girl."

"You know what I mean," Danielle countered, her tone serious.

"Point taken. There's obviously something wrong with the woman," Chris observed. "I don't know why anyone would go out of their way to piss off all their neighbors the first week they move in."

"She obviously doesn't like animals," Heather noted.

"That alone is a reason not to trust her," Walt pointed out.

AN HOUR after Chris and Heather returned to work, the front doorbell rang. Walt was sitting in the parlor reading, and Danielle was upstairs, so Walt went to answer the door. When he opened it, he found two women standing on the front porch. They were the same height, one with long blond hair and the other with short spiky brown hair. He was about to say hello when he noticed the blonde's vivid violet eyes. He had never seen eyes that color before. Without thought, he stared at her for a prolonged moment, failing to extend a greeting.

Focusing on the unusual eye color, he didn't notice the corners of the blonde's lips twitching upward in a smile. The woman with the spiky hair made a forced coughing sound and said, "Hello? This is Marlow House, isn't it? We have a reservation."

Startled out of his momentary lapse, Walt smiled sheepishly and said, "Oh yes, of course. Please excuse me. But I have never seen eyes your color before. They're quite striking. But I'm sure you hear that all the time." He opened the door wider.

"She's obviously wearing colored contacts," Marie said.

Startled by Marie's sudden appearance, Walt lurched in surprise, yet quickly reclaimed his composure. The two sisters exchanged curious glances as the blonde asked, "And who are you?"

"Walt Marlow. Please come in." He opened the door wider and flashed Marie an annoyed glare as he stepped aside, making room for the women to enter.

"Oh pshaw, don't give me that look, Walt Marlow," Marie scolded. "Danielle has told me about all the times you used to just pop in and startle her!"

Walt flashed Marie a quick smile and she chuckled. "That's better."

"Walt Marlow? Surely not the author?" the blonde asked as he shut the door.

"Yes. And I will admit, it still feels strange when someone recognizes my name."

"I bet it does," the blonde purred.

"My name is Rachel, and this is my sister, Claudia," the brunette introduced. "We left our luggage in the car. It was such a long drive, we thought we would check in first, maybe get a drink, use the bathroom."

"Certainly." Walt pointed to the powder room door. "There's a bathroom right there. I'll be happy to get you both something to drink, and you can wait in the parlor. Danielle should be down here in a moment, and she'll check you in."

"Parlor? You have a parlor?" Claudia chuckled.

"We do." Walt smiled. He showed them into the small room and before going off to the kitchen asked, "Would you like some iced tea —hot tea?"

"Iced tea would be wonderful," Rachel said.

"Yes, I would like that too," Claudia agreed.

Instead of going with Walt, Marie stayed with the women.

"He so recognized me," Claudia said with a snort after she was alone in the parlor with her sister—alone except for Marie. She walked to the sofa.

"He obviously doesn't have amnesia. He was utterly speechless when he opened that door and saw you." Rachel followed her sister to the sofa. "But I have to say, he is an excellent actor. He regained his composure and then pretended like he didn't know you."

"You knew Clint?" Marie blurted. Of course, neither woman could hear her.

Claudia dropped her purse to the floor and then flopped down on the sofa. "I suppose it's possible he did have amnesia, and seeing me jolted his memory. When he first opened the door and saw me, I got the feeling he was trying to place me, not that he was necessarily surprised to see me. And then he practically jumped out of his skin. I'd say that's the moment it clicked for him. This should be interesting."

"You might be right. Because you did register in our real names, so if he knew you were coming, I don't think he would act so surprised to see you."

"That's assuming this Boatman told him our names," Claudia reminded her.

"You think it's possible he recognizes you, but doesn't remember who you are?" Rachel asked, still standing by the sofa.

"Anything is possible at this point."

"I have to use the bathroom. I'll be right back."

"What are you two up to?" Marie murmured as she watched the spiky-haired woman leave the room.

Ten minutes later Rachel returned to the parlor as Walt came walking in with a tray carrying two glasses of iced tea, a sugar bowl and two spoons. Just as he set the tray on the coffee table, Danielle came walking into the room.

"Hello, you must be Claudia and Rachel Dane," Danielle greeted them just as Rachel took a seat on the sofa next to her sister. The two women looked to Danielle and smiled.

"Be careful with these two," Marie warned from the sidelines. Both Walt and Danielle glanced to Marie and then back to the women on the sofa. "They knew Clint. In fact, it appears to be the real reason they're here."

FOURTEEN

Claudia stood up and extended a hand to Danielle. "I'm Claudia Dane, and this is my sister, Rachel. I assume you're Danielle Boatman?"

Warily, Danielle shook Claudia's hand and then Rachel's. She glanced briefly at Marie, who shrugged in reply.

"Yes…I am. So what brings you to Frederickport and our B and B?"

"My sister and I had time off, so we thought a little escape from our hectic life might be relaxing," Claudia said as she sat back down and picked up a glass of tea. "The Oregon coast is such a lovely area."

"Pshaw, they didn't come for the Oregon coast," Marie said from the sidelines.

Danielle glanced from Walt to the empty chairs facing the sofa and gave a little nod. Flashing Danielle a smile, Walt sat down in one of the chairs while Danielle sat in the other one.

"We have another couple arriving this afternoon, also from Huntington Beach. Any chance they're meeting you here?" Danielle asked politely.

"Really?" Claudia frowned. She shrugged and said, "No. It's just my sister and me. Hmm…I guess this is a small world."

"Do we know each other?" Walt blurted.

Claudia glanced from Danielle to Walt and found herself

looking into his intense gaze. Refusing to look away, she stared back. "I don't know. Do we?"

If Danielle didn't know better, she would think they were having a blinking contest, and so far, there was no winner. Danielle cleared her throat and then said, "Walt has amnesia."

A smile curled Claudia's lips as she turned to face Danielle. "Does he?"

"Yes. He was in a car accident this past March. Before the accident, he lived not far from Huntington Beach," Danielle explained.

"And you look familiar," Walt lied.

"What did you do when you lived in California?" Rachel asked.

"I was a real estate agent," Walt explained.

"And now you're a writer?" Claudia asked.

Walt looked to Danielle and explained, "She recognized my name when I introduced myself."

"Now that you mention it, I do recall reading the author Walt Marlow had amnesia. Such a fascinating story," Claudia said as she sipped her tea.

"Do we know each other?" Walt asked.

"Wouldn't I have told you that?" Claudia asked with a smile. She set her glass back on the table. "I'm also a real estate agent, and I suppose it's possible our paths have crossed. But I meet so many people it's difficult for me to remember them all."

"How did you get amnesia?" Rachel asked. "I don't think I've ever met anyone who had amnesia. I thought it was something people only got on soap operas."

"As I mentioned, Walt was in a car accident," Danielle explained. "He was unconscious for a few days, and when he woke up, he didn't remember anything about his life."

"I also read you and he are engaged. Is that right?" Claudia asked.

Danielle nodded. "Yes. We're getting married on Valentine's Day."

Claudia arched her brows. "Isn't that a bit risky? What happens if he suddenly remembers he has another family somewhere—another wife?"

"She knew Clint. She knows perfectly well he wasn't married," Marie snapped. "She's here to start trouble!"

Walt studied Claudia a moment and smiled. "While I can't recall anything that happened prior to the accident, I know who I was, and I have a basic knowledge of what my life was like back then. Unfortunately, I can't recall any of the people I once knew, not even my fiancée, who was killed in the car accident."

RACHEL TOSSED her suitcase on one of the twin beds. "I'll take this one."

"I don't care. Take whichever one you want." Claudia dropped her suitcase on the floor and walked to the bedroom window. Moments earlier Danielle had shown them to the room they would be staying in. Claudia assumed she was alone in the bedroom with her sister. What she didn't know, the ghost of Marie Nichols sat perched on the dresser listening. Pulling back the curtains, Claudia looked out the window. "I want to know what kind of game Clint is playing."

"I'd like to know what kind of game you're playing," Marie asked as she watched the sisters.

"Why didn't you just tell them you know him?" Rachel opened her suitcase and started unpacking.

Claudia wandered back from the window and sat down on what would be her bed for the week. She faced her sister. "I'm waiting to have that conversation with Clint when we're alone."

"Maybe he really does have amnesia. The way he was looking at you, it was like he was trying to place you."

"That's what I thought after he first opened the front door. I don't think even Clint is that good of an actor. But I could be wrong." Claudia kicked off her shoes and pulled the pillows out from under the bedspread. She fluffed up the pillows, sat on the bed, and put her feet up on the mattress while leaning back on the pillows. She looked up to the ceiling. "I don't hear any footsteps up there. I don't think Clint's in his room."

Rachel finished hanging her clothes in the closet. "This entire thing is so bizarre." Rachel yawned.

"Tired?" Claudia asked.

"Exhausted. When we go home, you're driving. We should have flown."

"Whatever..."

"I'm going to take a nap." Tossing back the covers on her bed,

Rachel climbed under the blankets. "Let's talk later. I've got to get some sleep."

Marie sat in silence for a few minutes, watching as Rachel curled up in the bed with her eyes closed and her back to her sister, who lay silently on her bed, staring up at the ceiling.

"Well, this is boring," Marie said before disappearing.

Claudia stood up and started for the door.

Rachel opened her eyes. "Where are you going?"

"I'm going to go find Clint so we can have that conversation."

"If you can get him away from that Danielle for a few minutes," Rachel said with a yawn before closing her eyes again.

Claudia stepped out of the bedroom and looked down the hallway toward the stairs leading to the attic. According to what Danielle had told them when giving a quick tour of the house, Clint —or Walt, as Danielle called him—lived on the top floor. According to Danielle, the attic had been recently converted to a bedroom suite with a sitting area.

Claudia stared up at the ceiling. "How did you get her to remodel the attic for you, Clint?" She hadn't heard any footsteps overhead, so she was fairly certain Clint wasn't in his room. She just hoped she would be able to catch him alone, without Danielle.

Stepping lightly in her bare feet, Claudia started down the hallway, toward the stairs leading to the first floor. She paused a moment when she reached the closed door to Danielle's bedroom. Pressing her ear against the door, she listened. Someone was in the room, she could hear them moving around, opening and closing drawers. Claudia smiled. She didn't hear any voices, so she assumed Danielle was in the bedroom alone. Hopefully this meant she would find Clint alone downstairs, and the two of them could have a little talk. She continued down the hallway and to the stairs.

Holding onto the handrail, she made her way down to the first floor, careful not to make a sound. She wanted to surprise Clint— catch him off guard. Once she reached the first floor, she headed to the parlor and then the living room. Both rooms were empty. The downstairs bedroom was locked, but she didn't expect to find him in there, and no one was in the downstairs powder room. Just as she reached the doorway to the kitchen, she heard a woman's voice.

Claudia froze. A woman's voice meant Walt was not alone. The door to the kitchen was ajar; she stepped closer to listen. To her surprise it was Danielle's voice. She peeked inside the kitchen, hiding behind the partially closed door.

DANIELLE SAT at the kitchen table with Marie, drinking a cup of coffee and dissecting a cinnamon roll—popping each small piece into her mouth before breaking off another morsel.

"When they wake up from their nap, I'll go back up there and keep an eye on them," Marie told Danielle. "See what those two are up to."

"They must be the ones who sent that letter."

"That's what I'm thinking. Where's Walt?"

"He went upstairs to get those notes he left in my room. I imagine he's up in his room by now, working on his new book."

"Don't you think he should stay down here, keep an eye on those two?"

"Considering they're upstairs, not sure what good it would do. He can't really lurk around guest bedrooms—especially women guests. It's not like Walt's invisible anymore."

CLAUDIA STARED DUMBFOUNDED into the kitchen. At first she thought Danielle was on the telephone. But then she spied the cellphone sitting on the counter, plugged into a charger. The animated way in which Danielle carried on the conversation with her imaginary friend—the hand motions, the facial expressions—it made Claudia think she was talking to someone sitting at the table with her—not talking on the phone. But there was no one else at the table.

Of course, if Danielle was wearing a Bluetooth headset, it would be possible for her to talk on the phone while it was plugged in on the counter. Claudia frowned. From where she stood, it didn't look as if Danielle was wearing a headset. Curious, Claudia listened in for a few more minutes to the one-sided conversation. Unable to contain her curiosity a moment longer, she barged into the kitchen with a cheerful hello.

Danielle immediately stopped talking and looked up to Claudia.

"I thought you were talking to someone in here," Claudia said as she walked to the table, glancing around.

"Umm...sometimes I think out loud," Danielle muttered. "I thought you were taking a nap?"

"I was wondering if I could get a glass of water to take back upstairs with me."

"There's a pitcher of fresh iced water and glasses in your room, didn't you see it?"

"Is there?" Claudia smiled. "I must have missed that. Well..." Claudia yawned. "I think I will take that nap now. Thank you."

HER SISTER'S snoring was not the reason Claudia shook her awake a few minutes later. "Rachel!"

Groggily opening her eyes, Rachel glared at her sister. "Why did you do that?"

"Danielle Boatman is certifiable!"

Frowning, Rachel rubbed her eyes and sat up in the bed. "What are you talking about?"

"I went downstairs looking for Walt, and I found Danielle in the kitchen, talking to herself!"

Rachel shrugged. "I talk to myself sometimes."

"No. This was a full-on conversation. At first I thought she was on the phone."

"Maybe she was." Rachel yawned again, now fully awake.

Claudia perched on the edge of her sister's bed. "There was no cellphone in her hand, and she didn't have anything in her ears. She was having a conversation with an imaginary friend. It was not like someone just talking to themselves."

"So tell me, in this conversation, was she like asking herself questions and then answering herself? I worked with a woman who used to do that. A real weirdo."

Claudia shook her head. "No. It wasn't like that. It was a conversation—like something you might hear if she had been on the phone. You know, with missing pieces of the conversation so you don't know exactly what they're talking about. Like someone is answering her, or asking her a question. It was freaking bizarre."

"Does she know you overheard her?"

"Yes. I wanted to see if she was wearing a headset, so I walked into the kitchen under the guise of needing some drinking water."

Rachel glanced to the table with the pitcher of water and glasses. "We have drinking water."

"I know that. I forgot. But that's not the point."

"So what did she say?"

"She said she was thinking aloud."

"Maybe she was." Rachel shrugged.

Claudia adamantly shook her head. "No. You would have had to have been there. Danielle Boatman thought she was talking to her imaginary friend. She's off her rocker. No wonder Clint has been able to manipulate her."

"Aren't you making more of this than it really is? I mean seriously, lots of people talk to themselves."

"Do you know what she said? She said, 'It's not like Walt's invisible anymore.'"

FIFTEEN

Wrapped in a down parka jacket that was two sizes two large, Danielle looked up at the gray sky from where she sat on the porch swing. It wasn't much colder than it had been the day before, yet yesterday the skies were uncharacteristically clear, blue and sunny for January, making it feel warmer.

"What in the world are you doing out here in the cold?" Walt called to Danielle after he stepped out of the house a few minutes later. Danielle glanced over to Walt and patted the empty spot on the swing. He had put on a coat before stepping outside, so she wasn't worried about him freezing.

"I needed some fresh air," Danielle told him when he was close enough to hear without her shouting.

"Is Marie still eavesdropping on our new guests?" Walt asked when he sat down a moment later.

"Yes. Wish she wouldn't have left her post earlier." Danielle went on to tell him what had transpired in the kitchen.

When she was done with the telling, Walt gave a little shrug and chuckled. "So they think you were talking to yourself?"

"It was embarrassing." Danielle groaned.

"And Marie still doesn't know any more about them?"

"Maybe she does now. Like I said, she went back up to the bedroom after Claudia left the kitchen. I imagine Marie is listening to them discuss how crazy I am."

Just as Walt was about to respond, a car pulled up in front of Marlow House and parked.

"I wonder if that's the other guests." Danielle watched as a man and woman got out of the vehicle and looked toward Marlow House.

"They're coming this way," Walt said.

Danielle stood up. "According to Claudia, they aren't part of their group. So if whoever sent Clint that letter is one of our guests, I suspect they're the ones already upstairs, considering Claudia is obviously lying about knowing you."

Walt got up from the swing and walked with Danielle to the front door.

"Is this Marlow House?" the man called out as he and his companion neared Walt and Danielle. He carried a suitcase in each hand.

"Yes, it is. Welcome," Danielle greeted them as she stood with Walt on the front porch. She noticed the way the woman stared at Walt. It was as if she couldn't take her eyes off him. Danielle wondered if she was a fan of his book. She guessed the couple was in their late forties or early fifties. The man wasn't especially tall, maybe five nine—stocky with shortly cropped brown hair and brown eyes, and a clean-shaven face. He wore dress slacks and what appeared to be a button-up dress shirt under his leather jacket. The wife wore her coal black hair shortly cropped and heavily gelled. Danielle wondered if her legs were freezing under the baggy silky slacks she wore, yet suspected the snowy-white, faux-fur jacket was keeping her warm.

"Are you Danielle Boatman?" the man asked, setting down the suitcases and offering his hand to Danielle.

"Yes. I assume you are Mr. and Mrs. Thorpe?" Danielle shook his hand and then his wife's while Walt stood silently by her side.

Mr. Thorpe's eyes were on Walt when he told Danielle, "Yes, but please, call me Dirk. And this is my wife, Tanya."

"This is Walt Marlow. He's one of our full-time residents," Danielle explained, "and my fiancé."

"Marlow?" Dirk said, now shaking Walt's hand. "The same name as the bed and breakfast?"

"A distant cousin built Marlow House," Walt explained, now shaking Tanya's hand.

"And now you live here?" Tanya said.

Walt smiled. "Yes."

"So tell me, Mr. Marlow, what is it you do?" Dirk asked.

"Walt's an author," Danielle answered for him.

Dirk glanced to Danielle and back to Walt. "Really? Anything I might have read?"

"*Moon Runners*," Walt told him.

Dirk shrugged. "Sorry, I've never heard of it."

"Can we go inside? It's freezing out here!" Tanya whined.

"Oh yes, I'm so sorry. Please come in," Danielle apologized as she quickly opened the front door. Tanya hurried into the house while her husband picked up the two suitcases and followed her inside, Walt and Danielle trailing after them.

Once inside, Dirk set the suitcases on the wood floor and looked around, taking in the rich dark paneling and enormous entry hall. He let out a long whistle. "Wow, this is gorgeous."

"Why, thank you." Danielle smiled.

"So let me understand, this place was built by your distant cousin, but it belongs to Ms. Boatman here. Does this mean you're cousins or something?" Dirk asked.

"I don't think they could be getting married if they were cousins," Tanya told him.

Dirk shrugged. "I know of cousins who've married."

"No, no relation," Walt explained.

Dirk arched his brows. "Well, that's one way to get the old estate back in the family," he muttered, looking around the spacious entry hall again. "How is the housing market up here?"

Danielle shrugged. "I don't really know. But I have a friend who is a Realtor, if you're interested in looking at property while you're up here."

"Only if he does referrals."

"Referrals?" Danielle frowned.

"Dirk is a real estate broker in California," Tanya explained.

"Have you always been an author?" Dirk asked Walt.

Walt shook his head. "No. No, I haven't."

"Really? So what did you do before you started writing?" Dirk asked.

"Umm…I was a real estate agent," Walt said.

"Then I guess you know all about how referrals work." Dirk picked up his suitcases again. "Can you take us to our room, or do we have to sign in somewhere first?"

"You can leave your luggage here, and we can step in the parlor for a moment and take care of check-in," Danielle told him.

"Here, I'll take your luggage up to your room for you," Walt offered.

"Really? Imagine that, an author and a bellboy. Do I have to tip you?" Dirk handed Walt his suitcases.

AFTER LISTENING to her sister rant about crazy Danielle for fifteen minutes, Rachel finally said, "Hold that thought. I really got to use the bathroom." She jumped from the bed and dashed from the room. When she returned five minutes later, she was carrying a black cat in her arms.

"Where did you get that?" Claudia asked.

"He was standing outside the bathroom door when I walked out. Isn't he gorgeous? This must be the cat Danielle mentioned. I think she said his name is Max." Rachel sat on the edge of her bed, Max now on her lap as she stroked his back. The cat began to purr.

"Really, Max, don't turn traitor on us," Marie said from her perch on the dresser. Max looked up to the spirit and meowed. "Fickle feline."

"Just don't let him on my bed," Claudia warned. "I don't want to sleep with a bunch of cat hair."

"Look at his ears," Rachel said as she tweaked the white tips of Max's otherwise black ears. "I love these markings!"

"That one"—Marie nodded to Claudia—"knew Clint. I'm not sure about the one who's holding you...yes, Max, she seems nice, but I think they're up to something. They lied to Walt and Danielle."

"Oh, by the way, I think those other guests just arrived. I heard someone come in with Clint and Danielle."

"Clint is downstairs?" Claudia asked.

"I guess. I could hear them talking. They're obviously going to be staying in one of the rooms on this floor."

"Danielle said they're also from Huntington Beach. That's weird," Claudia said.

"All of this is weird," Rachel muttered.

Claudia walked to the door and opened it just a few inches, peering out into the hallway. She spied Clint going into a bedroom a few doors down, carrying two suitcases. A moment later, he came out of the room without the suitcases and headed back downstairs.

Claudia eased the door closed and turned to her sister. "Clint was just up here, but he went back downstairs again."

"I thought you wanted to talk to him?"

"I do, but he went back downstairs." Claudia walked over to a chair and sat down. "Are you going back to sleep?"

Rachel shrugged. "You already woke me up. I don't think I'll be able to fall asleep again."

"I'm sorry, but I had to tell you what I overheard."

The sisters chatted for another ten minutes—never once mentioning Walt, Clint, Danielle or their reason for coming to Marlow House. Growing bored listening to the tedious discussion, Marie focused her attention on a cat figurine sitting on a curio shelf. A moment later it toppled off, heading to the floor. Suddenly realizing the object might break on impact, Marie instantly reversed its direction, sending it back to the shelf, where it resumed its original position.

Rachel, who had been looking at her sister while discussing where they might go for dinner, caught a glimpse of the figurine from the corner of her eye. She looked over to it and froze. "Did you see that?"

Claudia frowned. "See what?"

Rachel pointed to the object. "That cat, it fell off the shelf for a moment."

"What do you mean it fell off the shelf for a moment?"

"It just like…dropped off the shelf and then went back up on it. All by itself."

Claudia stood up and rolled her eyes. "Rachel, maybe you should try taking a nap again. When you start seeing things, it's time to get more sleep." She started for the door.

"Where are you going?"

"I'm going to use the bathroom and then see if I can find Clint. I need to find him alone so I can let him know why we're really here."

"You…you aren't going to leave me here alone, are you?" Rachel looked with unease at the cat figurine.

Claudia chuckled. "I'm pretty sure you have more to worry about with the cat in your lap than the one sitting on the shelf." She picked up her purse from the floor, opened it and then removed a folded piece of paper.

"I suppose I could arrange it so you can talk to Walt alone. The sooner he does, the sooner we can find out what you're up to," Marie said before disappearing from the room.

Claudia stepped into the hallway, leaving Rachel alone in the bedroom with Max, looking nervously at the cat figurine.

SIXTEEN

Five minutes later Claudia washed her hands in one of the guest bathrooms on the second floor. She heard muffled voices in the hallway and figured it was the guests who had recently arrived—the ones whose luggage Clint had put in one of the other rooms. She heard a door open and close, and then the voices went silent. Assuming whoever it was had gone into the room where Clint had taken the suitcases, Claudia looked in the mirror and combed her fingers through her hair, fluffing it a bit to give it volume. Leaning closer to her reflection, she removed stray makeup from the corners of her eyes and pursed her lips, wishing she had grabbed her makeup bag.

Several minutes later Claudia stepped out of the bathroom into the hallway and about ran into Dirk Thorpe, who was just getting ready to try the bathroom door. They both jumped back in surprise.

"Dirk?"

"Claudia?"

The two stood in the hallway and stared at each other.

Claudia glanced around quickly to see if anyone else was in the area. She looked back to Dirk and asked, "What are you doing here?"

"I don't think you'd have to ask that question. I have to wonder, why are you here?"

"We had a deal," she reminded him.

"I didn't have one with Clint."

Glaring at Dirk, she asked, "Have you seen him yet?"

"Yes. And unless he's one hell of an actor, I think he has amnesia," Dirk said. "He had no clue who I was. Did he recognize you?"

Claudia shook her head. "No."

"And did you tell him who you are?" Dirk asked.

"Not yet."

They heard footsteps coming up the staircase.

"We can talk about this later." Dirk quickly slipped into the bathroom and closed the door behind him, locking it.

Claudia stood alone in the hallway, listening to whoever was coming up the stairs. A moment later she saw Clint.

"Hello, Claudia," Walt greeted her as he walked down the hallway toward her. What Claudia couldn't see was Marie, who stood at Walt's side.

"Okay, you're alone with him. Now out with it!" Marie demanded impatiently.

"I need to talk to you a minute. Alone," Claudia told Walt. "You see, I did recognize you."

"She didn't *recognize* you," Marie snorted. "She knows you and knew you were here when she made the reservations!"

"Are you saying we knew each other?" Walt asked.

"Can we please go somewhere alone? I would rather not risk someone overhearing us."

Walt nodded down the hallway. "You can come up to my room and talk to me there."

"I'll go warn Danielle so she doesn't barge in on you two," Marie said. "I'll be right back." The spirit disappeared.

Silently, Claudia followed Walt up the stairs to his room. Once she entered the remodeled attic, she looked around, taking in the attractive apartment.

"Wow. You really do have a fairy godmother," Claudia murmured, still absorbing her surroundings.

"Excuse me?" Walt frowned.

"Landing here. From what your golden goose told me earlier, this used to be just an attic before she fixed it up for you. Must have cost a pretty penny."

"Did she just call Danielle a golden goose?" Marie asked when she popped back into the room. Walt glanced briefly at Marie and then back to Claudia.

With her fingertips tucked into the back pockets of her jeans, Claudia strolled around the room, inspecting every detail.

"Danielle didn't remodel the room for me," Walt lied. "She remodeled it to rent it out, and when I decided to stay in Frederickport, I asked her if I could rent it from her."

"Find out what she's up to!" Marie urged. "I don't trust her as far as I could throw her…and now that I think about it, I might actually be able to throw her."

Walt glanced to Marie. Their gazes met. He shook his head.

Marie let out a sigh. "Okay. I will behave myself. But I heard what you did to the new neighbor's hat."

Claudia stopped pacing and turned to face Walt. "Interesting that you can afford this place, since you aren't working. From what I know, you don't have an Oregon real estate license. Just how are you managing to support yourself? Oh, right, I forgot, you wrote a book." Claudia laughed and resumed her pacing around the room.

"Exactly how did we know each other?" Walt asked.

"I can't believe you don't recognize me, Clint."

"I go by Walt now."

Claudia stopped pacing and looked Walt in the eyes. Silently, she studied him.

"What do you want?" Walt asked.

Claudia smiled. "So you do recognize me?"

"Why doesn't she just get on with it?" Marie grumbled.

Walt shook his head. "No. But you obviously want something from me. How do we know each other?"

"Let's see…we first met when we got into real estate. Started at the same brokerage. Which is why I know you didn't write that book."

Walt arched his brows. "Why would us working together convince you I didn't write *Moon Runners*?"

Claudia shrugged. "To begin with, that's when you confessed to me you have dyslexia."

"Dyslexia? Clint had dyslexia?" Marie asked. "The man was a real estate agent, surely that can't be true. Goodness, Adam has to read all sorts of contracts."

"Like I told you, I don't remember you—or anything prior to the accident. I don't remember having a problem reading. In fact, I read fine. Should I read something to you?"

"What scam are you pulling, Clint?" she asked.

"I go by my first name now—*Walt*."

Claudia smiled at him. "You can call yourself whatever you want. And if you marry Danielle Boatman, you can call yourself a bigamist."

"What are you talking about?"

"What is she talking about?" Marie parroted.

"I'm your wife, Clint. You can't marry Danielle Boatman, you're already married to me." Claudia handed Walt the paper she had been holding.

Marie moved quickly to Walt's side and watched as he unfolded the wrinkled sheet of paper Claudia had just handed him. Reading over his shoulder, Marie let out a gasp. It appeared to be a Mexican marriage license—uniting in matrimony Walter Clint Marlow and Claudia Jean Dane. "That scoundrel was married?"

"Hello, darling, happy to see me?" Claudia purred.

Expressionless, Walt handed the document back to Claudia. "You and I are not married."

"You think the license is fake?" Marie asked. "Or did Clint get a divorce? Did he ever mention a wife? Maybe a divorce or annulment? I would think before turning over his body to you, he would have had the courtesy to mention a wife!"

Claudia's smile vanished. Rage mounting, she shook the marriage license in Walt's face and shrieked, "What do you think this is? And I guarantee you won't find a divorce decree—or annulment. Not if you check every state in the Union and Mexico, because you and I are still married! And if you want to marry your golden goose Boatman, then you'd better be prepared to offer me a generous—and I mean very generous—divorce settlement!"

Walt took a step back from the raging woman, maintaining his calm. "Is this what this is about? An attempt to extort?"

"Oh, dear…and to think you're already married to Danielle. Does that make you a bigamist?" Marie muttered.

"I'm not a bigamist," Walt said aloud.

Claudia found herself about to hyperventilate. She told herself to calm down. Taking deep breaths, she regained her composure. Looking up to Walt, she asked in a calm voice, "Does this mean you're calling off the marriage to Danielle?"

"I think he was talking to me, dear," Marie said dryly

"No. I am marrying Danielle."

"Perhaps you don't care about being a bigamist, but I doubt

your precious *fiancée* will appreciate marrying a man who already has a wife."

"I don't believe you're my wife," Walt said calmly.

"How can you be so sure?"

"After my accident, some of my new friends tried to help me remember by researching my life in California and sharing the results with me. A wife never came up."

"That's because we never told anyone about our marriage. I would prefer to keep it that way. Of course, I know I can't stop you if you decide to tell people, which might be easier if you refuse to give me what I want, and I don't agree to a divorce."

"Another reason I don't believe we were married is because, from what I know, I was deeply involved with Stephanie. We were going to Europe together, where we planned to marry. I would not have done that if I had been married to someone else."

"I thought you didn't remember Stephanie?"

"Did you know her?" Walt asked.

Claudia stared at Walt for a few moments before answering, "Yes. I knew Stephanie."

"And did she know you claimed to be my wife?"

"No. You and I agreed to keep that between the two of us."

"Why would we do that if I was planning to marry her?" Walt asked.

Claudia studied Walt for a moment. "We had our reason at the time. But it doesn't matter anymore. Stephanie is dead, and you don't remember me—or so you say. And if you want to marry your precious Danielle Boatman, then you will need my cooperation in a divorce. And trust me, that won't come cheap."

Clutching the marriage license, Claudia turned abruptly and marched to the door. Just as she reached for the door handle, her free hand flew to her right cheek and she let out a gasp. Twirling around, she looked to Walt, her eyes wide. He stood a good ten feet from her, watching. Without a word, she turned back to the door, opened it, and hurried from the room.

As Walt listened to Claudia make her way down the stairs to the second floor, he looked at Marie and arched his brows. "You slapped her, didn't you?"

Marie shrugged. "She deserved it."

SEVENTEEN

Giving up on the idea of an afternoon nap, Rachel decided she would just have to go to bed early tonight. After Claudia had left to find Clint, Rachel changed her clothes, putting on soft yoga pants, fuzzy socks, and an oversized sweatshirt. Danielle's cat napped on the center of her bed while she sat in a nearby chair, reading *Moon Runners*. She had purchased the book after Claudia had told her the author was Clint Marlow. This was the first chance she had to actually read it.

Rachel wished her room had a fireplace like Danielle's bedroom. Marlow House might be a charming old Victorian, yet she found it rather damp and chilly. Wrapping herself in a throw blanket she had found in the closet, she snuggled up in the chair, book in hand.

She was already starting the third chapter. Clint—or whoever had written the book—definitely knew how to pull a reader into a story. Rachel knew her sister was convinced Clint hadn't written *Moon Runners*, but if he hadn't, then who was the author? And why would the author let Clint take credit for the book—especially one that was obviously successful? Her sister's theory made no sense to her, yet she wasn't about to argue with Claudia about it. The last time she'd tried arguing with her sister, it didn't work out—she ended up driving to Oregon. Rachel turned the page just as her sister burst back into the room.

BOBBI HOLMES

"I talked to Clint!" Claudia said, slightly out of breath, slamming the door closed behind her and locking it.

Rachel quickly shut the book and discreetly covered it with the blanket on her lap. She looked up to her sister and smiled. "How did it go?"

Just as Rachel asked the question, she frowned, her eyes on Claudia's face. "What happened to your cheek?"

Claudia furrowed her brows. "What do you mean?"

"Your right cheek, it's bright red," Rachel explained.

Tossing the marriage certificate on her bed, Claudia touched her right cheek and rushed to the dresser to look in the mirror.

"It's red," Claudia murmured as she looked at her reflection, gently caressing her cheek.

"What happened?"

Claudia turned from the mirror. "I have no idea. But when I was leaving Clint's room, it felt like someone slapped me."

"Did Clint hit you?" Rachel sat up straighter in the chair.

"Goodness no. He wasn't even near me. And for all his faults, Clint would never hit me. But I'll admit, I was pretty upset after we talked, and I just ran out of the room. I must have knocked into something and didn't even realize it."

"So tell me, what did Clint say?" Rachel asked.

"I showed him the marriage license. I told him if he wanted a divorce from me, I would expect a generous settlement."

"How did he take it?"

"He insisted we weren't married while claiming he still has amnesia and can't remember anything prior to the accident."

"If you showed him the marriage license, and he admits he can't remember anything, how can he say that?"

"Wishful thinking on his part," Claudia said with a snort as she flopped down on her bed and leaned against the stack of pillows.

Max lifted his head, looked at the far wall, and meowed.

"Hello to you too," Marie greeted Max. "I see you're still here."

"So what now?" Rachel asked. "Do you think he'll say anything to Danielle?"

"I seriously doubt it. But if he does, I wouldn't be surprised if she just tells him to pay me off to get rid of me. Which would be a good thing."

"Do you think you might be playing a dangerous game?" Rachel asked.

"What do you mean? Dangerous how? If you think they're going to call the cops and charge me with extortion, that's not going to happen. For one thing, I have so much on Clint, he doesn't want to go there."

"But he doesn't know that—I mean, not if he really has amnesia. And I wasn't talking about him going to the police."

"What, then?"

"What is to stop him from—you know—getting rid of you?"

Claudia stared at her sister a moment and then started laughing. "Oh, come on now, get real. Clint is not going to knock me off."

"I don't suppose he would," Marie murmured, knowing neither woman could hear her. "I doubt he would want your spirit hanging around. Can't say I would want it lingering either."

"But I have another problem," Claudia snarled.

"What?"

"Dirk Thorpe is staying here. I ran into him in the hallway."

Rachel frowned. "Who's he?"

"I thought I told you…" Claudia paused a moment and then muttered, "I guess not," before saying, "He's just someone who worked with Clint. Not someone I like. You might say we've had some issues in the past."

"Why is he here?" Rachel asked.

"I can only guess," Claudia said under her breath.

AFTER CLAUDIA HAD RUSHED out of the attic, Walt took the hidden staircase to Danielle's room. According to Marie, that was where Danielle was waiting for him. Instead of discussing the recent events there, the two returned to the attic. Danielle sat quietly and listened to Walt tell her what had transpired between Claudia and him.

"Where's the marriage license?" Danielle asked when Walt finished the telling.

"I gave it back to her."

"Why would you do that? We need to see if it's real."

"It's not real," Walt insisted.

"That's not the point. If it isn't real, we need the license to prove it's fake."

Walt sighed wearily. "I understand that. It just wasn't what I expected to hear her tell me, and I—well, I reacted. I just handed it back to her. After she left, I realized that was not the wisest thing to do. But I'm certain she isn't married to Clint."

"Why are you so sure?" Danielle asked.

"Because I remember how Clint felt about Stephanie. She was the reason he didn't want to stay. He wanted to be with her. They were to be married. He was desperately in love with her," Walt reminded her.

"So? Maybe that's why he and Stephanie were going to Europe. Maybe Claudia refused to give him a divorce, and that's why they were leaving the country," Danielle suggested.

"If Clint was married, don't you think he would have said something to us?" Walt asked.

"I don't know. Maybe not. Not if Claudia was one of the reasons he wanted out. Maybe he was afraid you wouldn't help him if you thought you'd have to deal with her."

"I still find it odd that this would be the first we're hearing of a wife," Walt said. "Remember, both Ian and MacDonald did a background check on Clint, and neither one of them came across a prior marriage."

"The marriage license was from Mexico. I doubt they checked for marriages down there. Maybe it was a quickie marriage where they eloped, and then it didn't work out and they never told anyone," Danielle suggested.

"Then why not get an annulment?" Walt asked.

"Maybe they did get one—or maybe you're right and the wedding never happened. Or maybe Claudia, for whatever reason, refused to let him out of the marriage, and that's why they were intent on leaving the country. But either way, we need to start with that wedding license."

"I'll ask Claudia to see the license again."

"If she shows it to you, immediately take a picture of it with your phone in case she won't let you keep it or make a copy."

"I wouldn't be surprised if she won't let me see it again. If it is fake, I suspect she won't."

"Then what do we do? Do you remember where in Mexico the license was issued?" Danielle asked.

"There is another option." Walt chuckled at the thought.

Danielle perked up. "What?"

"Marie." He grinned. "Now that she's harnessed her energy and can move objects, then there is no reason she can't get ahold of the license for us."

Danielle smiled. "True. I didn't consider that. You think she can do it?"

"I don't see why not. Moving a piece of paper is not as difficult as moving a chair."

"Or a pot of boiling water." Danielle cringed.

"Are you still upset about that pot of water I tried to move?" Marie asked when she popped into the room, overhearing the tail end of their conversation.

"No. We were discussing how you've managed to harness your energy, and we have a favor to ask you."

"Whatever you need, but first, I think you should know Claudia knows Mr. Thorpe."

"So they did come here together," Danielle said.

Marie shook her head. "No. Claudia was telling her sister about running into Mr. Thorpe in the hallway, and she was surprised to find him here."

"Well, they're in the same business and are both from Huntington Beach," Walt noted. "Not surprising they know each other."

"Mr. Thorpe also knew Clint. He's up to something," Marie told them. "According to Claudia, he works at the same office Clint did, and she doesn't like him."

"I think we need to keep all our guests under observation until we figure this out," Walt suggested. He looked at Marie and asked, "Perhaps you might find Eva and see if she can lend us her ears. There is no way you can be in two guest rooms at once."

"Or maybe tell us where we might find Eva," Danielle suggested. "I think Marie needs to stay here and keep an eye on at least one room."

"Oh my, I must say it feels rather good to be needed!" Marie smiled. "As for Claudia and Rachel, Rachel is alone in their room, reading, and Claudia just left to get them takeout. So until she returns, I won't be hearing anything from them. They're both tired after that long trip and plan to eat in and go to bed early. As for the Thorpes, when I checked their room, Mrs. Thorpe was in the shower."

"Then perhaps you can listen in to the Thorpes after his wife gets out of the shower, and see if you can find out why he's really here," Walt suggested.

"And we can go find Eva. Any idea where she might be?" Danielle asked.

"I'm fairly certain she'll be at the museum. She mentioned she was going over there this afternoon. Of course, she might not still be there. Now, what was that other favor you wanted to ask me?"

"You know that marriage license Claudia showed me?" Walt asked.

"Yes. Of course. What about it?"

"We need to take a closer look at it. I was going to ask Claudia if I could see it again, but I'm afraid she won't let me—especially if it's fake."

"I saw it when I was over in their room. It was on Claudia's bed. It was still sitting there when she left to get food," Marie told them.

Walt and Danielle exchanged quick glances, and then Danielle said, "Marie, you think you can get the license and take it to my bedroom?"

"Exactly how do I get it out of the room? I can walk through walls, but I certainly can't move paper through walls, and as long as Rachel is in the room, even if I managed to get the license without her noticing, I think she would notice the door opening to get it out of the room."

"Slip it under the door," Walt suggested.

EIGHTEEN

Pulled into *Moon Runners'* world, Rachel turned another page. The author had transported her back in time to the 1920s, along the Oregon coast, where prohibition gave birth to a lucrative industry of party boats and moonshine. The meow broke her concentration, and she looked up from where she sat in the chair, wrapped in a blanket. The black cat jumped off the bed and sauntered to the closed door. He began pawing it, as if playing a drum, persistent in his relentless pounding.

"Okay, okay, hold on. I get your message." Rachel turned down the top corner of the page she was currently reading and stumbled to her feet, tangled in the blanket. Max continued to pound on the door.

"Stop already. Danielle is going to think I'm holding you prisoner," Rachel said as she tossed the book on the chair and made her way to the door. As soon as she opened it, Max raced from the room, disappearing down the hall. Rachel closed the door and locked it. She made her way back to the chair. But instead of sitting down again, she snatched up the book and blanket and walked to her bed. Climbing under the sheets and adding the blanket atop the bedspread and blankets already on the bed, Rachel cuddled up against the pile of pillows and opened the book. She began to read.

Rachel had been reading for a good fifteen minutes in bed when motion from the empty bed next to her caught her eye. Frozen, she continued to hold the book before her as if reading as she discreetly peered over it. Her eyes widened as she watched the marriage license float up from the empty bed and hover in midair for a moment, as if some invisible force was reading it.

Unable to breathe, Rachel clutched the book tighter as she slunk down deeper into the mattress, her body disappearing beneath the blankets. Caught in her throat was a scream she was too terrified to release. She watched in horror as the paper began to float downward and slide across the wood floor, making its way to the door. Rachel's teeth began to chatter, and her hands shook, still gripping the book as if it were a lifeline. She heard the doorknob rattle. Someone was unlocking it.

The next moment the door flew open and Claudia stepped into the room carrying two small paper bags of take-out food. Rachel released the scream she had been holding, startling Claudia, who then dropped the sacks. They landed on the floor, atop the marriage license.

"Good lord, Rachel! What is your problem? I imagine the entire house heard you!" Claudia leaned down to pick up the sacks her sister had caused her to drop. In doing so she spied the marriage license and picked it up. Rachel remained huddled in bed, speechless, her complexion white.

"What is this doing on the floor?" Claudia asked as she shut the bedroom door. With her purse hanging from one shoulder, she held the take-out sacks in one hand and the marriage license in the other.

"I think this place is haunted!" Rachel finally squeaked out.

"What are you talking about?" Claudia dropped the sacks and purse on the bed. She then folded the marriage license and shoved it in her purse.

Rachel pointed to the purse. "It floated off the bed!"

Claudia frowned. She picked up one of the sacks, looked inside, and then tossed it to her sister. "What in the world are you talking about?"

"The marriage license, it floated off the bed and it just hung in the air for a moment and then it slid across the floor like it was trying to get out of the room."

Claudia scowled at her sister. "Have you been smoking some of that Oregon pot?"

"I'm serious! I think this place is haunted! First the cat figurine and now this!" No longer holding the book, Rachel grabbed the top of the blankets and pulled them up under her chin.

"Rachel, you seriously need to get some sleep. This old house is drafty. Obviously a draft blew the license off the bed onto the floor. Ghosts? Phssshh…get real." Claudia rolled her eyes and plopped down on her bed. She picked up her sack and opened it.

"What about the cat figurine?"

Claudia pulled a wrapped burger from the bag. "What about it?"

"I saw it fall off the shelf, and then before it hit the floor, it went back up on the shelf. I saw it!"

"Sure you did." After unwrapping the burger, Claudia took a bite.

"I want to go home."

Claudia shook her head and took another bite. After she swallowed, she said, "We are not going home until we finish what we came here to do."

"I don't want to stay in this room!"

"You're being silly."

Rachel jumped up from the bed and grabbed the sack of food. "I'm going to go eat outside."

"It's freezing out there."

"Fine, I'll take my coat!" Angrily, Rachel dropped the sack back on her bed and grabbed her coat. After she put it on, she picked up her sack of food and the book and stormed out of the room.

DANIELLE AND WALT had decided one of them needed to stay home while the other one went to find Eva. They didn't feel comfortable leaving their guests alone—considering some were at Marlow House under false pretenses. Even with Marie there, they felt one of them needed to stay.

Danielle insisted she be the one, while Walt went to find Eva. Her reasoning, she didn't want Walt to have to confront any of them again until after they could find out more about their motives. Walt, however, felt he needed to be the one to stay. While he didn't believe any of them were a physical threat to Danielle, he did not want to take any chances since they had lied to them. Walt ended up getting his way, and it was Danielle who went off to find Eva.

Walt sat in the side yard on one of the two patio chairs, sitting under a shade tree, intending to read a book. Because of the position of the late afternoon sun, the tree threw no shade, which suited him, considering the nippy weather. While most would probably find it too chilly to be sitting outside, he found the brisk air invigorating, reminding him he was alive—truly alive. He had just opened the book when Max came out the pet door from the kitchen. The cat joined him, making himself comfortable on Walt's lap.

A few minutes earlier Walt had spied Claudia's car pulling up in front of the house. Glancing up to the second floor, he could see Dirk walking around in the bedroom.

PEARL HAD JUST RETURNED the rake to the toolshed when motion from the neighbor's side yard caught her eye. Curious, she walked over to the property line separating her yard and Marlow House and looked through the wrought-iron fencing, concealing herself behind a large rosebush growing on the Boatman side of the property line. She spied Walt Marlow sitting on a patio chair with the useless black cat in his lap. They still let the thing come and go as it pleased; she often heard the swinging of the metal pet door. It was only a matter of time before it came back over in her yard and started digging up her flower garden and leaving behind disgusting droppings.

But a troublesome feline was not the only thing annoying Pearl these days. Cars had been coming and going all day long next door, and she resented the fact Marlow House had turned her neighborhood into a business district. Pearl had dreamed of owning her home—this particular home—for as long as she could recall. The dream did not include a wannabe motel just next door, in what should be an exclusive residential neighborhood.

The house she had just purchased had originally belonged to her maternal grandmother. Pearl cherished her childhood memories, spending summers with her grandmother in Frederickport. Back then, Marlow House had been vacant, and the house on the other side of the property had been occupied by an elderly couple. When Pearl was a teenager, her grandmother had passed away, and the property was left to her mother and her mother's only sibling, Aunt Sally. To Pearl's dismay, her parents could not afford the luxury of a beach house and had sold their share to Aunt Sally and her husband.

Pearl continued to visit the property, yet not as frequently as when her grandmother had been alive. While her aunt and uncle—and later her cousins—invited her to visit them at the beach house, she resented the fact her parents had sold their share of the property.

Her visits to the Frederickport beach house had ended five years earlier, with the death of Aunt Sally's last living child. The house then went to the grandchildren, who—according to all reports—did not get along. After five years of bickering over the property, they finally decided to sell. Pearl, who had always been open about the fact she would be willing to purchase the beach house if they ever decided to sell, was the first person they contacted.

However, they failed to disclose the changes in the neighborhood since her last visit. Marlow House was not only occupied now; it was an inn. Pearl was not happy with the changes. She wanted it to go back to how she remembered.

Standing on her tiptoes to look over the rosebush to get a better look, her nose practically sticking between two wrought-iron spires, Pearl peered into her neighbor's side yard. She could hear the breakers beyond the houses across the street, and when Walt Marlow started talking to the cat a moment later, she could hear that too.

NINETEEN

Walt could feel the temperature drop. Only about an hour of sunlight was left in the day, and then it would be time to start thinking of dinner. Chilly weather and meals to eat were in the category of shaving for Walt. Those were among the things he hadn't seriously considered for almost a century.

He glanced down at Max, who curled up on his lap, making himself comfortable. "What have you been up to today? I haven't seen you all afternoon." Walt gently stroked the cat's back.

Max looked up and blinked.

"Really? She took you in her room? Was she nice to you?"

Max rubbed the side of his face against Walt's left hand and began to purr.

"Did you see Marie when you were up there?"

Max meowed.

It wasn't necessary for Walt to talk out loud when communicating with the cat—it wasn't the words Max understood, it was the mental telepathy conveyed between the two. However, Walt had grown accustomed to vocalizing his end of the conversation, primarily for the benefit of Danielle or his friends who knew of his background. He, of course, never did this when around those who believed he had once been Clint. But he was alone now, out of earshot from curious listeners, or so he assumed, so he thought nothing of verbally expressing the thoughts he conveyed to the cat.

"Marie had something to lift from one of our troublesome guests. I hope she was able to get it out of the room without anyone seeing."

Max blinked at Walt.

"Are you sure? If she put it in her purse, it's going to be harder for Marie to get her hands on it."

Walt laughed at Max's reply.

"She told you all that? Where was she? Oh, spying on the other guests. I wonder if she's hiding in their room now." Walt laughed again. "Yes, hiding in plain sight."

Walt heard the kitchen door open and close. He stopped talking and looked toward the house while stroking the length of the cat's back. It was Rachel—Claudia's sister. She wore a heavy jacket and knit cap over her spiky hair, carrying a book in one hand and a paper sack in the other. She glanced around as if deciding where to sit. Walt didn't think she had noticed him yet—sitting under the tree, partially concealed by some shrubbery between him and the house. Her attention was focused on a portable yard swing located on the far side of the yard, near the fencing separating Marlow House from their unfriendly neighbor. It sat in the open sunshine. Rachel started walking for the swing.

"The seat will be wet," Walt called out just as she started to pass by him.

Jumping at his voice, she turned to face him.

"Sorry if I startled you," Walt apologized. "But I noticed you were heading to the swing, and I'm afraid its seat is always damp this time of year. I warned Danielle it will probably be moldy come spring."

"I didn't see you sitting there," Rachel stammered. She then noticed the cat sitting on his lap. Hesitantly, she walked toward him.

"You're welcome to sit here." Walt nodded to the empty chair next to him. "Non-upholstered chairs tend to be better this time of year unless you want a soaked backside. Plus, the sunshine feels pretty good."

"I thought you hated cats," Rachel blurted. She then cringed, regretting her hastily uttered words.

"So you and I knew each other too?" Walt asked in a quiet voice.

Rachel stepped closer and eyed the empty chair before looking back at Walt. "You really do have amnesia?"

"If not knowing anything about Clint's life before the car accident—aside from what I've been told—means I have amnesia, then yes." He nodded toward the chair again.

Rachel sat down, the book resting on her lap, and the paper sack atop it.

Walt glanced briefly to the book's spine peeking out from under the sack and then looked up to Rachel's face. "You're reading *Moon Runners*?"

Rachel blushed. "After Claudia told me about it, I was curious. I just started it today."

Walt smiled. "I hope you enjoy it."

Rachel clutched the book and looked sheepishly up to Walt. "I really am. Claudia doesn't think you wrote it."

"And what do you think?" Walt asked.

Rachel shrugged. "If you didn't write it, I would think the author would sue you. Especially now since they're making a movie out of it."

"Did we know each other well?" Walt asked.

"Not really. I only met you a couple of times."

Walt studied Rachel's expression. "According to your sister, she and I are married."

"That's between you and Claudia. I don't want to get involved." Rachel turned her attention to the sack sitting on her lap atop the book. She opened it and pulled out a wrapped burger.

"Did you go to the wedding?"

Rachel looked down at her food and shook her head. "She showed you the license. It's from Mexico. I've never been to Mexico."

"So we eloped? Was anyone else there? I'm afraid I didn't pay close attention to the license when she showed it to me. I wonder who the witnesses were."

Rachel took a bite of her burger and sat quietly for a moment. Finally, she said, "You'll have to ask my sister about that. I really don't know much more than what she has told you." She took another bite.

"If you didn't know me well, why did you say I didn't like cats?"

Holding her partially eaten burger, she looked over to Walt. "My sister doesn't care for dogs or cats. I remember once she told me you had that in common. I like animals. I never understood why

Claudia didn't, but I guess she found a soul mate in you in that regard."

"Interesting. I guess the amnesia made me forget my dislike for animals," Walt said with a smile, still stroking Max's back. "I'm rather partial to them now."

"Can I ask you a question?" Rachel asked.

"Go ahead."

"Have you told Danielle what Claudia told you today?"

Walt studied Rachel a moment before answering. "No," he lied.

"Don't you think she should know? I mean, if you have amnesia, then it really isn't your fault you don't remember being married. Doesn't Danielle deserve to know?"

"Does your sister expect me to tell her?" Walt asked.

Rachel shrugged. "I think she might tell her if you decide to ignore all this and go ahead and get married."

"If that's true, why didn't she tell Stephanie? Surely she knew Stephanie and I were on our way to Europe to get married."

"I don't know. Like I said, I really don't want to get involved. I shouldn't have asked you the question in the first place." Rachel shivered and pulled her jacket around her tighter while holding what remained of her burger in the other hand.

"I'm curious, why are you sitting outside in the cold eating, when you could be inside where it's warm? I believe there's a fire burning in the living room fireplace," Walt told her.

Rachel studied Walt a moment before responding. "You've lived here since your accident, haven't you?"

"Technically speaking, I lived here several weeks before the accident, but I don't remember that time. Why do you ask?"

"Have you ever noticed anything—umm—odd in the house?" Rachel asked.

Walt frowned. "Odd how?"

"Like objects moving on their own?" Rachel asked.

Walt smiled. "Can you give me an example."

"I'm not crazy. Claudia says I'm imagining things, but I swear I saw that cat figurine in our room fall to the floor—but before it got there, it went back on the shelf. And then right before my sister came back with the food, I saw a piece of paper floating in the air."

"Really?"

Rachel scowled. "You think I'm crazy." She took an angry bite of her burger.

"No, I don't. You're not the first person to claim to have seen unusual activity in Marlow House. You know—some say it's haunted."

"Are you making fun of me?"

"No," Walt said seriously. "A number of people have claimed the house is haunted."

"I suggested that to Claudia, and she thought I was being silly."

"You do know a number of people have been murdered in that house?" Walt glanced over to Marlow House and felt a twinge of hypocrisy, which he immediately dismissed. There was a time he would have been offended at someone exploiting the events that had transpired under his roof—no matter how true, especially when it came to his own death. One change he noticed about himself since rejoining this side, he wasn't as sensitive about his death as he had once been.

Rachel's eyes widened. "Murdered? Who was murdered?"

"I'm surprised you don't know. Most of our guests are familiar with the house's history before they even check in. Everything is online."

"Our guests? You talk as if you're already married to Danielle Boatman and this is your house."

Walt shrugged. "I am related to the original owners—and my name is Marlow—so I suppose I do feel a sense of ownership."

UPSTAIRS, Dirk stood at the bedroom window and looked out at the side yard. He watched Walt and Rachel, who sat together under a large tree. He wondered what they could be talking about. Sitting at the dressing table was his wife, Tanya, who was busy applying makeup and fixing her hair so they could go out to dinner. On the bed Marie sat quietly, waiting for them to say something she might find useful. So far, their conversation had been painfully boring and unhelpful.

"What are you looking at?" Tanya asked as she studied her reflection while running a brush through her hair.

"Clint is outside with Claudia's sister; they're talking." Standing with arms akimbo, Dirk continued to stare out the window.

"If Clint really has amnesia, what are you going to do?" Tanya asked.

THE GHOST WHO WAS SAYS I DO

"We spend the week refreshing his memory."

"And if he doesn't remember?"

"It would be easier for me if he remembers. But ultimately it really doesn't matter if he remembers or not. I'll simply show him the file."

"Remember what?" Marie asked, frustrated that they weren't elaborating.

"If you're going to take a shower before you go, you should probably do that now," Tanya told her husband.

Once Dirk left the room to shower, Marie saw no reason to stick around. If Danielle was able to find Eva, she might be following Dirk and his wife to the restaurant to eavesdrop, or perhaps they would want her to stay close to Claudia and her sister. But first—she needed to try for that marriage license again.

JUST AS CLAUDIA opened her bedroom door, she spied Dirk going into the bathroom. He didn't see her. He carried a change of clothes, and she assumed he was planning to take a shower. What she didn't see was Marie, who stood inches away in the open doorway, about to enter her bedroom.

Walking through Marie, Claudia stepped out into the hallway and closed the door behind her, locking it. She then headed downstairs.

Shivering over the unpleasant sensation of Claudia stomping through her illusion—more a mental than physical unpleasantness—Marie shook it off and was somewhat appeased by the fact Claudia hadn't been carrying a purse. Marie smiled and thought, *She must have left it in the bedroom.* A moment later Marie walked through the door into the bedroom, in search of the marriage license.

In the bathroom, Dirk had just finished unbuttoning his shirt when he realized he had left his shaving kit in the bedroom. Cursing the oversight, he hastily rebuttoned the shirt and made his way back to the bedroom to retrieve the shaving kit.

A few minutes later, on the return to the bathroom, movement down the hallway caught his eye. He stopped walking and looked to the source of the movement. At first he thought it was a mouse or some rodent scurrying along by the baseboard. It appeared to be a flash of white. But when he looked closer, he realized it was not a mouse—it was a folded piece of paper.

He assumed someone had simply dropped the paper, and a draft was now blowing it down the hallway. Intending to go pick it up, he stopped suddenly when the paper took a sudden right turn and flew under the door to Danielle's bedroom, as if it had been sucked into the room by some invisible force.

TWENTY

Danielle wanted to get to the museum before it closed for the evening. Yet, even if she did arrive before they locked their doors, there was no guarantee Eva would still be there. On the drive over she had called Chris to let him know she needed to talk to Eva. These days, the spirit didn't stray far from Chris. According to him, he had seen her that morning, and when she showed up again, he promised he would give her Danielle's message.

Stepping into the museum, Danielle was greeted by Millie Samson, who was on docent duty.

"You're here rather late," the elderly woman greeted Danielle. "Did you need to talk to me about something?"

"No. I was just in the neighborhood, and I thought I'd stop by and see the portraits before you closed," Danielle lied. "Chris mentioned there had been some changes to the exhibit."

"I must say, the portraits have been a boom for the museum. Ben would be so happy," Millie said with a sigh.

"At least he got to see the display open," Danielle reminded her.

"True. But it really is not the same without him. Ben is sorely missed."

"Yes, he is. He was a big part of the historical society." Danielle tried to be pleasant, but she wasn't sure she would ever feel the same about the members of the historical society board again, including Millie. It wasn't that she blamed them for their ancestors' sins, but she was deeply disappointed they had gone to such lengths to rewrite their history.

Millie nodded to the main section of the museum. "There's someone back there now, looking at the portraits. If you'll excuse me, I need to do something in the gift shop."

When Danielle arrived at the new section of the museum, which had been built to house the Bonnet exhibit, she found whom she was looking for. Eva sat perched atop her portrait, dressed in the same outfit she had worn when sitting for the painting. Unfortunately, she was not alone. Standing nearby, looking at the portrait of Walt Marlow, was a short little balding man Danielle had never seen before. Eva waved gaily at Danielle and, when doing so, sent pink snowflakes into the air. They floated down and disappeared before hitting the floor.

Hearing Danielle approach, the man looked her way.

"Hello," Danielle greeted the man. "Are you a fan of Jacque Jehan Bonnet?"

"Who is that?" the man asked with a frown.

Eva rolled her eyes and looked to Danielle. "He has been standing there for ten minutes cursing at that portrait."

Danielle frowned at Eva's comment yet said nothing. After all, the man could neither see nor hear Eva. She looked back to him and said, "That's the name of the artist."

He shrugged. "I don't really care about art. But I read about this portrait online, and I had to see it for myself."

Afraid Eva might decide to leave before she could talk to her, Danielle said, "I'm looking for my friend Eva. She was supposed to meet me here. You haven't seen another woman in here, have you?"

"You need to talk to me?" Eva asked.

Danielle nodded at the ghost and then glanced back to the man.

"Just the woman who works here," the man said, staring intently at the painting.

"May I ask why you're so interested in that portrait?" Danielle asked.

"It looks just like someone I know," the man said. "I still can't believe how much it looks like him."

"Really?" Danielle studied the man a moment. He continued to be mesmerized by the portrait. "You're not from Frederickport, are you?"

The man shook his head. "No. I'm not."

Before Danielle could ask him another question, he turned abruptly and left the exhibit.

"Such an odd little man," Eva said as she floated down from the portrait and landed her feet on the floor.

"I wonder who he knows that looks like Walt," Danielle muttered, looking to where the man had just walked off to.

"Clint of course," Eva said.

Danielle looked to Eva. "Clint? He knew Clint?"

"I have to assume so. When ranting at the portrait, he kept calling it Clint. I don't think they were friends."

Danielle let out a sigh. "What is going on? The last few days people from Clint's past keep popping up!"

Eva shrugged. "That was inevitable. Especially with all the publicity Walt has been receiving. If anyone knows what it's like to live in the limelight, it's me!" Eva threw out her arms dramatically, and in doing so bursts of light filled the room, reminding Danielle of camera lightbulbs flashing.

Danielle blinked her eyes, certain she was going to be seeing white flashes for the next hour. She suddenly missed the glitter. Maybe it did play havoc with her coffee, but flashing lights were more annoying.

"Now what did you need?" Eva asked.

"Can you come home with me, and I'll explain in the car on the way over?"

"Certainly."

"You didn't happen to catch that man's name, or where he's staying?" Danielle asked.

"No, but Millie brought him in to the exhibit, so I assume they may have chatted before he got here. I didn't hear their conversation. Right after she brought him to the exhibit, the phone rang in the back office, and she went to answer it. That's when he started ranting at the painting—when he thought he was alone."

"In his rants, what did he say exactly?" Danielle asked.

Eva shrugged. "He said he couldn't believe there were two of them, that one was too many, and that he was a snake oil salesman."

"Umm...no, I guess they weren't friends. Anything more specific, like why he thought Clint was a snake oil salesman?"

"Sorry, that was about it. Although I can understand his sentiment. Clint was running a scam on your Bonnets."

"Hmmm. Why don't I meet you in my car? I want to ask Millie something before I leave."

A few minutes later Danielle found Millie in the gift shop, preparing to shut down for the day.

"The exhibit is impressive, isn't it?" Millie asked when Danielle stepped up to the counter.

"Yes, it is. I was wondering, do you know who that man was who just left here?" Danielle asked.

Millie glanced up. "A tourist. He mentioned he was staying at the Seahorse Motel. Why?"

"Nothing really. He just looked rather familiar," Danielle lied.

"We had a nice chat, and he introduced himself. His name is Albert Hanson. Is that name familiar?" Millie asked.

Danielle shook her head. "Umm, no...it's not familiar."

"He's a good example of how the Bonnet exhibit has attracted new visitors to the museum."

"How do you mean?" Danielle asked.

"The Bonnet exhibit was the only thing he was interested in seeing. He told me he saw the portraits online, and since he was here for the week, he wanted to see them in person. He must be a Bonnet fan."

"Did he tell you that?" Danielle asked.

"No, but I have to assume. Of course, he might just be a fan of fine art. Either way, it's all good for the museum."

ON THE WAY home from the museum, Danielle picked up Chinese food for her and Walt. When she arrived back at Marlow House with Eva, Dirk's car was nowhere in sight, but Claudia's vehicle was parked out front. Danielle took the food up to the attic while Eva went into Claudia and Rachel's room to eavesdrop. According to Walt, Marie had tagged along with Dirk and his wife in hopes of learning why they were really in Frederickport.

Danielle sat at Walt's computer with a carton of chow mein, eating it with chopsticks while doing a little online sleuthing. Sitting next to the computer on the desk was the marriage license Marie had managed to lift. Danielle and Walt inspected the license, yet didn't learn anything new.

"What are you hoping to find now?" Walt asked from where he

sat on a nearby chair, a plate of Chinese food in one hand, a pair of chopsticks in the other.

"I'd like to find out more about our guests, but first I want to see if I can find something about that man I ran into at the museum. I can't believe all the people from Clint's past popping up right now. I suppose any of them could have sent you that letter."

She searched quietly for a few minutes and then said, "Nothing. I even searched images for Albert Hanson. Nothing comes up that looks remotely like the man in the museum. Let me search our guests now. Since they're both real estate agents, I'm sure they have some online presence." A moment later the results popped up. Danielle quickly clicked through the links. After opening the second webpage, she said, "Marie was right."

Walt looked up. "What did you find?"

"Dirk Thorpe works for the same brokerage Clint worked for before coming to Oregon."

"How long has he worked there?" Walt asked.

"According to this website, it looks like he's been there over ten years. He's an associate broker. Why didn't he just come out and say he knew you? Doesn't he know there's a good chance I might Google my guests to learn more about them? And then I would know he lied about knowing you."

"He didn't lie exactly. He didn't say whether he knew Clint or not," Walt reminded her. "Anything else interesting?"

"Not really. Let me Google Claudia now."

A moment later Danielle said, "Maybe she and Clint started at the same brokerage, but it looks like they haven't worked for the same real estate company for a few years. According to her webpage, she has been with her current broker for over five years. Both she and Dirk are active real estate agents."

EVA THOUGHT she was going to die of boredom. Which was of course redundant, considering she was already dead. Yawning dramatically, she reclined on an imaginary chaise lounge, floating in midair over the dresser while smoking a cigarette held in a long bejeweled cigarette holder. To ward off the boredom, she tried blowing smoke rings.

Rachel, who sat on her bed quietly reading *Moon Runners*, looked up and wrinkled her nose. "I thought this place was nonsmoking?"

Claudia, who lounged on her bed, reading a magazine, looked up and sniffed. "Someone is smoking."

Rachel jumped up from the bed and ran to the door. "I hope it isn't a fire!" She opened the door and stuck her nose out in the hallway and sniffed. A moment later she pulled her head back in the room and shut the door. "It's just in here."

"Someone must have smoked in here. I hate that." Claudia closed her magazine and tossed it on the end of the bed.

Hearing the discussion, Eva arched her brows. With a snap of her fingers, the cigarette and the smell vanished. "I'm rather impressed with myself. They actually noticed it!"

Claudia sniffed the air again. "I don't smell it anymore."

"Weird." Rachel closed her book and looked to her sister. "What are you going to do tomorrow? Just hang around and wait for Clint to do what you want? And now with Dirk here, sheesh, maybe we should just go home."

"I was thinking about that." Claudia jumped up and walked to the dresser where she had set her purse. She opened it. "Maybe I'll just show this to Danielle."

"The license?"

"Where is it?" Frantically, Claudia took her purse to the bed and dumped out all its contents.

"What's wrong?"

"I put the marriage license in my purse, and it's gone!"

"Are you sure?"

"Yes, I'm sure! Look yourself!"

Rachel got up from her bed and walked to Claudia's. "Calm down. It didn't just walk away—" Rachel froze at her own words and looked down at the contents of Claudia's purse strewn all over the bed.

"No, it didn't walk away. Someone took it! I bet Clint stole it!"

Rachel considered her sister's accusation for a moment. Finally, she said, "Claudia, Clint couldn't have taken it. Clint was downstairs in the backyard until Danielle came home. You were already up here in the bedroom. He would have had to have taken it while you were in the room."

Claudia stood silently, considering her sister's words. After a few moments of silent pondering, her eyes widened and she looked to the closed bedroom door. "Dirk!"

"Dirk?" Rachel frowned.

"The only people upstairs who could've taken it were Dirk or his wife. They were the only ones up here. Damn him. He stole the marriage license! This is not good!"

TWENTY-ONE

While Rachel and Claudia slept, Marie returned the marriage license to Claudia's purse. Danielle didn't feel it necessary to keep the original after making a copy of it, and she didn't want to cause a problem with Claudia when she noticed it missing. She had no idea if it was real, and despite her attempt to Google for the answer, she found nothing conclusive.

The next morning, Claudia woke up thinking about the marriage license, convinced Dirk was the one responsible for taking it. She was still thinking of the missing license when she stepped out into the hall and started for the bathroom just as Dirk was coming out of his room.

"Good morning, Claudia," he said briskly as he turned to the stairs.

"You were in my room," she accused.

Dirk stopped walking and turned back to Claudia. "Excuse me?"

"I want it back."

"I have no idea what you're talking about."

"What do you think you're going to do with it?" she demanded.

"Claudia, I have absolutely no idea what you're talking about. Get a grip." With that, Dirk turned and headed for the staircase again.

Claudia stood alone in the hallway, fuming as she watched him head downstairs.

"Ready to go down for breakfast?" Rachel asked when Claudia returned to the bedroom.

"If Walt and Dirk are going to be at the table, it will be pretty darn awkward," Claudia said as she grabbed her purse off the dresser.

"This entire week is going to be awkward," Rachel said.

With a shrug Claudia opened her purse, intending to retrieve her brush so she could straighten her hair before heading downstairs. She reached her hand in the purse and froze. "It's here!"

"What's here?" Rachel asked, standing by the door, waiting for her sister so they could go downstairs.

"The marriage license! It's here!"

Rachel's eyes widened. "It came back by itself?"

Claudia glanced up at her sister and rolled her eyes. "Don't be ridiculous. I must have overlooked it."

"Overlooked it? You dumped your purse out on the bed. How could you have overlooked it?"

"Obviously I did, because here it is." Claudia pulled the folded document from the purse and waved it at her sister before tucking it in a pocket of her handbag.

"There is something strange about this house." Rachel looked around nervously.

"Oh please, you're not going to start with the haunted thing again, are you?"

"Clint told me some believe this house is haunted. Did you know people have been murdered here?"

"Clint told you it's haunted? When?"

"I talked to him a little bit when I went outside to eat last night."

"Clint is just brimming with scams, isn't he? I guess the newest one—right after claiming he wrote a book he's incapable of writing—is that Marlow House is haunted. I imagine that would make a great tourist attraction."

"THIS IS GOING to be an uncomfortable breakfast," Danielle told Walt as she filled the pastry tray, and he poured freshly brewed coffee from the pot into the serving carafe.

"Sadly our two guests who didn't know my cousin have chosen to have breakfast with their family, so that just leaves the Dane sisters and the Thorpes."

"Perhaps they'll decide not to come down for breakfast?" Danielle said hopefully.

"I'm afraid not. Mrs. Thorpe is already sitting at the table, reading the newspaper and waiting for her husband to join her," Walt told her.

"Oh drat," Danielle grumbled.

"I'm a little tired of this game playing and everyone claiming to be someone they aren't," Walt told her as he picked up the carafe.

Arching her brows, Danielle turned to Walt. "What exactly do you mean?"

"Everyone pretending not to know each other. At breakfast, I'm going to let them know I know they knew Clint."

"Ummm…if you plan to—well, end the game playing—as you call it—you also intend to tell them you aren't really Clint? That you were a ghost and took over his body?"

Walt frowned at Danielle. "What, are you goofy?"

Danielle shrugged and picked up the pastry tray. "Just checking."

WHEN DANIELLE and Walt arrived at the dining room table, the Dane sisters and the Thorpes were already seated, drinking coffee.

"I brought more coffee," Walt said as he set the carafe on the center of the table with the pastries Danielle had just placed there. Their guests quietly watched as Walt and Danielle brought out the rest of the breakfast, which included scrambled eggs, bacon, hash browns, and biscuits and gravy. By their curious expressions watching Walt, Danielle suspected Clint had not been the type to help serve a meal.

"Do you always do all the cooking?" Dirk asked Danielle when she sat down at the table a moment later.

"No. I have a woman who works for me, and she does some of the cooking. But she wasn't feeling well, so I told her to stay home this morning," Danielle explained.

"And do you often help with the guests?" Dirk asked Walt.

Walt smiled at Dirk and said, "I try to help."

"Interesting," Dirk muttered under his breath as he piled scrambled eggs on his plate.

"I think it might be a good idea to clear the air—since you all intend to stay for the next week," Walt announced.

Dirk furrowed his brows. "Excuse me?"

"I still have amnesia, and I don't remember anything of my life prior to the accident; however, it has come to my attention that I knew all of you." Walt paused and then looked at Mrs. Thorpe. "I will amend that; I'm only assuming you and I have met since I worked with your husband." Walt smiled pleasantly.

"I don't understand. If you say you have amnesia, then how—" Dirk began.

"I told him," Danielle interrupted. All heads turned to face her.

"You? How would you know?" Dirk asked.

Danielle smiled at Dirk. "You've been in the real estate business for a while; don't tell me there hasn't been a time you were curious about one of your clients, so you Googled them to see if you could find anything?"

Dirk arched his brows and smiled at Danielle. "You Googled me?"

"Yes. And it seems you work for the same real estate office Clint worked for, so I have to assume you knew each other."

Dirk smiled at Danielle and glanced to Walt. "Yes, we worked for the same office. But I will have to say, we were not actually friends—simply colleagues. We never ran with the same crowd. And to be honest, I don't think we spoke with each other more than a couple of times—aside from having an occasional real estate deal together."

"Did you know Walt would be at Marlow House when you made the reservation?" Danielle asked.

Dirk looked at Danielle for a moment before answering. Finally, he said, "I knew Clint was staying here, yes."

"If you say you and Clint weren't really friends, then why did you come to Marlow House?" Danielle asked.

"I didn't say I came here because of him." Dirk picked up his coffee cup and took a sip.

Walt turned his attention to Claudia and said, "It seems Claudia and I were also acquainted in my other life."

"Other life?" Dirk chuckled.

"That's how it feels." Walt shrugged.

"And exactly how did you know Claudia?" Dirk asked.

"I suspect you also know her—but that's just a hunch on my part." Walt smiled. "But it seems she and I started out at the same real estate company."

Claudia glared at Walt but said nothing.

WHILE PEARL WAS STILL unhappy about the bed and breakfast next door, she was pleased there had been no sign of any cats rooting around in her yard since having a little talk with her neighbors. She also had not seen any stray dogs since she had been forced to lock the golden retriever in her toolshed.

Pearl dreamed of returning her yard to its former glory—including an addition of rosebushes to replace what her cousins had removed. She intended to devote Saturday morning to taking inventory of her plants, along with planning what needed to be added. Walking the perimeter of the property, Pearl came to the back of the yard. She looked over the fence at the garage her neighbors had added. She frowned. When she had been a young girl, there had been nothing back there. She remembered playing in the vacant yard with her cousins, believing it was their own private jungle. With a snort, she remembered what she had overheard Walt Marlow telling that woman about the house being haunted.

"Ghosts," she huffed. "What a bunch of poppycock."

Pearl noticed a withering rosebush on her side of the back fence, near the Marlow House property line. Walking to the bush, she knelt down and pulled the rose clippers out of the pocket of her gardening apron. The sad little plant had once been one of her grandmother's prized rosebushes. Determined to save it, she snipped off some of the dead foliage and then heard footsteps. Still kneeling by the bush, she looked up and spied Walt Marlow walking to the garage.

WALT GLANCED AT HIS WATCH. They had finished breakfast twenty minutes earlier, and now he was on his way to get his car so he could take it to the car wash. Before leaving, he had helped Danielle with the dishes, and with Eva and Marie at the house, he didn't feel uncomfortable about leaving her at home alone for an hour while he ran a few errands.

Just as he reached the side door to the garage, he heard someone call his name. Pausing, he looked back to his house and spied Claudia sprinting his way.

"Do you need something?" Walt asked when she reached him.

"I want to know what you intend to do about our marriage," Claudia asked.

"I need to think about it," Walt told her, telling himself he would stop by the chief's house and see if he knew how to help them determine if the license was real—and if Clint was still married.

"What is there to think about? If you want to marry Danielle Boatman, you can't do that until you divorce me," she said in a loud voice.

"Please, Claudia, can we talk about this when I come back?" he asked.

"I don't know what you're waiting for. Do you want a divorce or not?"

"You know that's not the point."

"Listen, Clint, if you don't make a decision about our marriage, then I will make that decision for you. I will show Danielle the marriage license and see what she wants to do. If she decides she doesn't want to marry some guy who already has a wife, then I bet you'll have to start looking for someplace new to live. And maybe I'll just let your fans know you were courting a woman while still married to someone else. I wonder if that producer will still want to make your movie if they know you're practically a bigamist!"

"You're being ridiculous. Everyone knows I have amnesia, and if you're really my wife, it's hardly my fault I didn't know I was married," he said in a low voice, practically a whisper.

"You don't seem anxious to get a divorce. I think you're just pulling another scam. You're good at scams, Clint Marlow. Just like that book of yours. Making everyone believe you actually wrote it, when I know for a fact you didn't write a single word of it!"

"You are being utterly ridiculous now," Walt snapped.

"Am I? I'll tell you what, I'm not going to wait around all week for you to make up your mind. If you want that divorce, then you'd better give me what I want."

TWENTY-TWO

Sitting on an imaginary sofa floating in midair, Eva leaned back leisurely and filed her nails while listening in on the conversation between Dirk and his wife, Tanya. So far, all she had overheard was the wife complaining about being stuck inside and wanting to go shopping.

"Clint isn't even here," Tanya reminded him as she sat at the dressing table and leaned closer to the mirror, applying more makeup.

"He just went to wash his car. You heard what he told Danielle, he's coming right back." Dirk sat on the edge of the bed, watching his wife.

Tanya turned around on the bench and faced her husband. "This is a nice little town and all, but it's hardly the ideal vacation getaway for January. Maybe if it was in the summer and there was at least a hint of sun, I wouldn't be opposed to spending the week here. I don't know why you can't show the paper to Clint and get on with it."

Eva looked up from her filing. "I agree with your wife. Out with it so I can find something more enjoyable to do."

"I explained it before. After seeing Clint for myself and talking to him, I believe he does have amnesia. He's not that good of an actor."

"So? It doesn't mean you can't just tell him what you know."

"But what if he doesn't believe me?" he asked.

"You have the proof. Show it to him. I don't care if he does have amnesia, he's still not going to want any of it to go public and risk going to jail."

"Do we really know that? At breakfast he talked about his time in California as if it was another life. Hell, he's even going by another name."

"So?"

"So instead of giving me what I intend to ask for—something that he can easily afford given his current turn of fortune—there is always the possibility he might go to the police instead. And then he's not the only criminal, I am too. Last I heard, blackmail is illegal."

"He wouldn't go to the police...would he?" She frowned.

"I honestly don't know. But I don't want to risk it. I believe that if his memory comes back—it will seem more real to him. At the moment, he's detached from his life as Clint—detached from his actions back then. I need to make him feel there's a real chance he'll be held accountable if he doesn't give me what I want."

"Then this might be a wasted trip. The man has had amnesia for almost a year now, and if he hasn't regained his memory, what makes you think he suddenly will now?" she asked.

"For one thing, he's been cut off from all the people he knew when he lived in California. Now that I think about it, it's probably a good thing Claudia is here. Being surrounded by people he once knew before he lost his memory might be what he needs."

"And just why is Claudia here?" she asked.

"I have to assume for basically the same reason we are."

"I just hope this entire thing doesn't blow up in your face."

"Come on, it worked out with Claudia, didn't it?" He grinned.

"Which is one reason I don't feel comfortable being under the same roof with her. You don't know what she might do."

"If she was going to do something, she would have already."

Tanya let out a sigh. "Do you have some plan to jog his memory, aside from us hanging around for the week?"

"Now that he knows we worked together, it will give me the opportunity to discuss the good old days with him."

"Good old days? You were hardly friends back then," she scoffed. "And if that's your plan, why didn't you just come out and tell him you two worked together when we first checked in?"

"I told you already. I thought if I seemed familiar, without telling him how we knew each other, it would get him to try to place me, which might help him regain his memory."

"Not sure this new plan will work any better than your old one."

"It might work if I bring up Jay Larson—talk about what a shame it is that he was murdered. That just might be the key to unlock his memory."

DANIELLE HAD JUST STEPPED out of the parlor when Tanya came down the staircase, wearing a coat and carrying a purse.

"Where are you off to?" Danielle asked when Tanya stepped on the first-floor landing.

"I thought I would do a little sightseeing. See what the local shops have to offer."

Danielle glanced up the stairs briefly. "Is Dirk going with you?"

"No. He's not much for shopping."

The doorbell rang, and both women glanced to the front door.

A moment later Danielle opened the door and found Chris standing on the front porch.

"Morning, Danielle," Chris greeted her cheerfully and then looked to Tanya and smiled. "Hello."

Tanya's eyes widened and she looked Chris up and down, a slow smile turning her lips.

"Chris, this is one of our guests, Tanya Thorpe. Tanya, this is a good friend and neighbor, Chris Johnson."

Chris offered his hand to Tanya, who took it, yet instead of shaking his hand, squeezed it lightly and said in a raspy voice, "Hello. If you were my neighbor, you could borrow a cup of sugar anytime."

Ignoring the comment, Chris smiled and said, "Nice to meet you, Tanya."

With a sigh, Tanya released his hand and then leaned over to Danielle and whispered, "Yummy," in her ear before saying her final goodbye and heading out the door.

"Looks like you made another conquest," Danielle teased after closing the front door.

"Oh, stop." Chris followed Danielle into the parlor. "I saw her wedding ring."

When they stepped in the parlor, they found Eva sitting on the sofa. "I saw you coming down the walk," she told Chris.

"Hello, Eva. I wondered if you were still here," Chris said.

"I see you're temporarily relieved of duty," Danielle told Eva.

Eva let out a sigh. "Yes, the wife went on a little shopping trip, so unless her husband is prone to talking to himself, I doubt it'll do much good watching him. Marie is still upstairs with the sisters."

"What exactly is going on?" Chris asked. "You never told me why you needed Eva."

Danielle spent the next ten minutes filling Chris in on what had been going on since the arrival of their current guests and answering his questions. She then looked at Eva and asked, "Did you hear anything that might shed light on what Dirk is here for?"

"My guess, he's planning to blackmail Walt. Not Walt, but Clint."

"For what? Is this about the supposed marriage to Claudia?" Danielle asked.

"I don't think so. But they mentioned someone who was murdered—a Jay Larson. Dirk seems to feel it's a name that might help Clint regain his memory. Which of course is impossible, since Clint has long since moved on."

"Did you say this guy was murdered?" Chris asked.

Eva nodded.

"If he was, I don't think Clint had anything to do with it. If he had a crime like that on his soul, I don't think he would have been able to move on with Stephanie," Danielle said.

"Maybe. But do you really know where he moved on to?" Chris asked.

Flopping down on one of the chairs, Danielle groaned. "I don't even want to consider that possibility." She looked over to her laptop sitting on the small desk. "I guess I should Google the guy."

"You do that. But one reason I stopped by is to let you know I'm taking off to California for a few days," Chris told her.

"Your uncles?" Danielle asked.

Chris nodded. "My uncle Simon has been asking to see me. I've decided to just go ahead and see what he wants."

"Is that wise?" Eva asked.

"He's locked up, and if he offers me a beverage, I'll decline." Chris flashed Eva a grin.

"I should go with you," Eva insisted.

"I'm a big boy, and I think Danielle and Walt need your help more than I do. I'll be back on Tuesday. Hunny is staying with Heather." Chris turned to Danielle and said, "After I see my uncle, I have to drive down to Costa Mesa, where I'm spending the night Monday before I head back the next day. That's not far from Huntington Beach, so you want me to see what I can find out about this Dirk character or Claudia, just let me know."

"How would you do that?" Danielle asked.

"I can always stop by their real estate offices under the pretense of looking for property. See if I can find out anything about them. Schmooze a little. Mention I know Clint."

"I would be curious to find out if Claudia and Clint actually dated before Stephanie, or what the relationship was between Dirk and Clint." Danielle stood up and walked to the desk. "Before you go, maybe I should Google this Jay Larson character."

A few minutes later, Danielle sat at the desk with her laptop on. Chris stood behind her, looking over her shoulder, while Eva lounged on the sofa, again filing her nails.

"Here's an article on a Jay Larson from Huntington Beach. He was murdered this past May in Los Angeles," Danielle said while focusing her attention on the computer monitor. "He could be the one Dirk was talking about."

"That's good news for Walt; whatever this is about, it's not about Clint killing the guy. Back in May, Walt was here stumbling around in a cast," Chris noted. "Does it say who killed Larson?"

"According to the article, it was a mugging. Hold on, let me see something." Danielle searched a few more minutes and then said, "It's still unsolved. According to one of the articles, Larson was a real estate appraiser."

UPSTAIRS, Claudia paced the bedroom while her sister sat silently on one of the two chairs in the room, reading *Moon Runners*. Marie sat on the other chair, wondering if the chief would be able to help Walt determine the status of Claudia's claim. But since it was Saturday, she didn't imagine they would be able to find out much today.

Rachel closed the book and looked up at her sister. "I don't know who wrote *Moon Runners*, but it really is a good book."

"It wasn't Clint," Claudia snapped as she walked to the window and looked down at the street.

"Can we go do something?" Rachel asked. "I can finish this book tonight. I would really like to get out today."

"I suppose we could do a little sightseeing," Claudia suggested as she gazed out the window.

"Maybe we could find someplace to have lunch. I would love a bowl of clam chowder."

Still looking out the window, Claudia caught sight of a man standing by the front gate, looking up at the house. She frowned. "Hey, Rachel, didn't you mention you saw a pair of binoculars in here?"

"Yeah. Over there." Rachel pointed to the shelf with the cat figurine.

Not budging from the window, Claudia held out her hand.

Rolling her eyes, Rachel tossed the book on the floor and reluctantly stood up and walked to the shelf. She grabbed the binoculars and then handed them to her sister. "What are you looking at?"

"A man," Claudia murmured, peering through the binoculars at the short balding man standing on the sidewalk. "It can't be. What is he doing here?"

Rachel looked out the window. "Who is he? Do you know him?"

"Unfortunately, yes. If I'm not mistaken, it's Albert Hanson."

"Who is Albert Hanson?" Rachel asked.

Claudia lowered the binoculars. "Another thorn in Clint's side."

TWENTY-THREE

Walt returned to Marlow House before noon on Saturday with a shiny black Packard. He parked it back in the garage and went to look for Danielle. He found her in the parlor working on her laptop computer.

"Was the chief of any help?" Danielle asked.

"You were right, he wasn't working today, and I went by his house, and no one was home." Walt dropped a kiss on Danielle's forehead. He had called her on the way to the car wash to tell her he was going to stop and talk to Police Chief MacDonald about Claudia's claim.

"Did you try calling him?" she asked.

Walt took a seat on a chair near the desk. "I didn't want to bother him when he's with the boys, and this is really something I would rather discuss in person, not on the phone."

"I don't blame you."

"What are you doing?" He nodded to the computer.

"Some online sleuthing."

"Find anything interesting?"

"A few things. Chris stopped by and—"

Walt interrupted Danielle and asked, "Before you tell me, where is everyone?" He glanced to the open doorway.

"Claudia and Rachel just left a minute ago. They said something about walking down to the pier. I suggested Pier Café for clam chowder. Didn't you see them outside?"

"I came up through the alley. What about Dirk and his wife?"

"The last time I saw Dirk, he was in the library checking out your portrait, and his wife left not long after you did to go shopping. She hasn't come back yet."

Walt stood up and walked to the door. "I think we should probably close this before you tell me what you found out. He could walk in on us anytime."

MARIE WAS happy to get out of the house and go for a walk. She followed Rachel and Claudia, who had just stepped onto the sidewalk in front of Marlow House. She heard a dog barking and glanced across the street. Lily was jogging over, with Sadie by her side. While Lily wouldn't be able to see Marie, Sadie would.

"Shouldn't the dog be on a leash?" Claudia asked when Lily and Sadie reached their side of the street.

"You can be so annoying," Marie snapped. Remembering how she used to pinch her son's ear when he was a little boy acting naughty, she tried the hands-free spirit version on Claudia.

"Ouch!" Claudia yipped, quickly grabbing her now sore ear. With a frown, she looked around, wondering what had just happened.

Ignoring her sister, Rachel said, "What a beautiful dog. Can I pet him?"

"Sure. This is Sadie. She's friendly." Lily smiled.

"That's what they all say before the dog takes a chunk out of you," Claudia snarked.

Kneeling in front of Sadie, offering pats in exchange for sloppy kisses, Rachel said, "Ignore my sister." She grinned at the dog.

"Hello, Sadie," Marie greeted her as Rachel scratched the dog behind her ears.

"I guess you're staying at Marlow House. I'm Lily Bartley. Sadie and I live across the street," Lily said cheerfully.

Rachel stood back up, giving Sadie a final pat. "Yes. I'm Rachel Dane, and this is my sister, Claudia."

Restless, Claudia asked her sister, "I thought you wanted to go to the pier?"

Rachel smiled apologetically at Lily and said, "It was nice to meet you, Lily. You have a beautiful dog."

A few minutes later the sisters were headed down the street toward the pier—Marie trailing behind them—while Lily and Sadie walked up to the front door of Marlow House.

"You didn't have to be so rude," Rachel told her sister when Lily was out of earshot.

"The woman is a friend of Danielle and Clint's. Danielle mentioned her this morning."

"So? There was no reason to be rude. She seemed nice."

"You just liked the dog. Admit it."

"And there is something wrong with that?" Marie asked deaf ears.

"Do you think Clint told Danielle about you?" Rachel asked.

"I seriously doubt it. He obviously told her that we knew each other; he practically admitted that at breakfast this morning. But about us being married? No way."

THE LITTLE MAN had been sitting at the booth for twenty minutes, and so far, all he wanted was coffee. Carla began refilling his cup and hoped he wasn't going to calculate his tip according to the price of one cup of coffee. Business was slow as it was at this time of year. With her spare hand she tucked a lock of her blue hair behind one ear.

"Do you know anything about that bed and breakfast down the street, Marlow House?" the man asked Carla after she finished refilling his cup.

"Sure. It's the oldest house in Fredrickport. You thinking of staying there?"

He shook his head. "No, I was just curious about it."

Carla set the pot of coffee on the counter and propped her left hand on one hip. "It's owned by Danielle Boatman. She inherited it from her great-aunt. The aunt's mother inherited it from Walt Marlow."

"The guy in the portrait?" he asked.

"You've seen the portrait?"

"Yes. I went to the museum yesterday and saw it."

"Those paintings used to be owned by Danielle Boatman—well,

at least the ones of Walt Marlow and his wife. The other one was owned by the museum. But the Glandon Foundation purchased them and now have them on loan at the museum. I guess they were painted by some famous artist—Monnet or Bonnet. Something like that."

"Yeah, I read about the paintings online."

"You want to know what's really wild?" Carla asked.

"What's that?"

"Walt Marlow has a distant cousin who's living at the house now, and he's a dead ringer for Walt."

"You mean Clint Marlow?" the man asked.

"Oh, so you've heard about him?"

"I know Clint Marlow," he told her.

"You do? Did you know him when he was Clint? He likes to be called Walt now. I know it's his first name, but still, it's a little creepy considering how much he looks like the other Walt." Carla shivered at the thought.

"Do you know him very well?" he asked.

"He comes in here fairly frequently. Normally with Danielle. They're engaged now. Actually, he's an alright guy. When I first met him, he seemed rather full of himself. Maybe the accident changed him. I don't know. He's also an author. A pretty successful one."

"Yes, I heard that too."

"You know what they say, it's not what you know, it's who you know."

"How so?" he asked.

"He was just pretty darn lucky he was staying across the street from Ian Bartley," Carla said.

"Who is that?" He frowned.

"He's a really big deal author. He writes under another name, Jon Altar. Lots of his stuff makes it to TV. I heard he read Walt's book and sent it to his agent. Everyone says there is no way it would have gotten published so fast if it wasn't for Ian. It was Walt's first book."

WHEN CLAUDIA and Rachel reached the pier, Claudia wanted to go into the café, but Rachel wanted to walk the length of the pier first. Reluctantly Claudia capitulated, yet grumbled the entire time.

Tired of hearing her sister complain, Rachel picked up her step so they could get to the café quicker. Once they walked in, they found most of the tables and booths empty, with one man sitting at the counter, his back to them.

"I thought Danielle said this place has good food," Claudia said while looking around deciding where to sit.

"I've never seen anyone who complains as much as you!" Marie said. "If you did marry Clint, it's no wonder the marriage didn't work out. I'm surprised you made it out alive. I wouldn't blame Clint if he had smothered you with a pillow." Marie then cringed, recalling that was exactly how she had been killed. "Perhaps that was a poor choice of words," she muttered.

"Who says it doesn't?" Rachel asked.

"Not very crowded in here." Claudia sat down in a booth.

"Danielle did say this was their off season," Rachel reminded while taking a seat across from her sister.

Marie took the empty spot next to Rachel and watched as the women each picked up a menu and began reading. Bored, Marie looked around the café to see if there was anyone she knew. She looked up at the counter and noticed the man who had been sitting there had just stood up. He looked in their direction and frowned.

Marie watched as the man walked toward them. She didn't recognize his face and was fairly certain he was not from Frederickport. Claudia and Rachel were both reading their menus and did not notice his approach. It was not until he was standing over their table did Claudia look up.

"Claudia Dane! It is you!" he shouted.

Rachel looked up from her menu and stared at the intruder. She was fairly certain he was the same man who had been standing in front of Marlow House that morning. Carla, who was just clearing his coffee cup from the counter, looked in the direction of the shout.

"Hello, Mr. Hanson," Claudia said in a soft voice.

"So you recognize me?"

"Umm...yes, how have you been?" she whispered.

"How do you think I've been? I always wondered if you were part of it. But here you are. You're staying at Marlow House, aren't you?"

Claudia stared at the man but did not respond. Standing behind the counter was Carla, listening to the man's every word. She wished the woman would speak up so she could hear what she was saying.

"Aren't you?" he shouted.

"Mr. Hanson, my sister and I are just in Frederickport for a little holiday, nothing more."

"Where are you staying?"

"What does it matter?" Claudia asked.

"If you're staying at Marlow House, I guess it just shows my hunch was right all along. I could kill both of you for what you did to me!" he yelled.

"Oh my," Marie muttered. "This does not sound good for Walt."

"Please, Mr. Hanson, I didn't do anything to you," Claudia whispered.

"You and Marlow destroyed me," he said at the top of his voice.

"Please, Mr. Hanson, a lot of people were hurt when the housing bubble burst. I can't be held responsible for that."

"Don't act so innocent. It was more than that, and you know it!"

"You might want to cool it." Rachel spoke up, nodding toward the front door.

Scowling, Albert Hanson jerked his head around to see what Rachel was referring to. A female police officer stood at the entrance to the café, looking his way.

Albert looked back to Claudia and whispered, "This isn't over." He turned and stormed from the café.

"Thanks for getting here so fast," Carla whispered to Officer Carpenter when she stepped up to the counter. "I can't believe you got here that quick. Pretty good service!"

"I was just down the street," Carpenter said. "What happened?"

Carla shrugged. "That man who just stormed out of here, he sat at the counter for the last half hour, drinking coffee and asking me about Marlow House." She nodded to Claudia and Rachel. "Those two women just walked in and sat down, and he went over there and started yelling at them."

"What about?" she asked.

Carla shrugged. "I don't know. That's why I called for you. He seemed pretty upset."

"I'll go talk to them."

"Afternoon, ladies," the officer greeted the women a few moments later.

"Officer." Claudia nodded.

"I understand there was a problem in here a minute ago?"

Claudia smiled up at her. "I'm sorry about that. We just happened to run into someone I know from back home, and he gets a little emotional sometimes. It sounded worse than it was. I apologize."

TWENTY-FOUR

Danielle left the door to the parlor open so she could hear when her guests were coming or going. She had spent most of Saturday at the computer, searching for information on her guests and the possible marriage of Clint. She hadn't seen the Russoms since they had left before breakfast, and she didn't expect them to return until later in the evening.

"You've been at that computer a long time," Dirk said from the doorway.

Danielle glanced up and smiled at him while quickly closing the search window. "How was dinner?"

"You were right. Pearl Cove has excellent lobster. Tanya was very impressed." He stepped into the room and glanced around.

"I'm glad you enjoyed it."

Dirk took a seat on a nearby chair and asked, "Where is Clint? I haven't seen him since breakfast."

"He's up in his room working on his new book." *And avoiding you,* Danielle thought. Walt wanted to learn as much as possible about Dirk before listening to whatever threat he had over Clint. "He also goes by his first name now."

"That's going to take some getting used to. I've always known him as Clint. But I'll work on it."

Danielle turned in her seat to face Dirk. "I'm curious, why didn't you just tell Walt you knew him when you arrived?"

Dirk shrugged. He uncrossed and recrossed his legs. "I intended to," Dirk lied. "But when you opened that door and he obviously had no clue, I felt a little foolish. So I said nothing."

"You also implied he's the reason you decided to stay here."

"Did I?" Dirk smiled.

"You did."

Dirk sat in silence for a moment before answering. Finally, he said, "My wife and I had been talking about taking a trip along the coast for some time. I saw Clint—I mean Walt—on television and I looked him up on the computer." Dirk smiled. "You did ask me if I ever Googled clients. He wasn't a client, but a colleague. I read about Marlow House and thought it looked rather quaint—and so here we are."

"January is a little cold to travel along the coast. Had you always planned to come up here this month? Or just after you saw Walt on television?" she asked.

Dirk shrugged. "I tend to be rather impulsive. I suppose Tanya would have been happier had I booked a room in the summer. But I never know what my schedule will be, and I had just sold my last listing, so I figured this would be an ideal time to take a trip, before business picked up again."

"I see..." Danielle murmured. *You mean you figured this would be a good time to blackmail Clint.*

"I must say, I am quite impressed with Cl—Walt's second career. I had no idea he was interested in writing. Who would have thought, from real estate agent to successful author?"

"IT LOOKS like the chief won't be back until Tuesday," Danielle told Walt on Sunday morning. They were alone in the kitchen, preparing breakfast for their guests.

"The boys missing school?" Walt asked.

"I guess. It's some family thing in Vancouver. He got my message and text messaged me this morning," Danielle explained.

"Perhaps we should be talking to a lawyer instead of the chief. I could call Melony," Walt suggested. "She should be able to find out if the marriage license is legit and what we need to do to get it annulled. I suppose I can afford to give Claudia a settlement if that's what it takes. Who knows, maybe I am a bigamist."

THE GHOST WHO WAS SAYS I DO

Holding a plate covered with a piece of paper towel in one hand, Danielle held a pair of tongs in the other while removing sizzling bacon from a pan. She began to laugh.

Looking up from the fruit he was cutting, Walt asked, "What's so funny?"

"Us making breakfast for your blackmailers. I mean, really, do we live in bizarro world or what?"

Walt flashed Danielle a grin. "It's better than making breakfast for Chris's uncles."

Danielle cringed. "So true. Now *that* was creepy. I wonder how it's going for Chris. He's supposed to see Simon today."

"He should have ignored the request."

In the dining room the guests—excluding the Russoms, who had already left for the day—gathered around the dining room table, waiting for breakfast. Claudia and Rachel had arrived first, followed by Dirk and his wife. Awkward silence permeated the room while Dirk waited for Claudia to finish with the coffee carafe so he could pour Tanya and himself a cup.

Standing by the table were Eva and Marie, who eyed the two chairs they wanted to sit in, but neither chair was pulled out from the table. Leaving the chairs where they were meant that everything from the waist down on the two ghosts would be hidden under the tabletop once they sat down.

"I suppose I can just do this..." Eva snapped her fingers and she was sitting in an invisible chair floating at the end of the table.

"That really isn't necessary," Marie told her.

"I will not sit in the middle of that table," Eva said.

"Give me a minute..." Marie looked at the four people at the table, and when she thought they weren't looking, she moved two of the chairs out from the table...one at a time.

Rachel was just about to take a sip of coffee when she noticed movement from the corner of her eye. Holding the cup to her lips, she sat frozen as her eyes darted to her far right. Now gripping the handle of her coffee cup, her eyes widened as she watched a chair move away from the table. Saying nothing, she blinked her eyes and turned to the chairs while gently lowering the coffee cup back down to the table. She continued to stare.

"Rachel, what's wrong?" Tanya asked. "You look like you've seen a ghost."

Licking her lips, Rachel swallowed nervously and then looked to the other people at the table. "Umm…did any one of you happen to notice if those chairs were tucked under the table when we sat down?" She pointed to the two chairs. What she couldn't see, they were now occupied—one by Eva the other by Marie.

"Obviously they weren't," Claudia said impatiently.

"I…I just saw one move. Didn't any of you see it?" She looked around frantically.

"I swear, Rachel, your imagination is working overtime," Claudia scoffed.

Fifteen minutes later, when Walt and Danielle were seated at the table and everyone was eating breakfast, Marie said, "I have to apologize. The reason poor Rachel seems so frazzled and out of sorts, I believe she saw me move these chairs."

"Marie dear, you say that as if you aren't quite certain she saw you. She did. The poor girl blurted it out, and now they're all looking at her as if she's a little daft," Eva corrected.

Danielle glanced from Marie and Eva to Rachel, who sat quietly pushing her food around her plate with her fork.

"I'm curious, Walt," Dirk said a moment later. "Have you been working with anyone to help get your memory back?"

"You mean like a psychologist?" Walt asked with a smile.

Dirk shrugged. "I would think they could do something to help you remember."

"I was told it will probably come back gradually."

"Rather hard to remember something you never knew," Marie scoffed.

"Have you been able to recall anything?" Dirk asked. "Like me or Claudia, are we a little familiar? Like someone you just can't place?"

Walt looked up from his plate, his eyes meeting Dirk's. "Not really."

After a few moments of silence, Dirk picked up a slice of bacon and said, "I suppose there are benefits to amnesia." He took a bite of the bacon.

"Benefits? How could there be benefits?" Tanya asked.

Dirk finished the rest of the slice of bacon and then said, "For one thing, when a friend dies, you don't have to be sad."

"If you're referring to Stephanie, I may not remember her, but I do feel sad she died," Walt said.

THE GHOST WHO WAS SAYS I DO

"Actually, I was thinking of Jay Larson." He picked up another piece of bacon and popped it in his mouth.

"Who's Jay Larson?" Danielle asked.

"He was an appraiser Clint—I mean Walt—used to work with a lot," Dirk explained. "He was killed last spring. Poor guy was mugged in LA."

"That's terrible. But what do you mean Walt worked with him a lot?" Danielle asked.

Dirk shrugged. "Larson was the appraiser for a lot of Walt's buyers."

"I don't know why we have to discuss business. After all, I'm on vacation," Claudia said abruptly.

Dirk looked over to Claudia. "Now that I think about it, didn't you have the seller's side of most of those sales that used Larson?"

"WHAT WERE YOU DOING AT BREAKFAST?" Claudia asked Dirk later on Sunday when she cornered him alone in the library at Marlow House.

"I have no idea what you're talking about. What are you rambling about now?" Dirk sounded bored.

"All that stuff about Jay Larson."

"I was just trying to help Clint regain his memory. I thought reminding him of people he once knew might help."

"If you tell Clint about Jay—about any of it—what's going to prevent him from going to the police? He has amnesia; he probably figures they won't hold him responsible for something he did before the accident."

"I seriously doubt amnesia is a get-out-of-jail card. But I tend to agree he might think it is, and I'd rather he not go to the police. I'd prefer he remembers for himself. I'm just trying to jog his memory."

"And if he doesn't give you what you want?"

Dirk shrugged. "I guess I'll have to make good on my threat."

"You can't do that!"

"Why can't I?"

"I paid you, Dirk. I sold my condo to pay you off. You took every penny. If you do this, you're reneging on our deal!"

"I guess you can always take me to court over it." He laughed.

"That's not funny."

149

The smile vanished from Dirk's face and he leaned close to Claudia and whispered, "Then perhaps you need to do what you can to convince Clint to give me what I want—for both of your sakes. From what I remember, you and he used to be pretty close, at least before Stephanie came into the picture. Who knows, maybe this will bring you two back together again, and he'll dump Danielle Boatman. But considering I intend to take a good share of his money, he might want to keep his rich little fiancée."

"This most definitely is about blackmail," Eva observed.

"Apparently so," Marie said with a nod.

The two ghosts sat on an imaginary sofa hovering in midair above the library's desk. They looked down at the arguing pair. Tears filled Claudia's eyes as she turned abruptly from Dirk and ran from the room. Dirk smiled and said, "Nice doing business with you, Claudia." He laughed and then went over to a chair and sat down. Picking up the magazine sitting on the end table, he opened it and began to read.

"I really don't like that man." Eva wrinkled up her nose. Waving one hand as if annoyed, she said, "Do something!"

"Do something what?" Marie asked.

"I don't know. That stuff you do. He needs a good swift kick!"

"Or...something more creative," Marie murmured.

Eva looked to Marie. "Creative how?"

"Slapping, pinching, and kicking are a bit adolescent, especially when the subject has no idea it's coming—or where it came from."

Eva arched her brows. "So?"

Cocking her head slightly, Marie studied Dirk. "I just think something a little more creative...he isn't a pot of boiling water..."

"Whatever are you talking about?" Eva asked.

"Watch," Marie said with a grin.

The next moment the chair with Dirk lifted up from the floor until the top of his head hit the ceiling. It then dropped back down to the floor, making a crashing sound—breaking one of the chair's legs.

"Oh dear..." Marie muttered.

TWENTY-FIVE

"Are you sure you feel up to going to work today?" Ian asked Lily on Monday morning. Sitting up in bed, he watched as she pulled socks from their dresser.

"I don't feel too bad this morning. That cup of dry Cheerios when I wake up seems to be doing the trick. What are you doing today?" Lily sat on the edge of their mattress in her underwear and started putting socks on her bare feet.

"I promised Danielle I would do a little online research. They emailed me a copy of the marriage license."

Socks now on her feet, still sitting on the bed, Lily turned to face her husband. "I don't know why they just don't talk to an attorney or at least hire a private investigator to check out that woman's story if Walt is so convinced it is a lie. But frankly, I have a sick feeling it's true."

"That feeling could be morning sickness. But I think that's what they're going to do. I spoke to Walt last night on the phone, and he told me he was thinking of telling Claudia that he's turning this over to his attorney and he wants a divorce—annulment if possible."

"He should have done that when she first sprung this on him," Lily said, "instead of dragging this out."

"I think you're being a little hard on him. Walt was blindsided when she dropped this on him. And this is more than simply getting a divorce or annulment, it means his marriage to Danielle is void, and that he is a bigamist. Not to mention, if he was legally married to this woman, will the courts decide she is entitled to half of everything he's made on *Moon Runners*? That's a lot to process."

"I suppose. Danielle told me Chris went to California to see his uncle Simon this past weekend—I don't know why he wastes his time on that piece of trash—and while down there, he's going to stop at the real estate offices Claudia and that other guy work at to see if he can find out anything about the charming blackmailers. But I just don't know why they can't leave this to a professional private detective," Lily grumbled.

"You of all people should understand why Walt and Danielle are reluctant to reach out to anyone regarding Clint's past. It's not the most conventional situation."

WHILE LILY FINISHED DRESSING for work, Chris sat at the window in the visitor's area of the prison in Southern California, waiting for them to bring in his uncle Simon. Initially the plan was to see Simon on Sunday, but wires got crossed somewhere, and he discovered if he wanted to see him, he would have to do it Monday morning. Fact was, Chris didn't want to see Simon at all, but he was growing weary of his uncle's attorney badgering him to see his aging uncle. He glanced at his watch and hoped he had enough time after leaving the prison to visit both real estate offices so he could help Walt and Danielle find out more about Clint's past. It was going to take him a couple of hours to drive from the prison to Huntington Beach.

He heard the sound of a heavy lock and steel door opening, and the next minute he saw his uncle through the glass window, walking in his direction, a guard by his side and handcuffs on his wrists. Simon took a seat on the chair facing Chris. They were just a few inches apart, but a wall and glass pane separated them.

Leaning closer to the window, Chris said, "Hello, Simon."

"I'm no longer Uncle Simon?" the elderly man asked.

"You stopped being my uncle when you tried to kill Danielle and me."

Simon nodded. "Fair point. But no matter how you feel, I am still your uncle. I am your father's brother."

"What do you want, Simon?" Chris asked impatiently.

THE GHOST WHO WAS SAYS I DO

"Did you hear Loyd has lung cancer?"

Chris shrugged. "I heard something about that. I also heard you cut a deal with the prosecutor to turn state's evidence on your brother so you could avoid the death penalty. I wonder how Loyd felt about that?"

"Loyd's dying anyway. He'll be dead before they ever execute him. He knows that. Loyd's the one who told me to do it."

Chris arched his brow. "Really?"

"It was also for you," Simon said.

"For me? For me how?"

"I guess you haven't heard yet, but we both pled guilty to all the charges in Oregon. That means there won't be a trial. I thought that would make you happy. You won't have to go through another court trial."

"You mean like when you tried to take my inheritance?"

"Please, Chris, can we just let it go?"

"Let it go?" Chris choked out.

"I'm in prison. I'll die behind these walls. So will my brother. That should make you happy."

"None of this makes me happy. Why would you even imagine it would?"

"I know you don't believe this, but Loyd and I deeply regret our actions."

"I imagine you do, considering you'll be spending the rest of your days in here."

"You're not going to make it easy on me, are you?" Simon asked.

Chris let out a sigh. "Go ahead and tell me what you want. Why did you want to see me?"

"It's about Loyd. He's in a lot of pain. He shouldn't be in here."

"We are talking about the same brother you flipped on?" Chris asked.

"I explained that. But the cancer has progressed, and he shouldn't have to spend his final days in here. I am begging you. He's in unnecessary pain. You could do it."

"I could do what?" Chris asked.

"See if you can have him transferred somewhere else—like a sanatorium. Somewhere where he'll be comfortable and taken care of."

"You do realize you're talking about the man who was perfectly fine with watching me die before his eyes? I don't recall any compassion coming from him when he thought it was my final hour."

"But you're a better man than him," Simon said.

"Is that it? Or maybe you want to see if I can get catered meals brought in for you? Or maybe a private cell?"

"I'm not asking anything for myself."

Chris stared at Simon, momentarily speechless. Finally, he said, "You're serious, aren't you?"

"He's my brother, Chris. He's your father's brother."

BACK AT MARLOW HOUSE, Dirk leaned on the dresser in his room and groaned. His wife sat on a nearby chair and watched as he flinched again, attempting to push back the pain.

"Dirk, take your medicine. This is ridiculous."

"I'll be okay. I just need to walk this off."

"You don't have to suffer like this," she argued.

"It's either this or have another hallucination," he told her.

"You don't know if that was from your pain medication," she said.

"I sure as hell hope it was! It was so real. I thought I was flying around in the library on a magic chair!"

"Oh hooey," Eva spat from where she sat on her imaginary chair, hovering nearby. "You did not fly around the room. The chair simply went up—and then down again. Let's not make more of this than it was."

"Rachel insisted the chair in the dining room moved on its own," Tanya reminded him.

Dirk looked to his wife, his expression humorless. "Oh, please, don't start with some ridiculous ghost theory."

"They do say this place is haunted."

"Why are you whispering, Tanya? Are ghosts hard of hearing? You don't want them to hear?"

"Don't be like that, Dirk. I'm just saying—"

"Yeah, yeah, I know what you're saying. But that's just ridiculous. I looked it up on my phone, and one side effect of the pain medication the doctor gave me is hallucinations. It's rare, but it has been known to happen. And it obviously happened with me. So until we get home and I can get a prescription for something else, I'll just have to tough it out."

"You're going to be a peach to be around for the next few days," Tanya muttered to herself.

Focusing on fighting the pain from his bad back, Dirk missed his wife's comment.

DOWNSTAIRS AT MARLOW HOUSE, Marie found Danielle in the kitchen cleaning up after breakfast.

"Can I talk to you a moment, dear?" Marie asked.

"Morning, Marie. I take it Walt is talking to Claudia, so you have been temporarily relieved of duty?"

"Yes, he asked her to take a walk with him, to discuss the divorce. But that's not why I need to talk to you. I have a confession."

Danielle turned from the counter to face Marie. "Confession? About what?"

"I was practicing my levitation skills…in the library…and I'm afraid I brought the chair down a little too fast. One of the legs broke off. I am so sorry. I would gladly pay for it. But I don't seem to have any access to money on this side. And while I tried putting it back together, it seems it needs a little more than what I'm capable of doing."

Danielle chuckled. "Accidents happen, and considering all the time you've spent helping us, consider it a trade. Don't worry about the leg. I'll get it fixed."

"Thank you, dear. Now, would you mind if I popped out for a while to see Adam? I haven't seen him since last week."

"No problem. Say hi to Adam for me."

Marie started to say okay and then paused. She looked at Danielle and said in a dry voice, "Funny, dear."

"SO, DO YOU WANT A DIVORCE?" Claudia asked as she and Walt stepped out onto the sidewalk in front of Marlow House.

"If we are married as you say, either a divorce or an annulment. Preferably an annulment."

"That's fine if you want an annulment, but I still expect a generous settlement."

"What do you see as generous?" he asked.

"I want half of everything you have—including half of whatever you make on *Moon Runners* in the future. After all, you wrote that book while we were married. Community property and all…"

Walt chuckled. "I thought you didn't believe I wrote the book?"

Claudia shrugged. "It doesn't matter what I believe."

The two continued to walk down the street toward the pier.

"I'll let our attorneys work that out."

Claudia stopped abruptly. "What attorneys?"

Walt stopped and looked at her. They stood in front of Pearl's house on the sidewalk.

"Naturally I'll turn this over to my attorney."

Claudia shook her head. "No. That is not the deal. We don't need attorneys!" she said angrily.

"Exactly how did you see us handling this?" Walt asked.

"There is no reason to get attorneys involved, and this way your fiancée never has to know she was engaged to a married man. You simply write me a check for half of what you have now."

"Oh really?" Walt laughed. He started back down the street.

"Don't laugh at me!" Claudia shrieked, running to catch up with Walt.

"Your suggestion is laughable; how can I not laugh? What happens, I give you half of everything I have, and then you decide you want to stay married to me?"

"No. If you would just listen to me. I will take care of the divorce and send you the papers to sign. And once it's official, you finalize the papers to ensure I get half of all future revenues from the book. So, see, if I fail to come through with the divorce, then I don't get half of the future revenues."

Walt laughed again. He paused and turned to Claudia. "But you would still be my wife, so I'm not sure how I'm protected."

"You have to trust me," she insisted.

"I don't even know you."

They started walking again.

"Clint, this will be—"

"I go by Walt now. Don't call me Clint," he snapped.

"Okay, Walt. This will save us money. Attorneys are expensive.

They are the only ones who make anything in a divorce settlement," Claudia insisted.

"Considering you and I obviously never lived together, I don't imagine I will end up owing you much of anything—maybe nothing at all."

"You're wrong. Because if you don't agree to the divorce under my terms, then I'm going to the police and turning over what I have on you. Who knows, maybe when they send you to prison, I'll end up with all your money. You won't need it when you're behind bars for the next twenty years. Of course, you can always write another book when you get out."

TWENTY-SIX

Chris popped two aspirins in his mouth as he drove the rental car to Huntington Beach. Grabbing the open bottle of water from the cup holder, he washed them down. Heather had made the appointments for him. First, he was meeting with a real estate agent from Claudia's office, and then four hours later, he would be seeing a second agent from Clint's old office. He felt a little guilty for taking the agents' time when he wasn't in the market for real estate. To assuage his guilt, each appointment was taking place at an upscale restaurant, where he would be picking up the tab. The first would be for lunch and the second meeting an early dinner. He had to eat anyway, so it seemed like a sensible thing to do.

Twenty minutes later Chris sat in a restaurant overlooking the ocean. He wasn't there long when an attractive thirtysomething professionally dressed woman was brought to the table. Chris stood up when she approached.

"Mr. Johnson?" she asked hesitantly.

Chris took her hand. "Yes, and you are Ms. Stockwell?"

"Yes, nice to meet you," she said while shaking hands. "But please, call me Jenny."

"And you can call me Chris," he told her as she took a seat at the table.

She flashed him a smile and then asked, "I hope you had a pleasant flight from Oregon."

"It was uneventful."

"That's always good." She grinned.

"But I must say, I forgot how crowded it is down here."

"True. But you can't beat that view." With her right hand she motioned toward the window.

"It is a lovely view." He wasn't going to argue and inform her his ocean view from his back patio at home was far more impressive—and far less people. Instead he said, "If you don't mind, before we get to my real estate questions, perhaps we might chat a little—get to know each other while we have lunch. I always feel more comfortable doing business with someone I know something about—plus, I'm starved. I missed breakfast."

"Why certainly!"

A few minutes later after ordering drinks and looking over the menu, Jenny said, "The woman I talked to—I think she said her name was Heather Donovan—tells me you're out scouting for properties on behalf of the Glandon Foundation?"

Chris nodded. "That's true."

"I confess, after she called, I looked up the Glandon Foundation. Rather impressive the philanthropic work you do."

"It's not me—I just work for the organization. But I have to say, I am proud of what they have accomplished."

A few minutes later the server took their order. As they chatted, waiting for their food to arrive, Chris ordered Jenny another cocktail. As she finished her second drink, he thought he might need to call her a cab to take her back to her office. She seemed a little tipsy. While he never intended to get her inebriated—hardly a gentlemanly thing to do—he thought it might be a good time to pump her for information.

"By the way, I have a friend who knows someone who works with you."

"Really? Who is that?"

"Claudia Dane."

"No kidding? I've known Claudia for years. We started at the same real estate office. How does your friend know her?"

"Claudia's staying at her B and B right now. When I told my friend what real estate office I was talking to, she mentioned one of her guests was an agent there."

"Did you say your friend owns a B and B?"

"Yes."

"Surely you don't mean Marlow House?" Jenny asked.

Chris feigned innocence. "You've heard of it?"

"Why yes. You don't know Clint Marlow, do you?"

"Yes. Do you?"

"Oh my god, what a small world!" Jenny laughed. "I read all about what happened to Clint. Do you know if he still has amnesia?"

"He does. Were you good friends?"

"Not really. But I've known him for years. He started at the same office Claudia and I started with."

"Were Claudia and Clint close?" Chris asked.

"They used to be real estate partners. Quite the power team. But then they each went off on their own and ended up in different offices."

"Why did they break up their team if they were—a power team —as you describe?" Chris asked.

Jenny shrugged. "I have no idea. One spring they went to Mexico together, and when they came back, their partnership was over."

"What happened in Mexico?" Chris asked.

"Not a clue. Just between you and me, sometimes I got the feeling they were—you know, more than just a real estate team. Especially when they took that trip to Mexico—just the two of them. But it obviously didn't work out."

"Did they remain friends?"

"I suppose they did. They certainly did a ton of real estate deals together afterwards. Hmm…maybe that's why she's up there. Now that Stephanie's gone, maybe she thinks she has a second shot at him."

"Clint—or Walt as he goes by now—he's engaged to my friend."

"I did read about that too." Jenny took another sip of her drink.

"When you said they did a ton of real estate deals together, what did you mean? I thought they stopped being a team?"

"They weren't a team anymore. But Claudia started flipping properties. She did pretty good at it for a while. That girl had a knack of picking up a house dirt cheap, throwing some paint on it, and then turning around and making a hefty profit. To be honest, I thought her listings were way overpriced. I was always shocked that she typically got what she asked."

"And what was Clint's part in this?"

"He brought the buyers."

BACK AT MARLOW HOUSE, Eva, like Marie, had been given a reprieve from her duties as ghostly snoop. Tanya had taken the car for a drive to Astoria, leaving her husband at Marlow House alone. He insisted the pain in his lower back was just too severe to sit in a car for any length of time.

"Do you have any aspirin?" Dirk asked Danielle when he found her in the kitchen.

"Yes, there's some in the downstairs bathroom medicine cabinet. Help yourself."

"Thank you. Where is everyone, by the way?"

"Rachel drove into town to see a movie."

"Alone?"

Danielle shrugged. "Unless she knows someone in Frederickport she hasn't told us about. Claudia went for a walk."

"Where's Walt? I want to talk to him. Seems like I keep missing him. I thought maybe if I tell him some stories about work, it might help him regain his memory."

"Walt had some errands to run. I don't know when he'll be back," she lied.

"I'll just have to catch him when I come back." He turned and headed for the door, his hand on his lower back as he hunched over.

"Are you okay?" Danielle asked.

Dirk paused a moment and turned to face Danielle. "I have back issues. The medication I use normally knocks out the pain."

"If you're out, maybe you can get a refill at the pharmacy?" Danielle suggested.

Dirk shook his head. "I'm not out of it. But I had a bad reaction to it yesterday, so until my doctor can give me something else, I'll just have to make do with something over the counter."

Danielle cringed. "Oh...I hope it wasn't too bad. Had a friend once whose face about doubled in size after an allergic reaction to medication."

"In my case it was flying around your library."

"Excuse me?"

Dirk chuckled. "Yesterday when I was in the library alone, sitting on one of your chairs, I thought the chair took flight. My head about touched the ceiling. Or so I thought at the time. I confess it had me pretty freaked out, but then I realized it was a hallucination, and either I was going crazy—or there was a logical explanation. There was. A reaction to my medication."

After Dirk stepped out of the room and headed to the downstairs bathroom, Danielle shook her head and said under her breath, "Marie failed to mention someone was sitting in the chair when she was practicing her levitation skills."

AFTER TAKING TWO ASPIRIN, Dirk headed to the library. He hadn't been back since his little episode. Stepping into the room, he looked at the chair he had been sitting in when it took flight—or so he thought at the time. With a frown, he noticed the chair sat lopsided. Glancing down at its legs, he immediately knew why. One of them was snapped in half. A chill went up his spine.

He stared at the chair and then slowly approached, his focus on its legs. Kneeling down in front of it, he looked at the wood floor and noticed several dents along the planks. Leaning over, cringing a bit as pain shot up his spine, he rubbed his palm against the floor and over the indentations. Moving the chair slightly, he noticed the dents lined up perfectly with the chair legs—with the deepest dent lining up where the broken leg would have landed. It was as if the chair had been dropped down from the ceiling, breaking a leg on impact.

Shaking his head at the thought, he stood back up, struggling a bit to get upright again.

"I need to get this settled with Clint and then get the hell out of this place before I start believing this really is a haunted house."

Determined to put some space between himself and Marlow House so he could clear his head, he decided a walk to the pier might be what he needed. Walking sometimes helped alleviate the pain in his back, whereas sitting acerbated the problem. Leaving the library, he headed toward the front door, grabbing his jacket from the coatrack along the way.

ALBERT HANSON SAT at the counter and waited for the server to bring his food. It was the same woman who had waited on him the last time he had been at the café. He watched as she pulled the plate with the burger and fries from the pass-through window and headed his way. A moment later she set the plate before him.

"Can I get you anything else?" she asked.

"No, this looks good." He picked up his napkin and put it on his lap. He looked at her name tag. She hadn't been wearing one the other day. It said *Carla*.

Lingering on the other side of the counter, Carla twirled a lock of her blue hair around one finger and said, "You were sure upset the other day."

"Yeah. Well, sorry about that." He took a bite of his burger.

"Something happen between you and Clint Marlow? I assumed that was the Marlow you were talking about," Carla asked.

"Let's just say Clint Marlow is nothing but a scam artist and crook."

"Clint Marlow, he was the reason you were so interested in Marlow House the other day, wasn't he?"

"I heard he was staying there."

"You know, he has amnesia. He can't remember anything about his life when he was Clint," Carla told him.

Albert looked up from his burger. "Do you really believe that?"

Carla shrugged. "I guess. I know he seemed kind of sleazy when I first met him. But I think he's changed. Are you here to see him? Is that why you're here?"

"I wanted to talk to him. Yes. But I don't know if I will. What good will it do if he really can't remember anything?"

"If you want to talk to him, maybe now is your chance. Right before I came in here, I saw him walking down the pier, talking to that lady. You know, the one you got upset with when you were here the last time."

"They were together?"

"Yeah."

Albert dropped his burger on the plate, stood up abruptly, and then jerked his wallet from his back pocket. From the wallet he pulled out a twenty and slammed the bill on the counter. "This should cover it."

Carla watched as Albert rushed from the diner while attempting to shove his wallet in his back pocket. But in his haste, the wallet dropped on the floor.

"Wait!" Carla called out from behind the counter. Ignoring her cry, Albert disappeared out the door. Carla hurried around the counter and picked up the wallet from the floor.

"Waitress!" a customer called from the other side of the restaurant.

About to go after Albert, she paused when the customer called for her a second time.

Shoving the wallet in the pocket of her apron, she muttered, "He'll be back," before heading for the customer calling her.

TWENTY-SEVEN

January's late afternoon sky was as gray as the ocean, making it difficult to see where the horizon began or ended. Standing alone at the end of the pier, wrapped in her wool jacket, Claudia looked out to sea and for a brief moment felt compelled to simply jump into the icy waters and end it all. This was not how it was supposed to go down. She had fully expected Clint to simply write her a check and send her on her way; the old Clint would have done that.

Claudia did not want to go to jail, but the walls were closing in on her, and without money to help her start a new life, in another country—like Clint was going to do—then she could possibly face ruin. If Dirk hadn't shown up, it might have been easier. Dirk complicated matters and made her nervous, never knowing what he was going to tell people. Then to make everything worse, Albert Hanson was in Frederickport. Who else from her and Clint's past would be showing up?

It was all Clint's fault. It had been his idea, all of it. Looking back, it was actually pretty cheeky of him to approach her with the idea, especially after what he had done to her in Mexico. Of course, Clint never understood why she had been so upset at the time. He had accused her of lacking a sense of humor.

A gust of wind made her shiver. Seeking warmth, she dug her hands into her coat's pockets. Her right hand hit something cold and hard, and then she remembered she had put it there. Her small pistol. Wrapping her hand around the gun, keeping it in her pocket, she wondered if she had the courage to take care of those who threatened her freedom.

"Where did Clint go?" came a familiar voice behind her.

Startled, she twirled around to face the person and without thought pulled the revolver from her pocket.

"HOW DID IT GO WITH CLAUDIA?" Danielle asked Walt when he returned to Marlow House.

"Not good. Maybe we should go up to my room and talk?" he suggested.

"Why? We're all alone in the house." Danielle smiled. Sitting on the parlor sofa, she closed the book she had been reading and patted the empty spot next to her.

"Where is everyone?" Walt asked as he sat down.

"Well, I haven't seen the Russoms since they left early this morning. They must be having fun with their family; they never stick around here. Rachel isn't back from the movies yet. I assume Tanya is still in Astoria, and Dirk took off not long after you left with Claudia. Where is she, by the way?"

"She was pretty upset. I left her down at the pier."

"So it didn't go well?"

"According to her, I might have more problems than just an unwanted marriage." Walt leaned back in the sofa and put his arm around her. "Remind me, the next time I move into someone's body, make sure I thoroughly check them out."

Danielle chuckled and leaned back into Walt, resting her head against him. She propped her feet on the coffee table. "Don't make me laugh; none of this is funny."

"Remember what I told you, sometimes we just have to—"

"Laugh," she finished for him. "Yes, I know. So what did Clint do?"

"I have no idea. According to Claudia, it's something that I could spend the next two decades in prison for."

"Considering Dirk is intending to blackmail you about something, I suppose we shouldn't be too surprised. We're supposed to be planning our wedding, not dealing with all this."

"I'm sorry." Walt kissed the top of her head and hugged her briefly.

"Walt, it's not your fault. You are hardly responsible for anything Clint did."

"I understand that. But it is strange, sometimes I do feel responsible."

"Well, you're not."

"I just heard someone at the front door," Walt whispered in Danielle's ear.

The next moment someone called out from the entry hall, "Hello?" It was Rachel's voice.

"We're in here, Rachel, in the parlor!" Danielle called out.

"Didn't I ever tell you it's unladylike to scream in the house?" Walt teased.

Gently elbowing Walt, Danielle countered with, "Oh hush!"

"Hi," Rachel said when she walked into the parlor a moment later.

"How was your movie?" Danielle asked.

"It was okay." Rachel shrugged. "I wish Claudia had come with me. Is she upstairs?"

"I don't think she's back yet," Walt told her.

"Back from where?" Rachel asked.

"Rachel, maybe you can come sit down for a minute. I'd like to talk to you before Dirk and his wife get back," Walt told her.

"Umm...okay." Rachel looked curiously from Walt to Danielle and then sat down.

"I just thought you should know, I told Danielle everything your sister told me about us being married."

Rachel's eyes widened. "You did?"

"He told me on Friday, right after your sister told him. I knew all along," Danielle said, still snuggled up at Walt's side.

"But you said you hadn't told her," Rachel said.

Walt flashed her an apologetic smile. "Sorry, I lied. But I preferred to play my cards close to the vest until I figured out what I intended to do."

"And what do you intend to do, if I may ask?"

"I'm going to let my lawyer take care of it."

"Your lawyer?" Rachel squeaked. "You haven't told Claudia that yet, have you?"

"Yes. We had a little talk this afternoon, and I told her what I had decided to do. I really don't know why I waited so long to come to that decision; it was the obvious one. But I will admit, your sister's announcement came as a complete shock, and it took me a few days to process it."

"What did she say? I don't think she wanted to use a lawyer."

"Maybe not, but I certainly would not handle an annulment any other way."

"Annulment?" Rachel asked.

"If possible. If not, then a divorce," Walt said.

CHRIS HAD to give Heather credit. The two restaurants she had selected each had excellent ocean views. Maybe he was partial to his view back home, but this second restaurant was even nicer than Pearl Cove. He had ordered a cocktail while waiting for the real estate agent to arrive. It didn't take long.

"Chris Johnson?" the agent greeted him, extending his hand.

"I assume you're Andrew Drake?" Chris countered as he stood up.

The two men shook hands and exchanged pleasantries. While briefly discussing what Chris might be in the market for, Andrew confessed that he—as had the prior agent—had Googled Glandon Foundation. By his attitude and enthusiasm, Chris knew the man was impressed—and willing to do about anything to garner the foundation's potentially lucrative business.

"May I ask how you happened to call me?" Andrew asked.

"Actually, an acquaintance recommended your office," Chris explained. "He used to work with you."

"Really? Who is that?"

"You knew him as Clint Marlow. He goes by Walt Marlow now," Chris explained.

"Seriously? I heard Clint has amnesia or something. He must not if he recommended the office. How can you recommend something you don't remember?"

Chris shrugged. "He *says* he doesn't remember."

"You don't think he has it?" Andrew asked.

"He's engaged to a good friend of mine. I just find it odd he can't remember anything. When I told him I was coming down here, he mentioned your office and suggested I call. I suppose he might have just recommended it because he knows he used to work there—not that he actually remembers." Chris picked up his cocktail and took a sip.

"Maybe he does have amnesia." Andrew chuckled. "When Clint left, he had a few choice words for our broker. They had some issues. So I don't imagine he would actually recommend us. But I hope you won't hold that against us."

"Of course not." Chris smiled. "Were you friends?"

"Colleagues."

"According to my friend, another one of your colleagues is staying at the same B and B where Clint is currently living. A Dirk Thorpe?"

"Dirk?" he practically choked out.

"I haven't met him," Chris said. "Danielle just mentioned he was staying there."

"Well, that should be interesting." Andrew took a swig of his drink.

"Interesting how?"

"Clint and Dirk were not exactly friends. Not saying they had some feud going on or anything. Actually, I don't remember them even talking to each other. But Dirk was pretty critical of Clint."

"Critical how?"

"Let's just say Dirk didn't believe Clint had his clients' best interests at heart. But hey, from what I understand, Clint is no longer in the business, and from what I hear, he's doing pretty good as an author. Which I think is great!"

GETTING READY TO GO HOME, Carla started to remove her apron. While checking her pockets, she found the wallet she had put there—and had forgotten.

"Dang, he didn't come back for it," she grumbled. Opening the wallet, she looked through it. Tucked in with the bills was a credit card receipt for the Seahorse Motel. "Well, at least I know where you're staying—" Carla pulled out his driver's license and looked at it "—Mr. Hanson."

Twenty minutes later, Carla was walking into the office of the Seahorse Motel. She found Sam sitting at the front desk.

"Since when do they have you working in the office?" Carla asked Sam.

He shrugged. "I'm just helping out for a couple of hours. What can I do for you, Carla?"

"I'm looking for one of your guests, an Albert Hanson. He left his wallet in the café, and I want to give it back to him. I can't believe he hasn't missed it yet."

"Hold on…" Sam punched a few keys on the computer and then looked up at Carla. "He's staying in room seven."

"Thanks, Sam."

A few minutes later, Carla stood in front of room seven and knocked on the door. There was no answer. She knocked again. Holding the wallet, she looked down at it and asked herself, "Do I leave it with Sam or take it with me? Or maybe I should take it back to the café?"

TWENTY-EIGHT

Rachel finished reading the last page in *Moon Runners*. Holding the book open on her lap, she looked down and smiled. She had only read it out of curiosity, but it turned out to be her new favorite. It also piqued her curiosity about the author. Had the man she once knew as Clint written it—or was there some mysterious ghost writer out there who wanted to preserve his anonymity, and why? As much as she enjoyed the book, she didn't think she would share her opinion with her sister.

Thinking of her sister, she glanced up from where she sat on the sofa and looked to the living room window. It was getting dark outside. *Where is Claudia?*

Earlier Claudia had mentioned going downtown to see what the quaint beach community of Frederickport had to offer in the way of shops. Rachel assumed that was where she had gone after leaving Walt. It wasn't a far walk from the pier to the downtown district, and Rachel had the car, so wherever Claudia went, it had to be by foot. Closing the book and setting it on the coffee table, Rachel glanced at the time.

Picking up her cellphone off the table, she called her sister's number. She listened to it ring—and ring—until Claudia's voicemail came on, telling her to leave a message.

"I hate when you ignore my call!" Rachel grumbled, turning off her phone. Standing up, she picked up the book and headed for her room to dress for dinner. They had planned to go to Pearl Cove tonight. Rachel figured she would go ahead and get ready.

A few minutes later Rachel found herself alone on the second floor. Dirk and Tanya hadn't returned to Marlow House, and Danielle was downstairs in the parlor with Clint—or Walt, as she kept reminding herself to call him. Since she had the entire second floor to herself, Rachel went ahead and took a shower, not worrying about someone waiting for the bathroom. Staying at a bed and breakfast, where you didn't necessarily have your own bathroom, always made Rachel feel a little uncomfortable.

Thirty minutes later she was in her bedroom getting dressed. Claudia had still not returned. After finishing applying her makeup, Rachel picked up her cellphone and called her sister again. She waited for it to ring and then was surprised a moment later when she heard ringing coming from the dresser.

Holding the cellphone in one hand, Rachel walked to the dresser and used her other hand to open the top drawer. In it she found her sister's purse, and by the ringing coming from the purse, Rachel was fairly certain Claudia had left her cellphone behind.

With a groan, Rachel turned off her phone. The purse stopped ringing. Rachel looked in her sister's purse, and just as she expected, Claudia's cellphone had been left behind. She then rummaged through the purse and found Claudia's wallet was missing.

"At least she remembered to take her wallet with her," Rachel said aloud as she shoved the purse back in the drawer.

"EXCUSE ME, can I talk to you a minute?" Rachel asked from the doorway of the parlor.

Walt and Danielle, both of whom were sitting on the sofa reading, looked up.

"Sure," Danielle said.

When Rachel walked in the room a moment later, Danielle said, "You look nice. Where are you and Claudia going for dinner?"

"That's what I want to talk to you about; Claudia hasn't returned yet. I'm getting worried about her."

"Did you try calling her?" Walt asked.

"Yes. But my sister left her cellphone behind. Which doesn't really surprise me. She doesn't always take it with her, especially if she wants to disconnect from real estate. At least she has her wallet with her."

"So what did you want to talk to us about?" Danielle asked.

Rachel looked at Walt. "I wanted to know, when you left my sister earlier, did she say anything to you about where she was going afterwards?"

Walt shook his head. "Sorry. She was pretty upset. She wasn't thrilled I intended to use an attorney."

"I bet," Rachel muttered under her breath.

"She started rambling a bit—making threats. I just told her when she calmed down, we could talk later, and I came back here."

"Where were you at the time?" Rachel asked.

"We had just arrived at the pier," Walt told her.

"If you're worried about her, do you think you should call the police?" Danielle asked.

Rachel quickly shook her head. "Oh no. If Claudia was as upset as Walt says, that would just make it worse. Claudia and I have been living together for about seven months now. When she first moved in with me and stayed out late, I would try calling her. And if she didn't answer her phone—like now—I would get worried and start calling around and asking her friends where she was. I soon learned not to do that. No, that would just make her mad. If she was really upset after she left Walt, it's entirely possible she's sitting in some bar right now having one too many cocktails and will be calling me to pick her up."

Danielle flashed Rachel a smile and said, "Well, if there's anything we can do, just let us know."

"Thanks." Rachel started to leave the room, but paused a moment and turned around to face Walt and Danielle. "Since Claudia left her phone here, she's going to have to borrow someone's if she wants me to pick her up later. I think I'm going to go get something to eat by myself. But in case she comes back here without calling me, will you please tell her to call me?"

Danielle nodded. "Certainly."

"I CAN'T BELIEVE you have three rooms rented and you have the house to yourself tonight!" Lily said. She sat on Marlow House's living room sofa with Ian, with Walt and Danielle sitting across from them in the two chairs. Max napped under the coffee table while Sadie sat nearby, eyeing the cat.

"You just missed the Russoms," Danielle said before taking a sip of her wine.

"They only come by to take a shower or sleep," Walt added. "They haven't even made it to a single breakfast."

"Which is insane. They obviously have no idea what they're missing," Lily said.

"Walt likes it. Means more cinnamon rolls for him," Danielle teased.

"On our way over, Lily told me you talked to Chris tonight. I hope he was more helpful than I've been," Ian said.

"It was kind of interesting." Danielle set her wineglass on the side table. "The agent he talked to from Claudia's office had known both Clint and Claudia for a long time; they all started in real estate with the same broker. She didn't know if Clint and Claudia dated, much less had a secret marriage. But both agents confirmed Claudia and Clint had been a real estate team early in their careers."

"What exactly does it mean to be a real estate team?" Lily asked.

"Just that, they're a team. Like a partnership, where they work together with clients," Ian told her.

"Do you know why they broke up?" Lily asked.

"Not really, just that they went to Mexico together—just the two of them—and when they came back, they ended their partnership and each went to different real estate offices," Danielle explained.

"Mexico? It couldn't have been when they were married, could it?" Lily asked.

"In my gut, I don't believe they were married," Walt insisted.

"No one mentioned a marriage. But the team breaking up didn't mean they stopped working together. Claudia started flipping properties. She would buy a fixer-upper, put it on the market, and typically Clint brought in the buyer. I guess they did this until about six years ago," Danielle explained. "Chris also found out a little about Jay Larson."

"Isn't that the person your potential blackmailer was bringing up with Walt?" Lily asked.

Danielle nodded. "Yes. Jay was always the appraiser for the buyers Clint brought for Claudia's listings. Both agents felt Claudia listed them on the high end, and they told Chris they were always surprised when they appraised at full price."

"I don't understand how they always got the same appraiser," Lily asked. "That's not even possible."

"Not now," Ian said. "But it was back then—providing Clint steered his buyers to the same lender, and that lender requested Larson. You can't do that now because the lending laws have changed because of the housing crash."

"According to the agent at Clint's old office, Dirk had a meltdown once when his buyer used Larson, and the property didn't appraise."

"Some properties won't; that's just part of the business," Ian said.

"The problem, Dirk felt Claudia's listings were wildly overpriced, and didn't believe they should have ever appraised at full price. And then when one of the properties his client made an offer on—one he felt was priced right—did not come in at the listing price, he was furious."

"I can understand that," Lily said.

"Interesting. If they were still a team, working at the same office and flipping properties, they would have to disclose to the buyer they were not just a dual agent, but that they were in fact the seller. But if they were each working for separate brokers, then when Clint brought in a buyer, he could make it look like his fiduciary duty is to the buyer—and not disclose he has an interest in the property. If that was in fact what was going on," Ian suggested.

"Considering what Clint tried to do with Danielle's portraits, we all know he was not above pulling a scam on someone," Lily reminded them.

"If Clint and Claudia were somehow getting an appraiser to overvalue property and Dirk knew that—or if Clint and Claudia were violating their fiduciary duties to their clients, that might all be illegal, yet I doubt it's what Dirk is trying to blackmail me over," Walt said.

"Why do you say that?" Lily asked.

"Statute of limitations?" Danielle asked.

Walt nodded. "We would have to look it up, but I suspect if all of this happened over six years ago, the statute of limitations would be up, making it impossible for anyone to charge Claudia or Clint."

"I thought it was seven years?" Lily asked.

"It varies," Ian said. "And if I'm not mistaken, I think it's something like three years for real estate fraud."

DANIELLE STOOD at the window of the attic, looking outside at the near moonless night.

"Are you coming?" Walt called out to Danielle from the bed, patting the empty spot next to him.

"No one is back yet, not even Rachel." She continued to stare out the window.

"That probably means Claudia got ahold of her," Walt suggested. "And it's my guess they're at a bar somewhere getting blotto."

"Blotto?" Danielle chuckled.

"Would you prefer splifficated?" Walt asked.

"Oh, I like splifficated better." Danielle turned from the window and walked to the bed. Walt pulled back the covers so she could crawl in with him. When she did, he pulled her close, the two cuddling under the blankets.

"Dirk must have called Tanya to pick him up," Danielle said. "I hope when they come home tonight, they don't wake us up."

"Maybe if we're lucky, none of them will come back," Walt said.

"I just realized who else didn't come back today like they promised."

"Marie and Eva?" Walt said before pulling Danielle closer.

TWENTY-NINE

Reluctantly, Danielle opened her eyes and rolled over to face the nightstand. She looked at the time on the alarm clock. With a moan, she stumbled out of bed and made her way to the bathroom. A few minutes later she returned to the bedroom and looked out the window, rubbing her eyes.

"Come back to bed," Walt called out.

"I gotta make breakfast," she groaned.

"No, you don't. Joanne is coming this morning, remember?"

"You're right," Danielle said with a relieved sigh, turning from the window.

"Plus, someone is going to see you standing at my bedroom window early in the morning, and then there will be a scandal," he teased.

Crawling back into bed, under the sheets and blankets, she said, "I just wanted to see if our guests made it home last night."

"And?" Wrapping his arm around her, Walt pulled her close, spooning Danielle, resting his chin against the top of her head.

"All the chicks are tucked in—or at least all three cars are parked in front of the house."

"I was rather hoping the Dane sisters and the Thorpes had decided to move on."

"No such luck. But today we can go talk to the chief, he is

supposed to be back, and see if we can get together with Melony and get that marriage of Clint's taken care of."

Walt pulled her tighter. "It isn't true. I can't believe Clint had a wife."

Turning so she could face him, Danielle placed her hands on his shoulders and looked in his blue eyes. "It is what it is. It's Clint's marriage, not yours. I know legally we need to deal with it, but considering everything, you need to stop letting it bother you so much."

"But if Clint was married to Claudia, then we're not legally married."

Danielle brushed a kiss across Walt's mouth and said, "Don't be silly. You were never married to Claudia, so it really is a nonissue. Hopefully, if Clint was married to her, Melony can get the marriage dissolved before our wedding next month, and then we'll make it not just official but legal. And if you have to pay Claudia something, so what? In the big scheme of things, you know as well as I do that there are some things money simply cannot buy—and you and I have that."

"I love you, Danielle Marlow," Walt whispered before pulling her closer.

MORNING RUNS along the beach were typically brisk, but during winter months, they could be brutal. With the drop in temperature, Heather had started wearing long underwear under her jogging clothes. Considering the damp cold January weather, if she didn't add layers, she would be freezing to death about now. As it was, she was cold in spite of the fact she had been running for a good thirty minutes. She had left the headphones at home and wasn't listening to music. This morning she had a running partner—Hunny—Chris's pit bull.

The pair ran down the beach, Hunny staying close at Heather's side without a leash. Heather had a leash; it was rolled up and in her jacket pocket along with her cellphone. Every so often Hunny would get a little ahead of Heather, but a simple whistle brought the dog back to her side.

Anyone who met the pit bull was instantly impressed with how well trained she was. More than one person had asked Chris if he

THE GHOST WHO WAS SAYS I DO

had a private trainer—or perhaps he had sent Hunny to puppy boot camp. Chris had done none of that, and if they had told any of those people the real reason the dog was so well trained, they would never believe it. Chris had a pet whisperer—*Walt*.

It was fairly easy to train an intelligent dog if one had an interpreter. No reason to ply a dog with treats to make him or her understand what you want. Walt simply explained to Hunny the meaning of basic commands. This didn't mean Hunny understood the meaning of every word. After all, she was a dog. Learning by Walt's method of training didn't deny Hunny her treats. In fact, Chris tended to overindulge her. It was one reason Heather took Hunny with her on the run—the dog could afford to lose a pound or two.

Jogging south on the beach, Heather spied Chris's house ahead. Chris was still in California, but he was supposed to be back today. She and Hunny had already passed the house once, but now she was on the way back home, which was just beyond Chris's house, on the other side of the street. They were about three hundred feet from Chris's house when Hunny took off running. Heather whistled. The sound of the waves washing up on shore along with the growing morning breeze drowned out the whistle. Heather wasn't overly concerned; she figured Hunny would simply stop at Chris's back porch and wait for her there. However, Hunny ran past the porch and veered away from the house and headed to the ocean.

"No! It's too cold to go swimming!" Heather cried out, breaking into a full run in hopes of getting to the dog before she jumped into the icy water.

Instead of taking a dip, Hunny stopped just at the edge of the sand as it met the incoming waves. The dog began to bark at what appeared to be a tangle of seaweed. Hunny continued to bark, and when Heather got closer, within hearing distance for the dog, Heather's stern command to come did little to dissuade Hunny. Holding her ground, the pit bull stood guard over the ocean debris and continued to bark.

"Walt's going to have a stern talk with you!" Nearing the dog, Heather was now out of breath. She looked at the seaweed that had so captured the dog's attention, and her heart sank.

"No..." Heather groaned. Stomping her right foot repeatedly in the sand, she shouted, "No! No! No! This always happens to me!"

Tangled in the seaweed that so had the dog's attention was a human foot—and attached to the foot was a body. An obviously dead body.

WHEN DANIELLE STEPPED out of her bedroom on the second floor Tuesday morning, she found Rachel standing by her door.

"Good morning," Danielle said brightly. She took a deep breath and could smell bacon cooking.

"I knocked on your door several times, but you must be a deep sleeper," Rachel said.

It was then Danielle noticed Rachel's serious expression. The fact was, Danielle had forgotten to turn on the baby monitor in her room when she went to bed the night before. It was something she normally did if guests were staying in the house. That way, if they came looking for her in the middle of the night because of an emergency, she would hear them. Everyone assumed she slept in a bedroom on the second floor. What they didn't know, Danielle slept in the attic room with her secret husband—and she got up to the attic by way of the hidden staircase in her closet.

"I'm sorry, is there a problem?" Danielle asked.

"It's Claudia, she never came back last night! I'm so worried." Rachel started to cry.

Danielle was still comforting Rachel in the hallway when Walt started coming down the stairs from the attic bedroom a few minutes later.

"Let's go downstairs, get you a cup of coffee," Walt suggested, "and Danielle can call the police."

"The police?" Rachel started crying harder.

Patting Rachel's back and guiding her down the hallway, Danielle said, "I'm a good friend with the police chief. Let me call him."

Once they were downstairs, Walt went to the kitchen to get some coffee while Danielle tried to calm Rachel. While calling the police, she didn't need a sobbing woman in the background. In the kitchen Walt found Joanne preparing breakfast.

"Morning, Joanne, I just came to get some coffee," Walt told her as he grabbed three mugs from the overhead cabinet.

"Did I hear someone crying?" Joanne asked.

"Yes. One of our guests is upset because her sister never came home last night," Walt told her as he filled one of the cups with coffee.

"Oh dear. I hope she's okay." Joanne stood at the counter, cutting up a melon.

"Has anyone else been down this morning yet?" Walt asked.

"I met the Russoms. They seem like a nice couple. They said they're having breakfast at his cousin's house, but they did take a couple of cinnamon rolls with them."

"What about the Thorpes?" Walt asked.

"The Russoms were the only ones who have been down this morning—except for you."

WHEN POLICE CHIEF MacDonald arrived at Chris's house, he found Heather sitting on the back patio with Hunny by her side. On the beach nearby, several officers stood by what he assumed was the body.

"Morning, Heather, I see it happened again?" MacDonald greeted her.

"I am cursed," Heather groaned.

"Do you recognize the person?" he asked, glancing from Heather to his officers down by the water.

Heather shook her head. "Fortunately, no. Tripping over dead bodies is bad enough, but I'd rather not know them."

"Have you seen…umm—"

"Any ghosts?" Heather finished for him.

"Have you?"

Heather shook her head. "Not yet. It's possible the spirit has already moved on—or is lingering near the actual place of death."

With a nod, MacDonald left Heather and walked down to his officers and the body.

The first thing he noticed, the eyes were closed. He always felt a corpse looked more peaceful with the eyes closed; while open—they looked more dead.

"Do we have any idea who it is?" MacDonald asked.

Brian Henderson, who had been kneeling by the body, stood up and handed the chief a wallet. "This was in the coat pocket."

"Does it look like a drowning?" the chief asked, flipping through the soaked wallet.

"Considering the bullet hole in the chest, I don't think so," said one of the responders from the coroner's office, who was inspecting the body.

MacDonald pulled a California driver's license from the wallet just as his phone began to ring—it was Danielle. Believing she might be of some help if this was murder, and because she only lived a few doors down, he took the call.

"Morning, Danielle," he answered.

"Chief, I hate to bother you so early in the morning, but we have a situation…"

MacDonald studied the license as he listened to Danielle, comparing its photograph to the face of the corpse. "Yes?"

"One of our guests is missing. She didn't come home last night. Her name is Claudia Dane, and she's thirty—"

"Danielle," he interrupted.

"Yes?"

"I'm afraid I may have found your missing guest."

"What do you mean?" Danielle asked.

"A body washed up on the beach last night, in front of Chris's house. If you look out your front window, you'll see all the police cars. It's a woman, and according to the driver's license we found in her wallet, her name is Claudia Dane."

There was silence on the other end of the line. Finally, the chief asked, "Are you still there?"

"I'm sitting here with Claudia's sister, Rachel. She's pretty worried about her sister, and I told her I would call you."

"And you don't want to just blurt out her sister is dead—I get it. This wasn't a drowning, Danielle. She has been shot. I'll need to talk to the sister. How about if I come over there?"

"That might be a good idea."

THIRTY

Danielle continued to hold the phone by her ear, even though MacDonald had already hung up. She needed to collect her thoughts, dreading what she was going to have to tell Rachel. After a moment, she let out a sigh and lowered the cellphone.

"What did he say?" Rachel asked anxiously.

Setting the phone on the nearby table, Danielle turned to Rachel and took her hand. "I am so sorry to have to tell you this…"

Rachel began shaking her head in denial, and before Danielle could finish her sentence, she sobbed, "No!"

"I am so, so sorry, Rachel." Danielle squeezed her hand gently, helping the crying woman to a nearby chair.

"What happened?" Walt asked as he walked into the library with a serving tray carrying three cups of coffee and three cinnamon rolls.

Standing by Rachel's side, her hand on the crying woman's shoulder, Danielle looked at Walt. "The chief is on his way over to talk to Rachel. They found Claudia—her body washed up on the beach near Chris's house."

"What happened?" Rachel asked between sobs. "This morning I woke up and she still wasn't back, and I just knew something was wrong. Twins know. What happened?"

"Police Chief MacDonald should be here any minute," Danielle told her. "And he can tell you what he knows."

Stifling her sobs, Rachel wiped the tears away with the back of her sleeve. Her red-rimmed eyes looked up at Walt. "Did you do this?"

Startled by the question, Walt said, "Good God, no. I barely knew the woman. Why would I hurt her?"

"Because she was blackmailing you. That's what it was. I told her it was dangerous, but she insisted you would never hurt her."

Kneeling by Rachel's side, Danielle took hold of her hand and looked into the grieving woman's face. "Walt didn't hurt Claudia."

"But did Clint?" Rachel choked out, flashing an angry glare to Walt.

"Why would he? The marriage was no secret from me, and considering his amnesia, no one is going to hold it against him for having a wife he didn't remember. We told you he intended to let his lawyer handle it. Hurting your sister makes no sense."

"But she's dead. And he was the last one who saw her!" Rachel sobbed.

The doorbell rang. Danielle looked up at Walt. "That's probably the chief now."

"I'll let him in," Walt said, turning to the door.

POLICE CHIEF MACDONALD sat alone with Rachel in the library of Marlow House.

"Can you tell me when the last time you saw your sister was?" he asked.

"Right before I left for the show yesterday. I asked her to go with me."

"And she didn't call you anytime after that?" he asked.

Drying the corners of her eyes with a tissue, she sniffled. "No. She left her phone here."

"Was that common for your sister to leave her phone behind?"

Rachel shrugged. "Sometimes. Especially when she wanted to disconnect from work. She is—was a real estate agent."

"Her wallet was in her pocket. Do you know if she took a purse with her?"

Rachel shook her head. "Her purse is upstairs, with her phone. She didn't like carrying things. If we walked somewhere instead of taking the car, it was pretty common for her to put her wallet in her pocket.

"Last night when she didn't return, were you concerned?"

Holding the damp tissue in her hands, she looked down and absently twisted it. "I feel a little guilty. I accused Clint of hurting her. But I think I know what happened."

The chief arched his brows. "You do?"

Still twisting the tissue, she nodded. "When I came home from the movies, Clint—I mean Walt told me he had taken a walk with Claudia so they could talk. They, umm…well, used to know each other…before his accident. He can't remember."

"So what do you think happened?"

"I don't think the conversation went as Claudia expected. I loved my sister, but she could act impulsively. Knowing her, she got angry, found a local bar, had too much to drink, and since she didn't have her phone on her, tried to walk home and somehow fell in the ocean."

"Rachel, your sister did not just fall into the ocean."

Rachel looked up, her eyes wide. No longer twisting the tissue, she asked, "What do you mean?"

"Your sister was shot. We won't know for sure until after the autopsy, but it looks as if she was shot and then thrown into the ocean."

"Shot?" she squeaked. "Who would shoot her?"

"That's what I was hoping you might be able to tell me—who would want to hurt your sister?"

Licking her lips, she furrowed her brows and considered the question. "Maybe I was right."

"Right about what?"

Rachel glanced to the closed door and then back to the chief. "Maybe it was Walt. He was the last one to see her alive."

"Why do you think Walt would want to hurt your sister?"

"My sister was—she was—umm—I don't know. They had a past, she and Clint. I just know she was trying to get him to take responsibility for it."

"You're being a little vague."

Claudia shrugged. She glanced back to the closed door. "And then there's Dirk."

"Dirk?" he asked.

"Dirk Thorpe. He's staying here too. My sister knew him from back home, and she was upset when he showed up. Something went on between them, but she wouldn't tell me what." Closing her eyes, Rachel shook her head. "Why is all this happening?"

"Why did you and your sister come to Frederickport?"

Opening her eyes, she looked at the chief. "My sister saw an interview with Clint on television about *Moon Runners*. Until then, she had no idea he had supposedly written the book. The last time she heard anything about him was after his accident. We heard Stephanie had been killed and he had amnesia. She didn't believe he had written the book and was convinced he was pulling some sort of scam. That's why we came. Which was obviously foolish, because now she's dead."

JOANNE BROUGHT Rachel a plate of food and stayed with her in the library while the chief went into the parlor with Walt and Danielle. MacDonald spent the next fifteen minutes listening to them update him on what had been going on since the Dane sisters and the Thorpes had arrived on Friday. He already knew some of it from a few phone calls he'd had with Danielle, but this was the first time he was getting the complete story. He sat in one of the chairs facing the sofa, a small pad of paper in hand as he jotted down notes.

"I find it interesting she didn't once mention you and Claudia were married," the chief said.

"You mean Clint and Claudia," Walt corrected.

"Sorry—Clint and Claudia," the chief conceded.

"Obviously from what she told you—or what she didn't tell you—she didn't want to come out and say her sister had been blackmailing Walt," Danielle said. "Although technically speaking, I don't really think a wife demanding a large settlement before agreeing to divorce is legally considered blackmail."

"I thought you had Eva or Marie keeping an eye on Claudia?" the chief asked.

"We did. But after spending the last four days eavesdropping, even spirits get restless," Danielle said. "And frankly, we didn't see the point in constantly monitoring Claudia; we figured we already knew everything she wanted from Clint. That was, at least, until she started alluding to crimes Clint supposedly committed. And frankly,

THE GHOST WHO WAS SAYS I DO

I did expect Eva and Marie to come back last night at the very latest."

"You haven't seen them?" the chief asked.

Danielle shook her head. "No."

"Maybe when they come back, they'll tell you they saw something that might help figure this out," the chief suggested.

"Or maybe Claudia will come back and tell us what happened," Walt interjected.

"You said Heather hasn't seen her, so it's always possible her spirit passed over already," Danielle said.

Walt shook his head. "Wishful thinking on your part, Danielle."

The chief glanced at the notes he had just written and then scratched something out. "I really need to pay more attention," he muttered under his breath.

Looking curiously at the pad of paper in the chief's hand, Danielle asked, "What do you mean?"

"I was talking to myself," the chief explained.

"And?" Danielle asked.

"My notes. I don't need anyone looking at them and asking me who Marie or Eva are."

"SHOULDN'T my wife be in here too?" Dirk took a seat on the sofa. The police chief sat in a chair facing him, notepad in hand.

"I'd prefer to speak to you alone. Can you please tell me about your day yesterday—and when you might have seen Claudia Dane."

Dirk shook his head and said, "I can't believe she's dead. I mean —I just saw her yesterday at breakfast."

"Please tell me about yesterday."

Dirk shrugged. "Got up, had breakfast here. I saw Claudia then. Everyone was there. Afterwards, my wife decided to drive to Astoria to do some shopping. I stayed here, and then I got a little bored and decided to walk to town."

"Did you see Claudia on your walk?"

Dirk shook his head. "No. I didn't see her. I ended up at a bar. I had too much to drink. Called my wife, and she picked me up on her way back to town, and the two of us went to get something to eat. We got back here, and everyone was in bed already. I noticed

Claudia's car out front, so I assumed she was asleep upstairs with her sister."

"I understand you and Claudia didn't get along."

"We weren't exactly friends. But we weren't enemies. I barely knew her."

"You also work at the real estate office Clint once worked at, is that correct?"

Dirk nodded. "Yeah."

"Were you and Clint friends?"

"Friends?" Dirk smiled. "No, not really. Business associates."

"So why did you come to Marlow House? In January?"

"Don't people come in January? I'm not the only one staying here."

"True. But why did you decide to stay at a bed and breakfast where someone you didn't really get along with was now living?"

"I never said I didn't get along with Clint," Dirk argued.

"What do you know about Jay Larson?" the chief asked.

Startled by the question, Dirk frowned. "Excuse me?"

"Jay Larson. I understand you brought him up at breakfast yesterday morning, and Claudia seemed a little upset about it."

Licking his lips, Dirk shrugged and said, "Jay was an appraiser. Clint used him a lot. I just thought if I brought up people he used to know, it would help with his memory issues. I was just trying to be helpful."

An hour later, Dirk was up in his bedroom with his wife, comparing notes on what questions the police chief had asked each of them.

"I can't believe Rachel didn't tell that cop about Claudia and me." Absently combing his fingers through his hair, he sat down on the edge of the mattress and faced his wife, who sat at the dressing table.

"Just because she hasn't said anything doesn't mean she won't," Tanya said.

"Maybe she doesn't know," he suggested.

"You think that's possible?"

"It must be the reason."

"It doesn't matter," Tanya said. "It just meant Claudia had a motive to kill you, not that you had a motive to kill her."

"Last I heard, blackmail is against the law."

THIRTY-ONE

About the same time that Police Chief MacDonald was talking to Rachel, Eva and Marie appeared on Chris's back porch. Heather barely flinched at the sight of the two women—an elderly gray-haired one, wearing a spring dress, straw hat and sneakers, and a second much younger woman, who looked like a dead ringer for Charles Gibson's Gibson Girl from an earlier century—as they floated down from above, each holding umbrellas like a pair of Mary Poppins wannabes.

Sitting at Chris's patio table, her chin propped on a balled fist, Heather didn't budge an inch as she glanced up and watched the pair come in for a landing. Hunny was not so nonchalant in greeting the new arrivals, with her butt in full tail wag.

"Really?" Heather said dryly after the pair landed before her and the umbrellas disappeared.

"We were just heading back to Marlow House, and we noticed all the commotion. What's going on with all the police cars?" Marie asked.

Heather nodded toward the beach. "A dead body. A woman."

Marie turned to Eva. "Oh, you were right! Something was going on!"

Eva glanced out to the beach, where the police officers and other responders gathered. "I can always sense when someone has moved on to this side in Frederickport."

"What are you doing here?" Marie asked.

"What do you think?" Heather lifted her chin off her balled fist and folded her hands on the tabletop. "I found the body, of course."

Marie glanced briefly to the police officers down on the beach and then back to Heather. "Oh my. You are rather good at that."

"It's a gift." Heather shrugged.

"Have you seen her spirit?" Marie asked.

"That's pretty much why I'm sticking around. If I see her, I was hoping she would tell me what happened. According to the chief, she was shot."

"Shot?" Marie gasped.

"Yep. And then dumped in the ocean. It would be nice to find out who did it. I'm not too keen on living in a neighborhood with a killer on the loose."

"Is she anyone you know?" Eva asked.

Heather shook her head. "No. But from what the chief said, it's someone who was staying at Marlow House. He's over there now."

Eva and Marie looked at each other, and the next moment they were no longer standing on the patio, but were on the beach standing amongst the officers, looking down at the body.

Hunny began to bark.

"Quiet already! Let's go home. I'll let Eva and Marie take it from here. I'm tired of waiting for a new ghost to show up." Heather stood up, removed the leash from her pocket, and hooked it on Hunny's collar.

EVA LOOKED down at Claudia's lifeless body. "It's the one who claimed to be Clint's wife."

"Oh my, I should have stayed with her. Maybe I could have saved her." Marie glanced around. "Do you see her anywhere?"

"No. But I have a horrible feeling this could cause some problems for Walt and Danielle. Let's see if we can find her."

The two spirits floated up into the air and then each began moving in opposite directions—Eva traveling south while Marie ventured north, on the lookout for Claudia's newly departed spirit.

THE GHOST WHO WAS SAYS I DO

PEARL STOOD on her front porch looking up the street, wondering why all the police cars were parked up the road. Curious, she slipped back in her house for a moment and grabbed her jacket. After putting it on, she headed down to the sidewalk.

A few moments later she was just passing Marlow House when she came face-to-face with her neighbor to her south—Heather Donovan—the one with the long black braids and straight-cut bangs. Pearl knew she had a cat, but she had no idea she had a dog.

Pearl froze. "You have a pit bull!"

Heather paused a moment and looked Pearl up and down. "So? What's it to you? She's on a leash."

Pearl looked down at the dog, seeing only beady eyes, ignoring their kindness and not noticing the wagging tail or goofy dog grin. "Don't let her near me!"

"Then I guess you're going to have to cross the street because I'm walking down the sidewalk to go home."

"You don't have to be so snotty!" Pearl huffed.

"Aren't you the one who threatened to shoot my cat?" Heather countered.

"I have a right to keep cats out of my yard so they don't turn my flower garden into a litter box."

"And I have the right to walk down the sidewalk with my dog on a leash." Without another word Heather continued on her way, the dog by her side.

Seeing the pit bull coming in her direction, Pearl quickly made her way across the street, practically running to where she saw the police cars parked.

A few moments later, Pearl stepped onto the sidewalk across the street just as the responders from the coroner's office were bringing what appeared to be a body up from the beach to their van. A sheet concealed its identity. They were about six feet away. She stopped and watched as they started to load the body in the vehicle, when a gust of wind came up and blew the top portion of the sheet to one side, revealing the dead woman's face.

Pearl's eyes widened. "Oh my!"

"Mrs. Huckabee, you should probably go home," Brian Henderson said when he spied her watching. He had just come up from the beach. Joe Morelli trailed after him.

"What happened?" Pearl asked Brian. "That's the woman staying at Marlow House."

"Do you know her?" Brian asked.

Pearl turned away from the van; the body was already inside and they were closing the doors. She looked at Brian. "She was staying at Marlow House. That's Walt Marlow's wife."

"Excuse me? You're mistaken. Walt Marlow is not married," Brian told her. "In fact, he's engaged to your neighbor Danielle Boatman."

"No." Pearl shook her head emphatically. "I heard them arguing. In fact, more than once."

"You heard her arguing with who?" Joe asked.

Pearl looked from Brian to Joe. "With Walt Marlow. He's a tenant at Marlow House."

"Yes, I know who Walt Marlow is. Why were they arguing?" Joe asked.

"She wanted to know if he wanted a divorce, and he said he preferred an annulment. But then she told him she wanted half of all his money. He didn't seem happy about that. But who would be?"

Brian and Joe exchanged glances.

"Are you sure you heard that correctly?" Brian asked.

"The last time I heard them arguing, they were standing right in front of my house. It was hard not to hear them. They were both screaming at each other—although her voice was the loudest. They both seemed pretty upset. But I definitely heard them right. She asked him if he wanted a divorce. He said he preferred an annulment. But I suspect she didn't want either one."

"Why do you say that?" Brian asked.

"I've always felt that if someone wants out of a marriage, you certainly aren't going to make angry demands of your spouse before you agree to sign the divorce papers. What happens if he doesn't agree? You might get stuck in the marriage—but maybe that's what she wanted. Plus, she seemed pretty upset that he was going to call his attorney. How much can you want out of the marriage if you don't want to contact an attorney? No, I think ending their marriage was all his idea—not hers. And considering he has been running around with another woman, it's not surprising. The poor thing. I felt sorry for her. He seemed rather callous about it all."

"When was this last argument?" Joe asked.

"Yesterday, early afternoon. They walked down to the pier

together. I went upstairs, and when I looked out my window, I could see they were all the way up the street, not far from the pier."

"Thank you, Mrs. Huckabee, we might be stopping by your house later to ask you some more questions," Brian told her.

"That's fine. You didn't tell me what happened to her."

Brian and Joe exchanged glances again. Brian then looked at Pearl and said, "It appears she was shot."

"She was murdered?" Pearl gasped.

"It might have been an accident or perhaps self-inflicted. We'll know more after the coroner finishes with her," Brian explained.

"He killed her! I know he did!" Pearl insisted.

"Who killed her?" Joe asked.

"Walt Marlow, of course. You should see how he carries on with that Danielle Boatman. I live right next door, and I see what those two are up to! And to think he was a married man all this time. No wonder he got rid of his wife."

"Mrs. Huckabee, this is an open investigation, and at the moment Walt Marlow has not been charged with anything—nor is he currently a suspect. So please, I would appreciate it if you do not spread that rumor."

"I am not spreading rumors! I'm simply telling you what I saw. I would think the police would want the help of witnesses in a matter like this!"

"Yes, of course," Brian said patiently.

"Plus, I think Walt Marlow is crazy."

"Crazy?" Joe frowned. "Why do you think he's crazy?"

"I heard him tell that other woman that Marlow House is haunted. What a crazy thing to say! And the way he talks to that cat. It's like he believes it understands him."

"Thank you, Mrs. Huckabee, but I do think you should probably go home now," Brian urged.

With a huff, Pearl turned and marched down the street, back toward her house.

Joe and Brian watched her walk away. Finally, when she was out of earshot, Joe asked, "Could she be right? Was she Marlow's wife?"

Brian shrugged. "I find that highly unlikely. But considering he has amnesia, I imagine she came as quite a shock to him if she was."

"Enough of a shock to want to get rid of her?" Joe asked.

"But kill her? I had a couple of wives I got rid of. It was called divorce, not murder."

"I wonder what she really overheard regarding Marlow claiming the house is haunted," Joe asked.

Brian shrugged. "Who knows what Mrs. Huckabee really overheard."

"Is she the one who locked Sadie in the toolshed?" Joe asked.

Brian nodded. "Yes. It's not that I'm ignoring what she just told us, and we'll need to go back and get an official statement from her, but she does tend to jump to conclusions."

"You think she misunderstood what they were arguing about?" Joe asked.

"We both checked out Clint Marlow, and we never came across a wife. We know he had a fiancée; however there was nothing about a wife or previous marriage. But Huckabee did say she heard them arguing. And the fact Walt Marlow was seen in a heated argument with the murder victim within hours of her death—then maybe I spoke too soon when I told Mrs. Huckabee he wasn't a suspect."

THIRTY-TWO

Watching Pearl return to her house, Brian said, "One of us should probably walk over to Marlow House and let the chief know what Huckabee just told us, while the other one finishes up here."

"To be honest, I don't want to be the one to bring this news to Marlow House," Joe said. "Not weeks before Danielle's wedding."

"I suppose Boatman's used to me raining on her parade, so I'll do it. But to be honest, I think Huckabee heard it wrong. But either way, the fact she heard them arguing right before the woman was killed, that's not good for Marlow."

Before he could respond, Joe's cellphone rang. He looked at it and then glanced up to Brian and said, "It's the chief," and then answered it.

"What was that about?" Brian asked a few minutes later when Joe ended the phone call.

"When we finish up here, he wants some men over at Marlow House to search the room Claudia was staying in. Danielle has already given permission, and the sister of the victim said it was fine, so we don't need a search warrant. I mentioned you were going over there anyway—that you needed to talk to him"

Fifteen minutes later Brian was at Marlow House, being led to the library by Joanne, where he found the police chief alone with Walt and Danielle.

"Are you about finished up at the beach?" the chief asked when Brian entered the room.

"Joe's down there getting everything wrapped up. But I need to talk to you." Brian glanced at Walt and Danielle and then looked back to the chief. "Alone."

Danielle stood up. "We'll be in the kitchen. We missed breakfast, so I'm going to grab something to eat. You both are welcome to get something to eat too when you're done in here."

Walt stood up with Danielle, and they gave Brian a quick hello and goodbye before leaving him alone with the chief.

"What is it?" the chief asked.

Brian then went on to recount the conversation he and Joe had had with Danielle's new neighbor. "Personally, I think she heard it wrong," Brian told the chief when he finished the telling. "But the fact they were arguing, that is something we need to look into."

"Matches what Walt already told me. I think she heard the conversation just fine." The chief pointed to a chair, as Brian was still standing.

"Are you telling me Marlow admitted to being married to the woman?" Brian sat down in a chair next to the chief.

"Not exactly. When the woman showed up on Friday, she claimed to be Walt's wife and demanded a large sum of money if he wanted a divorce. She showed him a marriage license. Of course, he doesn't remember anything about his life as Clint. I've known about this since Saturday."

"You have?" Brian asked in surprise.

"Walt didn't believe her story. He wanted to see if I could find out if it was really true. It was a Mexican marriage license, and she still has the original. Which is one thing I'm counting on them finding in the search."

"Wow." Brian leaned back in the chair. "So he wasn't trying to hide the marriage after he found out about it?"

"Absolutely not. He told Danielle right away. I've been gone, so I couldn't really help him. But they had decided to just turn this over to Melony and, if the marriage was valid, see about getting it dissolved as soon as possible. That's what Walt told Claudia when they had the argument. According to him, when they got to the pier, they each went their own way. He came home, and he has no idea where she went."

"We know where she ended up."

LATER, since he had not had any breakfast that morning, MacDonald accepted Danielle's offer of something to eat while his officers searched Claudia and Rachel's room. When they were done and on their way, the chief stayed behind and talked to Walt and Danielle for another fifteen minutes. He was about to ask Danielle to get Rachel and Dirk for him before he left for the station. However, it wasn't necessary to find Rachel; she found him.

"Police Chief MacDonald, I just finished going through the room after your people were done, and I wanted to know if they took the gun."

"Gun? What gun?" the chief asked.

"Claudia's. She had a little .38, usually kept it in her purse, but sometimes, if she didn't take her purse with her, she would keep it in her pocket if she had one. She used to tell me it was dangerous for a real estate agent to show empty properties. I had forgotten about the gun, and then when I was thinking how you said she was shot, I thought, if only she had had her gun with her, and then I remembered when I had checked her purse yesterday, when I called her phone, I didn't remember seeing the gun. So I looked again after your people finished searching our room, and when it wasn't there, I went through the luggage, closet, everywhere. I even checked under the mattresses. But it's nowhere to be found. So I thought maybe they took it."

"No, there wasn't any gun. If she had it with her and it was in her pocket, it's possible it came out when she was in the water," the chief suggested.

"Oh dear…" Rachel frowned.

"Ms. Dane, I'm glad you're here. I wanted to talk to you anyway. I need you to come down to the station this afternoon. I have some more questions for you, and I think it would be best if we do it down there."

"Yes—of course. But, well—I was thinking of leaving, going home. I don't really want to drive home alone. I was going to try to get a flight. That drive up here was just so long, I don't think I can do it alone. But I'm not sure what to do with the car. It's Claudia's."

"I would really appreciate it if you could stay a few more days," the chief asked.

"I suppose I need to think about making arrangements for Claudia's body…" Rachel began to tear up again.

"When I see you later today, I'll see if I can find out when the coroner thinks they'll be able to release your sister's body."

"I, umm…well, I know Claudia always said she wanted to be cremated." Holding a damp tissue in her hand, Rachel looked down and twisted it as she talked. "I suppose I should see about having her cremated here. I imagine it would be expensive to have her body taken back home. And then I…" She began to sob. "Oh…I will be going home with Claudia's ashes instead of her!"

AFTER RACHEL ARRIVED at the police station later that afternoon, Joe took her to the interrogation room and then went to find the chief. He was in his office talking to Chris Johnson.

Joe popped his head in the chief's office and said, "Rachel Dane is here. I went ahead and put her in the interrogation room."

"Thanks, Joe. I'm going to be a few more minutes. I need to finish talking to Chris."

Chris glanced over at Joe and waved. "Hey, Joe."

Joe nodded in return. "Chris."

"Could you please see if Ms. Dane would like some coffee or something to drink? I'll just be a few more minutes."

When the chief was alone with Chris again, he asked, "So that's about everything?"

"I'm pretty sure. If I were you, I'd look a little closer at that Dirk fellow. From what I found out, he was no fan of Claudia or Clint. And from what Eva and Marie have overheard, he intends to blackmail Walt over something."

"WHAT'S TAKING the chief so long?" Brian asked. He stood with Joe in the office next to the interrogation room, watching Rachel through the two-way mirror. She was drinking the cup of coffee Joe had brought her.

Joe glanced over to Brian. "The chief was talking to Chris. Seemed important."

"Heather mentioned Chris was in California when I was talking to her today."

Joe looked back to Rachel. "So Marlow might be married?"

"That's what Claudia Dane told him. And they found a marriage license in her room. It was a Mexican license."

"Wow...can you imagine what it would be like to have people pop up in your life and you have no idea who they are because you have amnesia?" Joe asked.

"Marlow doesn't believe it, because he was intending to marry Stephanie. And I have to agree with him. When any of us checked into his background, there was nothing about a wife."

"But if she had a marriage license?" Joe asked.

Brian shrugged. "If it is legit, I suspect there's already a divorce decree out there waiting to be found."

"I'M sorry to keep you waiting."

"That's okay, Chief MacDonald. I have nowhere to go anyway. Do you know anything more about what happened to my sister?"

"No. Which is why I need to talk to you." He took a seat at the table, a manila folder in his hand. He opened the folder and removed a sheet of paper and slid it across the table to Rachel. "Have you ever seen this before?"

Rachel stared at the document and then nodded.

"Why didn't you tell me about it?" he asked.

She looked up to him. "Why would I?"

"Don't you think it might be important, the fact your sister was married to Clint Marlow?" he asked.

"He likes to be called Walt now," Rachel said as she pushed the document back to him. "Anyway, it's not real."

"It isn't?"

"No. My sister and Walt were never married."

"Did you know she was blackmailing him with this?"

Rachel shrugged. "It wasn't going to work anyway. I told her so. Even if he agreed to her terms, once they started with the divorce, he would find out they weren't even married. She wouldn't listen to me. I...I didn't want to say anything because I didn't want to be accused of being part of it."

"Where did she get the license?" he asked.

Rachel smiled sadly and looked up at the chief. "From Clint."

The chief frowned. "I don't understand."

"They used to be a real estate team. She was crazy about him, but he wasn't interested that way. Oh, not to say he didn't accept her *hospitality* once in a while. Their broker had a place in Mexico and offered it to them after they closed some big deal. It was in the spring, the very end of March. The two of them went down there, and Claudia, well, she thought it was going to turn into something."

"What happened?"

"She got really drunk their last night, too much tequila. When she woke up the next morning, that marriage license was sitting next to her in bed. She really thought they had gotten married while they were both drunk. And by the way it was on the pillow next to her, with a flower, she immediately thought sober Clint was happy about it. But she forgot it was April first. They always played pranks on each other every April first. He never understood why she got so upset. Afterwards, when they came back from the trip, Claudia told him she didn't want to work with him anymore, and she moved to another office."

"But they started working together again?"

"Yes. She missed him. He came to her with an idea of fixing up properties and then flipping them. She listed the properties, and he brought the buyer. To be honest, it wasn't exactly ethical. I loved my sister, but she liked taking shortcuts. They made pretty good money for a while, and then the housing market crashed."

"Has your sister ever mentioned a Jay Larson?"

"No. But Dirk mentioned that name at breakfast the other day. Someone Clint—I mean Walt—knew."

"Do you know anything about him?"

She shook her head. "No."

"What do you know about Dirk Thorpe?"

"I know my sister hated him."

"Why?"

"I have no idea. She was just really upset after he showed up here. I know he used to work at the same office as Clint."

"Was your sister being blackmailed?" he asked.

"Blackmailed?" Rachel frowned. "No. I don't know why you would ask me that. I know it seems like she was trying to blackmail Walt, but it wasn't going to work."

"About that..." The chief leaned back in the chair, his eyes on Rachel. "I can understand why your sister didn't find the April Fool's joke funny. But why after all this time, especially when he doesn't even remember what he did, would your sister decide to try extorting money from him? After all, she obviously once cared for him. And it seemed she put the incident in Mexico behind her when they started working together again. Why now? Was it just because he came into money?"

Nervously fidgeting with her hands on the tabletop, Rachel looked down and shook her head. "I don't know all the details. I just know that after Clint left, something came up with the real estate department regarding the listings she had sold to Clint's buyers. At the time, she thought Clint had gone to Europe with Stephanie, because that's what she'd heard. And when she tried to contact him, she learned about the accident and how he had amnesia. Since he was in no position to help her, she ended up selling her condo and paying whatever fines there were herself."

"She felt Clint owed her because of those fines she had to pay?"

Rachel nodded. "Yes. Clint had given up his real estate license, so he really didn't have to worry about getting fined. But she had to keep working, and needed to keep her license, so she had to pay them. She didn't think that was fair, especially because she believed it was Clint's fault they got in trouble."

"Her plan was to indirectly get the money she thought he owed her by pretending they had been married?"

"I know it sounds really lame. But yeah. That's pretty much it."

"Do you know of anyone who might have had an issue with your sister?" he asked.

She shook her head. "No. And certainly no one here, aside from Walt and Dirk." Rachel paused a moment and then added, "But there was that guy."

"What guy?"

"He was a guy my sister knew whom we ran into while we were here. She told me he was a disgruntled client of Clint's who had bought one of her listings. She first noticed him standing in front of Marlow House. And then a couple of days later, we ran into him at that diner on the pier. He approached us and said Clint ruined him and then accused her of being part of it."

"What happened?"

"A police officer walked in and then the guy left. Claudia didn't seem that upset. She said he was Clint's problem."

"Do you know who he was?" the chief asked.

"No."

THIRTY-THREE

Dirk and his wife arrived at the police station a few minutes before the chief finished talking with Rachel. They asked them to sit in the waiting area until they were ready to see them. The chief walked Rachel out, and before taking Dirk's wife to the interrogation room, he took Joe and Brian aside and asked, "I need one of you to find out what fines the California Department of Real Estate levied against Claudia and why. Also, see what complaints were ever brought against Clint or Claudia."

"You mean against Walt?" Joe chuckled.

"No. It was Clint back then. Walt's a different man," the chief said.

After MacDonald walked down the hall with Tanya while Dirk remained sitting in one of the chairs in the waiting area, Joe looked at Brian and said, "I don't understand why he feels he can't turn the interrogations over to us. We were first on the scene; it's not like we're new at this. But he always does this with anything involving Marlow House."

"I suspect there's information about this case he hasn't had a chance to share with us yet. He was at Marlow House for a long time this morning and then had that discussion with Chris. From what I understand, he had some information pertinent to the case."

"I suppose."

"If you don't mind looking up that information for the chief, I'm going to head on down to the pier. Carla should be at work by now," Brian said.

"HOW WELL DID you know Claudia Dane?" the chief asked Tanya. The two sat alone in the interrogation room.

"Not well. I saw her a few times at open houses I attended with my husband."

"Did you know she was going to be at Marlow House before you arrived?" he asked.

"No. But why would I? Like I said, I barely knew the woman. I certainly wasn't informed of her travel plans."

"How well did you know Clint Marlow?" the chief asked.

"Just a little better than I knew Claudia. He worked at the same office as my husband, so I would see him at business functions, like the Christmas party, that sort of thing."

"Did you know Clint Marlow would be at Marlow House before you arrived?" he asked.

"I assumed he would be there. We saw that interview with him on the morning show. To be honest, that's why we came in the first place. Dirk was curious."

"Curious why?"

Tanya arched her brows and smiled at the chief. "Seriously? Wouldn't you be curious if someone you worked with suddenly became famous—well, semi-famous—and supposedly had amnesia? We needed to get away for a few days anyway, and Dirk thought it would be a kick to come here. I think he wanted to see if Clint really has amnesia. But it isn't like we planned the trip just for that, we were intending to go somewhere this week. We just happened to decide on Frederickport."

"Tell me what you did yesterday and the last time you saw Claudia."

"At breakfast. That was the last time I saw her. I wanted to do a little sightseeing in Astoria, and Dirk didn't want to go. I was heading back to town when I got a call from Dirk telling me he was at some little bar and wanted me to pick him up when I got back so we could go have something to eat. So that's what I did."

"Do you know what time that was?" he asked.

"I didn't pay any attention to the time. But it was about an hour before the sun went down. I was already on my way home when he called. I picked him up at the bar; we had a couple of drinks; then we went to get something to eat."

WHEN IT WAS Dirk's turn in the interrogation room, the chief again asked him about what he had done the previous day. His version of the events matched his wife's.

"What can you tell me about the fines Claudia had to pay the real estate department to keep her license?" the chief asked.

Dirk shrugged. "I have no idea. Claudia and I didn't work in the same office."

"Do you know of any issues Clint had with the real estate department?"

"No. But agents who have issues with the real estate department tend not to broadcast it. And Clint and I weren't exactly friends."

"You had some issue with him working with Jay Larson, didn't you?"

Dirk stared dumbly at the chief a few moments and then asked, "What are you talking about?"

"According to some agents who work with you, you had an issue with Larson and Marlow. Can you tell me about it?"

Dirk shifted uncomfortably in the chair. "I don't know what that has to do with Claudia's death."

"I understand you brought up his name at breakfast yesterday morning."

"So? I was just trying to help Clint jog his memory. I figured if I started tossing out the names of people he knew, something might stick. I was just trying to help."

"But why Larson's name? And I'd like you to tell me what issue you had with him and Clint."

"Larson was a real estate appraiser. Clint used him all the time."

"I thought appraisers were technically chosen by the buyer's lender, and even then, the lender can't say which appraiser they want, it has to come out of a pool?"

Dirk shrugged. "That's how it is now. But it used to be a lender could call his favorite appraiser to make sure the appraisal came in at sale price. If Clint got his buyers to use his lender, then he knew the listing would appraise. That's because his lender always used Larson."

"I understand why you may not know if an agent was sanctioned by the real estate department. But I also know it's fairly easy to look up that information. I find it curious you would know who appraised the properties Clint sold, but you never bothered to check his status with the real estate department."

"Why would I? Anyway, when a property comes up on the MLS, any agent checking will see it, along with the listing price. Claudia's listings were always ridiculously overpriced, yet they always sold at full price and appraised. That's information any agent is going to come across when doing a CMA. I couldn't believe her listings kept appraising, so I did a little checking and discovered Larson was the appraiser. Of course, with the new rules in place, a lender can't cherry-pick his appraiser anymore."

AFTER DIRK and Tanya left the police station, Joe met with the chief in his office.

"What did you find out?" the chief asked as he sat down behind his desk.

"I didn't find anything on Claudia. Nothing. She's never had any issues with the real estate department. No complaints, nothing. Marlow had a few complaints, but they were minor and all resolved. He's never been fined by the department either."

"So what was Rachel talking about?" The chief frowned.

Joe shook his head. "I have no idea."

"Where's Brian?"

"He went down to the pier to talk to Carla. She hadn't come in to work yet when we stopped there earlier. But they told us she pulled a double shift yesterday and would have been there at the same time Walt and Claudia walked down to the pier. We're hoping she saw something," Joe said.

"I'm going back to Marlow House and talk to Claudia's sister again. While I'm there, I'd like you to check into that condo Claudia sold. See if there's any way to find out what she did with that money. If she didn't use it to pay real estate fines, then where did it go? Her reason for coming here in the first place seems to be tied to that. We need to know who she gave that money to, and does it have anything to do with her murder?"

WHEN THE CHIEF arrived at Marlow House late Tuesday afternoon, he was greeted by Danielle at the front door. She took him to the living room, where Walt, Chris and Heather were sitting, with Hunny napping on the floor next to her human.

"Actually, I came to talk to Rachel," the chief said after saying hello to everyone.

Danielle stood up from where she sat next to Walt on the sofa. "She's upstairs packing, but I'll go get her for you."

"Packing? I thought she agreed to stay in Frederickport for a few more days?" he snapped.

"Oh, don't worry, Chief, she's not going far. She got a room at the Seahorse Motel."

"Why? Doesn't she have a room here for the rest of the week?" he asked.

"Seriously, Chief? Do you blame her? As far as she knows, Walt or Danielle gunned down her sister and tossed her body in the icy ocean," Heather said. "Too creepy to stay under the same roof with them."

"Gee, thanks, Heather," Danielle said dryly.

Heather shrugged. "Well, it's true. She doesn't know who killed her sister. And who had a better motive than the man she was blackmailing, or the woman getting rid of her fiancé's wife."

"Glad the chief understands you," Chris told Heather.

"Actually, Heather has a point," the chief conceded.

Heather flashed a smug grin to her friends.

"Let me go get her. I'll take her to the parlor. I assume you want to speak to her alone," Danielle said.

"Before you go, I wonder, have any of you seen Claudia?" the chief asked them.

"No, that's what we were just talking about," Chris said. "But according to Heather, Marie and Eva are out looking for her."

"They didn't actually tell me they were looking for her, but when I saw them each flying around over the beach like a couple of witches from *The Wizard of Oz*, I assumed that's what they were doing."

"DANIELLE SAID you wanted to talk to me again?" Rachel said when she entered the parlor. The chief stood up to greet her and then motioned for her to sit down in one of the chairs.

"I understand you're moving over to the Seahorse Motel?"

"Yes. I have to say, Danielle was really very nice about it. In fact, she refunded all my money. I told her that wasn't necessary, but she insisted." Rachel took a seat.

"Under the circumstances, I suppose I can understand why you might feel uncomfortable staying here."

Rachel nodded. "So what did you want to talk to me about, Chief MacDonald? I thought we covered everything."

"You told me your sister sold her condo to pay real estate fines."

"Yes. But I'm not sure what that has to do with her murder."

"Considering that was the motivation for her coming here, I believe it could be relevant. But the problem, we checked. And your sister has never been fined by the real estate department. In fact, she's never had a complaint against her."

"She paid the fines, so that's probably why nothing showed up," Rachel suggested.

"It doesn't work that way. If she paid a fine to the real estate department, there would be a record of it."

Rachel frowned. "But I know she paid it. When she sold her condo, she made a little over a hundred thousand. She started paying off the fine, and within a month all the money was gone."

"A hundred thousand? That's a pretty big real estate fine."

Rachel shrugged. "That's why she wanted to get Clint to pay his share."

"So she didn't pay it off all at once?" he asked.

"No. The only reason I know that, one day after she came home from work, I went in her room to talk to her, and I found her counting money. It was five thousand dollars. I knew she was tight with money because of the fines she had paid, so I was naturally curious why she had all that money. She told me she was taking it down to the real estate department."

"Didn't you find it odd she was paying in cash? Or paying in installments if she already had the money?"

"I just figured she wanted to pay in cash so they would give a receipt for cash, and not chance having the check getting lost in the mail. And paying in installments, I don't know. I just figured she wanted to hang onto her money as long as possible before she had to hand it all over, you know, in case an emergency came up."

"Does the department of real estate have an office close to you?"

"I assume so."

"Do you know if she has receipts for these payments?"

"I never saw any." Absently chewing on her lower lip, Rachel frowned at the chief. "You don't think she paid that money to the real estate department, do you?"

"No, I don't."

Rachel looked down at her lap and sniffled. "I tried to be there for my sister, but I knew enough not to get too much in her business. It always irritated her if I asked too many questions. That's why I didn't call the police when I went to bed last night and she wasn't there. I figured she was probably at a bar somewhere letting off steam, and if she thought I was checking up on her, she would just get mad. But now, I wish I would have called. Maybe I could have saved her life."

THIRTY-FOUR

It started to sprinkle. Rachel sat alone in the car in the parking lot of the Seahorse Motel, looking at the weathered old buildings. She hadn't checked in yet, but she didn't have an umbrella, and she didn't feel like getting wet. Maybe it would stop raining if she just sat here for a few more minutes.

"I have been looking all over for you! When I told you you could use my car, I certainly didn't expect you to just take off with it!" Claudia ranted from the passenger seat.

Rachel began to cry.

"Seriously? You're going to cry about that? Sometimes you can be so emotional."

Rachel pulled a tissue from her purse and began dabbing the tears away.

"Let's go back to Marlow House. I really want to change my clothes," Claudia told her.

The rain stopped. Rachel looked up through the windshield. With a sniffle, she unhooked her seatbelt and removed the key from the ignition.

"Where are you going?" Claudia asked.

Grabbing her purse off the passenger seat, Rachel opened the car door.

Claudia looked down and frowned. *I didn't notice her purse sitting on my lap*, she thought.

Annoyed, Claudia followed her sister from the car to the front office of the motel.

"What are you doing here?" Claudia asked.

"I have a reservation, Rachel Dane," Rachel told the man sitting at the front desk.

"Welcome, Ms. Dane. We have room six all ready for you."

"What do you mean you have a reservation? We already paid for a week at Marlow House!" Claudia demanded.

A few minutes later Claudia followed her sister from the office back outside. "Would you stop ignoring me! I'm serious, Rachel. You are really starting to annoy me! What's gotten into you?"

Fuming, Claudia stood by the side of her car and watched as her sister pulled a suitcase out of the car's trunk. She then noticed her own suitcase.

"Wait a minute, what is my suitcase doing in there?"

Rachel slammed the trunk shut, leaving her sister's luggage behind.

"How am I supposed to change my clothes if you leave that in the car? And just why are we here? What happened at Marlow House? Did Danielle Boatman find out who I am? Is that it? Did she kick us out? Is that why you won't talk to me?"

Claudia followed her sister to the door of room six. Just as Rachel put the key card in the lock, the door to room seven opened and out walked a man. He was busy hanging the do-not-disturb sign on his door and wasn't paying attention to his new neighbor.

Seeing the man, Claudia gasped. "I don't want to deal with you again!" She vanished.

As Rachel unlocked the door and started to open it, she glanced to the next room over. The man who had just stepped from the room looked directly at her. Their eyes met. She recognized him.

KELLY BARTLEY SAT with her brother in a booth in Pier Café. She'd talked him into meeting her there for a predinner slice of pie, and the chance to pump him for information on what had gone on not far from his house just that morning. Joe would fill her in when he got home, but she was too curious to wait, and she couldn't bother him at work, not when he was in the middle of investigating a murder.

"Did you see the body?" she asked ghoulishly.

"Thankfully, no." Ian shook his head at the question and took a sip of his coffee.

"But it was someone staying at Marlow House?" she asked.

"That's what Danielle told me when I talked to her on the phone."

"I don't know why anyone stays at Marlow House. Seriously." Kelly shivered.

Ian frowned at his sister. "What is that supposed to mean?"

"That place is a death trap. I can't even count how many people who've stayed there have been murdered—sometimes even right there on the property. Even a few attempted murders. Honestly, Ian, if I were you, I don't think I would've bought a house right across the street from it. It's bad luck."

"I don't think the woman's death had anything to do with Marlow House. And Lily seemed to get out alive," Ian smirked.

"It's not funny, Ian. I'm serious. I think you should do an article on that place."

Ian was just about to tell his sister he had no intention of writing such an article about his friend's bed and breakfast when Kelly said, "Oh look, Brian is here. I wonder if he knows anything more about the woman's death?"

CARLA SAT with Brian in a booth on the other side of the restaurant. No one was seated on either side of them.

Holding a photograph in her hand, she shook her head sadly. "So that's the poor woman who was killed?"

"Do you remember ever seeing her?" he asked.

"Oh yeah. I saw her a couple of times. The first was over the weekend. It caused quite a ruckus. In fact, I called the police. That female cop showed up."

"Officer Carpenter?" he asked.

"Yeah, I think that's her name. But as soon as she walked in, he took off."

"Who?"

"The woman—the one in the photograph—was sitting over there with another woman." Carla pointed to a booth. "Then this man comes in, I remember his name because he left his wallet in here and—" Carla stopped and looked at Brian. "I think he might be the one who killed her!"

KELLY COULDN'T KEEP her eyes off the booth with Brian and Carla.

"Maybe you should learn how to read lips," Ian suggested.

Kelly looked to her brother and frowned. "What?"

"It's killing you that you can't hear what they're saying."

"Carla obviously knows something. Look how Brian seems to be hanging on every word!"

Shaking his head at his sister, Ian took a bite of his pie.

Fifteen minutes later, after finishing their pie and Brian had left the diner, Carla came back to their table to see if they would like anything else.

"Any news on that woman they found this morning?" Kelly asked just as Carla picked up their dirty plates.

"You mean the one Heather Donovan found," Carla said as she set the plates back on the table, stacking one atop the other and shoving Ian over in his seat so she could sit down.

Rolling his eyes, Ian moved over, making room for Carla, who continued to address Kelly. "You know, if Heather Donovan ever asked me to go jogging with her, I would tell her hell no! It's like dead bodies are attracted to her."

"Do they know anything more?"

"Well, just between you and me, I think they might have found the one responsible. Brian is going over there right now, so I can't really say who. But I think the lid is going to be blown off this case by nightfall."

Ian arched his brow. "Really?"

"And it's not Walt Marlow. Although, when I realized who the woman was, that was my first thought," Carla said.

"Why in the world would you imagine Walt was responsible for that woman's death?" Ian asked.

"Because she was his wife—a wife he obviously wanted to get rid of," Carla whispered.

"Wife?" Kelly gasped.

Ian groaned.

Carla nodded. "Yep. When they searched her room over at

Marlow House, they found the marriage license. She and Walt Marlow were married in Mexico."

"Who told you that?" Ian asked. "I can't believe they would discuss what they found in the search."

"They didn't tell me." Carla shrugged. "But two of the cops who searched the room stopped in here later to get something to eat, and I overheard them."

BRIAN HAD JUST PULLED up to the Seahorse Motel when his cellphone rang. It was the chief.

"I just got a call from Rachel Dane. She's pretty upset. That man her sister knew, who approached her at the diner, he's staying in the room next to hers. Room seven."

"I'm there now." Brian went on to brief the chief on what Carla had told him.

Just as Brian got off the call, he spied a short balding man heading to room seven, carrying what appeared to be a paper sack with take-out food. Brian quickly got out of the squad car.

"Albert Hanson?" Brian called out just as the man was about to put his key card in the door.

Albert turned from the door and looked up at Brian. "Yes?"

"Are you Albert Hanson?"

"Is there a problem, officer?"

"I need to speak with you for a moment."

A few minutes later, Brian sat on a small sofa in the motel room while Albert sat on a chair facing him.

"I understand you left your wallet in Pier Café yesterday."

"Yes. I picked it up this morning. Is that what this is about?"

"I also understand you had an argument with a woman in there on Saturday," Brian said.

"Is she pressing charges or something?"

"She's dead."

Albert's eyes widened, and he slumped back in his chair. "Dead?"

"When was the last time you saw her?"

Albert noticeably swallowed. "Yesterday afternoon."

"Tell me about it. And when you do, I would like to know what issue you had with her and Clint Marlow."

Albert licked his lips and nodded. "Clint Marlow was my real estate agent. My parents had passed away and left me a couple of hundred thousand. I thought it would be wise to invest in real estate. So I went to Marlow. He pointed out if I paid cash, I would only get one property, but if I used my inheritance as the down payment, and my good credit, I could secure loans and he could find me at least three houses to buy, which I could rent out. It seemed like a great idea at the time. But when the market crashed, I was upside down in all the loans, and lost everything."

"A lot of people lost money when the housing market crashed," Brian noted.

"Yes. But I later discovered those houses were never worth what I paid for them, even when the market was good. Marlow had to know that. But he just wanted me to buy more houses so he could make a commission."

"So what happened the last time you saw Claudia Dane?"

"When I first saw her, I thought it was a sign that they were in it together somehow. I mean, here she was in Frederickport. I'd seen an interview with him on TV, how he was this big-shot author now, and I just wanted to confront him. But then there she was, the agent who had listed the properties."

"So you were angry with her?"

"Yes, but mostly with him. He's the one that was supposed to be looking out for my best interest. I know I shouldn't have gone off on her in the restaurant like that. But I sorta snapped when I saw her. And then yesterday, that waitress, the one who found my wallet, she told me that woman was on the pier with Clint Marlow, so I went out to find them."

"Then what?"

"They didn't see me. They were arguing. Then she took off, went walking down the pier."

"What did you do?"

"I followed Marlow. I was going to confront him. But...well, I chickened out. I followed him back to his house, and he didn't see me. He went inside, and I just stood out there like an idiot. I didn't do anything. Finally, this woman next door, she asked me what I was doing out there, so I just took off."

"Next door? The neighbor to the north or south of Marlow House?"

He considered the question a moment and then said, "The neighbor to the south."

"So you never talked to Marlow?" Brian asked.

Hanson shook his head. "No, but if people are getting killed, maybe I should tell you something."

"What?"

"Before I came here, I sent Marlow a letter—an anonymous letter. I…I wanted to scare him. Make his life feel uncertain like he made me feel. But I realize he doesn't even remember any of it. And legally, well, my lawyer said there's nothing I can really do. Not unless I want to spend a lot of money on a costly court case I can't afford and would likely lose. You need to know I'm the one who sent that anonymous letter, but I had nothing to do with that woman's death, I promise."

THIRTY-FIVE

When Marie had been a little girl, she believed that when a person died, they would then become an angel with wings. The notion appealed to her, not because angels were ethereal creatures, but because anything with wings could fly. She would have been just as happy to learn that when a person died they became a bird.

What she had learned since death was that when a person died, they became a ghost—and while an experienced ghost might fashion wings, they would only be an illusion, in the same way as Eva's glitter and Walt's cigars had been. However, she didn't rule out the possibility of advancing to an angel someday, because she still didn't know what really happened once she chose to move on to the other side and leave her ghostly self behind.

In spite of being bereft of wings, she discovered to her delight that a ghost could fly. Perhaps it was not flying in the traditional sense, because the body she wore—one she was capable of changing by adjusting her age or wardrobe—was only an illusion, and when she soared above the rooftops, it was only her conscious spirit adjusting its perspective on the world.

All afternoon she had been observing Frederickport from an eagle's view, searching for the spirit of Claudia Dane. Marie felt guilty for it all, wondering if the poor woman might have been saved had she returned to Marlow House the previous day. Marie also felt a hint of shame for the slap and pinch she had given the woman, in spite of the fact she still believed she deserved it.

However, Marie could still remember how she had felt when newly departed, wandering the streets of Frederickport, having no idea she had died. She felt compelled to help this confused soul, remembering the frustration of bewilderment, not understanding what was happening to her.

Marie was just about to turn back and return to Marlow House, wondering if perhaps Claudia had gone back there, when she spied the spirit in question. From this distance she wasn't certain the blond woman below was in truth the wayward ghost. But then she witnessed a Cadillac drive straight through her. The driver of the vehicle had no idea what he had just done, and continued on, but Claudia—and Marie was now convinced it was Claudia—raised her fist and started shouting at the car as it sped away. Still standing in the middle of the road, Claudia was driven through by a second vehicle, this time a pickup truck, and again its driver didn't flinch, but now Claudia was furious. From above, Marie watched as the newly minted ghost marched angrily up the road.

THE PLACARD on the door said Police Chief MacDonald. Claudia wasn't sure how she got here exactly, standing alone in a corridor, inside a building that was obviously the police station, considering the plaques hanging on the wall.

"Can I help you?" came a female voice behind her.

Claudia turned quickly and found herself looking into the face of an elderly woman wearing a sundress and straw hat. She thought it odd attire for January. "Do you work here?"

"Not exactly. My name is Marie. And you are Claudia?"

Claudia frowned. "How did you know that?"

"Perhaps you should stand over here, away from the door. I believe there's someone coming, and you're in their way. And trust me, he won't go around you." Marie motioned for Claudia to join her a few feet from the entrance into the chief's office.

"But I need to talk to a policeman," Claudia said as she walked to Marie. "Two different vehicles almost ran me over a few minutes ago. They didn't even stop. I think they need to do something about that intersection."

"I'm afraid they're rather busy right now," Marie said. "They're investigating a murder."

"Murder? Who was murdered?"

"Shh, let's be quiet and listen." Marie pointed over Claudia's shoulder. Claudia turned around and watched as an attractive police officer came walking their way. Tall and husky, he had warm brown eyes and dark wavy hair.

"That's Sergeant Joe Morelli," Marie explained. "I believe he's on his way to talk to the police chief."

"But I need to talk to him. That's why I'm here."

"You're going to have to wait. The murder and all," Marie explained.

They watched as Joe knocked on the chief's door and then went in a few seconds later.

"Let's see what's going on," Marie whispered. She motioned toward the office and started following Joe.

"We can do that?" Claudia asked.

"They won't mind if we're quiet," Marie promised.

With a shrug Claudia followed Marie.

"Any updates from the coroner's office?" Joe asked.

"The bullet was from a .38," the chief told him.

"Isn't that what the sister said she carried?" Joe asked.

"A .38? I have a .38," Claudia murmured.

"Her gun hasn't been found. She also had defensive wounds. It looks like she was in a struggle before she was shot," the chief said.

"You thinking someone tried to take it away from her, and she got shot with her own gun?" Joe asked.

"It's possible, but if we can't find the weapon, we aren't going to know for sure. Did you find out anything about the funds from the sale of her condo?" The chief, who was sitting behind his desk, motioned to an empty chair.

Joe sat down. "It went into her bank account, which she depleted by withdrawing five thousand dollars a day until it was all gone."

Claudia frowned. "What's going on? I don't understand."

"You need to listen and try to remember, Claudia," Marie whispered. "But it's going to be okay. I'm here and will help you."

"No idea where that money went?" the chief asked.

"That's where the paper trail seems to stop," Joe said.

"I wonder if our killer will have a bank account with regular five-thousand-a-day deposits?" the chief asked.

"Chief, I don't know why you seem to think someone was blackmailing her. Her sister certainly didn't think that was the case. Maybe she had a gambling problem, and that's why she was going through all that cash. But as far as the murder goes, we do have one prime suspect, one who was seen with the victim right before her death, and who had a motive to want her dead."

"I don't believe Walt Marlow is the killer," the chief said.

"Walt Marlow? Why are they talking about Walt Marlow?" Claudia looked frantically from Marie to the police chief.

"First of all, she wasn't really his wife. Her sister told us that marriage license was fake, and for the record, I have since verified that fact. Claudia Dane and Clint Marlow were never married," the chief explained.

Claudia gasped. "Why are they talking about me?"

"Chief, after I looked into the money, I decided to follow up a hunch of mine," Joe told him.

"What hunch?"

"I never intended to pass this on, but considering the circumstances, I don't have a choice," Joe told him.

"Pass what on?" the chief asked.

"Danielle is pregnant," Joe announced.

"Who told you that?" the chief demanded.

"Pregnant?" Marie gasped. "Oh, how wonderful!"

"I don't want to say right now. Because of the fact she's pregnant, I started wondering if maybe she and Walt decided to go ahead and get married now. They could still have the ceremony on Valentine's Day."

"Joe, this isn't the 1950s," MacDonald reminded.

"You sound like Brian," Joe retorted.

"Are you saying Brian knows about this?"

"Brian knows about Danielle's pregnancy, yes," Joe said. "But he doesn't know they're already married."

"What are you talking about?" the chief asked.

"Having a wife show up before your marriage can complicate things, but as you said, the marriage can be dissolved. But if he was already married to Danielle, then Claudia's claim made him a bigamist. I decided to check to see if since learning of Danielle's pregnancy, they had gotten married."

"What are you saying?" the chief practically groaned.

"Yes, what are you saying?" Claudia asked.

"They are married all right. Fact is, they got married months ago," Joe told him. "This changes everything."

"No, it doesn't," the chief argued.

"I know you're close to Danielle, but—"

"Are you suggesting I would shirk my duty because of my feelings for Danielle?" the chief asked.

"No, sir, it's just—"

"Sergeant Morelli, Walt Marlow has absolutely no motive to murder Claudia Dane. And even if he had been legally married to Ms. Dane, I seriously doubt any prosecutor would pursue bigamy charges against a man who had amnesia and had no knowledge of the marriage. And you keep forgetting, Walt and Danielle informed me of Claudia's claim the day after she made it, so if Walt had any intention of getting rid of a troublesome wife, he certainly would not have told the police chief of her existence."

A knock came at the door. Joe turned around to see Brian standing at the open doorway.

"I'm dead," Claudia muttered.

"I'm sorry, dear," Marie told her. "I wanted to come right out and tell you, but I'm rather new at all this. I thought perhaps it might be the best way. Let you ease into the idea."

Looking past Joe, the chief asked, "What did you find out, Brian?"

"I think we're back to square one," Brian said. "I don't think Hanson had anything to do with Dane's death, and he provided Walt an alibi."

"How did he do that?" the chief asked.

"He admitted to being down at the pier when Walt was there with Claudia. When the two parted ways, he followed Walt back to Marlow House."

"What are you talking about?" Joe asked.

Brian then went on to recap his conversation with Carla and then with Hanson. When he was done, he added, "Before coming back here, I stopped at Pearl Huckabee's house. She confirmed Hanson's story. Huckabee saw him standing outside Marlow House and asked him what he was doing."

The chief looked at Joe. "Well, what did I tell you?"

"Did they think Albert Hanson killed me?" Claudia asked.

"They're trying to find out who is responsible for your death. Why don't you tell me?" Marie urged.

Claudia looked at Marie. "Who is responsible for my death? That's easy. Clint Marlow." The next moment, Claudia vanished.

THIRTY-SIX

Danielle's head felt as if it were about to split in two. If Walt hadn't gone for a walk along the beach to see if he could find Claudia's ghost, she would get him to change the stupid lightbulb. Heck, he could do it without getting on the ladder or even touching the lightbulb. Reaching up to the fixture, she stood on her tiptoes and unscrewed the burned-out bulb.

"Danielle, what in the world are you doing on that ladder?" Marie asked when she appeared in the kitchen.

"I'm changing a lightbulb, what does it look like? If I knew you were going to be here, I would have waited a few minutes and had you do it." Danielle finished unscrewing the lightbulb and then climbed down off the ladder.

"Let me finish!" Marie shooed Danielle away from the ladder.

Danielle shrugged. "Fine. Give it a shot, but please try not to break the bulb. It's my last one." Danielle picked up the good bulb and handed it to Marie. She watched as it lifted from Marie's hand and floated to the ceiling, where it screwed itself into the socket.

"That's actually pretty cool," Danielle said. "You're doing a lot better."

"Thank you."

"Heather told me you were off looking for Claudia. I take it you didn't have any luck?" Danielle walked over to the counter and opened one of the overhead cabinets. She pulled out the bottle of aspirin and unscrewed its lid.

"Danielle, what in the world are you doing?"

The bottle of aspirin flew out of Danielle's hand, sending aspirin flying out of the container onto the floor, with the bottle landing on the table.

Wide eyed, Danielle turned to the ghost. "Marie? Why did you do that?"

"I don't believe it's wise for you to take those. Not in your condition." Marie glanced down, looking for the aspirin. They began floating up from the floor, making their way back to the aspirin bottle on the table.

"Not sure I want to take them now, after they've been on the floor," Danielle grumbled. She looked at Marie and frowned. "What do you mean, my condition?"

"The baby, dear," Marie whispered.

"What baby?" Danielle frowned.

"Yes, what baby?" Walt asked as he walked into the kitchen.

Danielle looked to Walt. "You didn't see her?"

Walt shook his head. "No. But what is this about a baby?"

"Are you saying you aren't pregnant?" Marie asked.

"Why would you think I was pregnant?" As soon as she asked the question, Danielle looked down at her stomach. Touching the waist of her jeans, she asked, "Do I look fat?"

"No, you don't look fat," Walt scoffed. "You look perfect."

"Are you saying you aren't pregnant?" Marie asked.

"No, I'm not pregnant. Why did you think I was?"

"Joe Morelli said you were," Marie told her.

"Joe?" Walt frowned. "What would Joe know about if Danielle was pregnant or not?"

"He also knows you two are married."

"What?" Walt and Danielle chorused.

"I also saw Claudia," Marie added.

PULLING the curtain to one side, Heather looked out the window. The sun was beginning to set. If there wasn't a killer on the loose, she would be tempted to slip on a jacket and walk down to the beach and watch it. With a sigh, she let the curtain drop back in place. Her teapot began to whistle.

Wrapped in a throw blanket, she made her way from the living room to the kitchen, dragging one corner of the blanket along the floor. It was chilly in the house, but she was attempting to conserve energy. Once in the kitchen, she set the blanket on a chair and walked to the stove. Picking up the kettle, she began filling her teapot when a woman walked through her wall into the room. Heather froze. It was the same woman she had found on the beach that morning, Claudia Dane.

"Do you always walk into people's houses uninvited?" Heather snapped.

"You can see me?" Claudia asked.

"Yes, I can see you." Heather picked up her teapot and empty cup and headed for the kitchen table. "Everyone has been looking for you."

"Are you dead?"

Setting the teapot and cup on the table, she then picked up the blanket and wrapped it around herself. Sitting down in a chair, she said, "If I were dead, I wouldn't be freezing my butt off right now. So, who shot you?"

"How do you know I was shot?" Claudia asked.

"That bullet hole in your chest is a big clue."

"You aren't very kind to someone who just died. Are you a demon or something? Am I in hell?"

Heather cocked her brow and looked at Claudia. "Do you deserve to be in hell?"

"Maybe...I haven't always done the right thing."

"I suspect few people always do the right thing. It's more the summation of your life."

"So this isn't hell?" Claudia asked.

Heather shrugged. "Some think it is."

Claudia groaned.

Picking up her teapot, Heather started to fill her cup. "I would offer you some, but ghosts don't drink tea."

"Is that what I am, a ghost? She said I was dead, but she didn't say I was a ghost."

"Seriously, you have to be told? You just walked through my wall, know you are dead, and basically admitted some people can't see you. If that isn't the definition of a ghost, what is?"

"Am I always going to be a ghost?"

"No. When you move over to the other side, I don't think you'll be a ghost anymore. Who were you talking about when you said *she* told you you were dead?"

"She said her name, but I don't remember. Too much to process. She was an old woman—"

"Straw hat and sundress?" Heather asked.

"Yes!'

"Ahh, Marie!" Heather sipped her tea.

"You know her?"

"She's another ghost," Heather explained. "So tell me, who shot you?"

"Marie asked me who was responsible for my death, and I told her. Clint Marlow."

"Clint Marlow is dead, so unless he's come back from the grave, I don't think so." Heather frowned and then muttered, "*Technically there was no grave, but whatever.*"

"What do you mean he's dead? Did someone kill him too?"

"If you're talking about Walt Marlow, he's still alive," Heather told her.

"It's the same person," Claudia argued.

"Nope, it's not. Why don't you sit down, and I'll tell you the story of Walt and Clint Marlow." Setting her teacup on the table, Heather reached over and pulled out a chair for Claudia. "And then you can tell me what happened to you."

HEATHER SAT ALONE in her kitchen. Claudia had just left. She picked up her cellphone and called the police chief.

"Heather? Have you seen her?" the chief asked when he answered her call.

"Yes. She was just at my house." Holding the phone to her ear, Heather glanced to the kitchen window. It was dark outside.

"Does she know who murdered her?"

"She wasn't murdered exactly," Heather said.

"What do you mean?"

"People are funny when they die."

"I don't follow you," the chief said.

"Sometimes they're more candid than they would be if you

asked them the same question when they were alive. I'm not saying all dead people tell the truth. Not that I've talked to as many dead people as Danielle, but that's what she told me."

"Heather, please, will you get to the part where Claudia gives you the identity of the killer?"

"It's more a reluctant killer. You see, Claudia admitted she was the one who pulled the gun on her would-be killer. And for a moment she seriously considered pulling the trigger. The other person didn't feel like waiting for Claudia to make up her mind."

"There were defensive wounds. The person who shot her was trying to get the gun away from her, right?" the chief asked.

"Pretty much. Of course, when the gun went off accidentally, it doesn't sound like there was much effort to try to save Claudia. When all this went down, she was on the end of the pier. One minute she's wrestling with someone she considered killing; the next thing she knows, she's in the ocean."

DANIELLE LEANED against Walt's shoulder. They sat alone together in the library, watching flames dance and crackle in the fireplace. The Russoms had stopped by briefly to change their clothes. They were on their way to Astoria, where they planned to spend the night. Marie had taken off shortly after they left. Dirk and his wife had gone out to dinner, so Walt and Danielle were alone in the house.

Walt draped an arm around Danielle, his right hand caressing her bare arm. Staring into the flames, he asked, "I wonder what Claudia meant when she said Clint was responsible for her death."

"Probably because if it wasn't for her and Clint's past, she wouldn't have come here," Danielle suggested. "And then she would still be alive."

"You're correct," came a female voice from behind them.

Abruptly Walt and Danielle sat up and turned around, coming face-to-face with Claudia's ghost.

"You can see me. Heather said you could both see ghosts. She was right."

"You've seen Heather?" Danielle asked.

"Yes, I just left her. I told her what happened. And I wanted to apologize to Walt. None of it was his fault." Claudia walked toward them, making her way around the sofa and taking a seat on a nearby chair.

"You know?" Walt asked.

"That you're masquerading as Clint?" Claudia smiled. "But now that I really look at you, there is something different. For one thing, you look a little younger."

"He is." Danielle smiled.

"Where are Dirk and his wife?" Claudia asked.

"They went out to dinner," Danielle explained.

"Dirk plans to blackmail you."

"That's what we figured," Danielle said.

"Yes, Heather told me you've been keeping an eye on us."

"What does Dirk have on Clint?" Danielle asked.

"Dirk found out Clint and I had been working together getting buyers to purchase my flips, inflating the prices, and paying off the appraiser." Claudia cringed. "When I pass over, I wonder if I'll go to hell for real estate fraud?"

"I imagine there will be some penance, but here on this side, you would be beyond the statute of limitations. From what I understand, they couldn't bring any charges against you now—or against Walt. So I'm not sure why Dirk imagines he can blackmail anyone. Does he think Walt would be willing to pay just to save his reputation?"

"That's not why Dirk is going to blackmail Walt. He has something on Clint—on both of us—that could mean some serious prison time. The only reason he hasn't approached him yet, he wants Clint's memory to come back. Of course, that's not going to happen because Clint's already gone. But I imagine Dirk's not going to let amnesia keep him from making what he believes to be a lucrative score. Unfortunately, he has the documents to prove what Clint and I did. And trust me, you don't want him sending them to the authorities."

THIRTY-SEVEN

"Do you think she moved on?" Walt asked Danielle. Alone again, they were in the kitchen, cleaning up after dinner. Danielle stood at the sink, handwashing the dishes while Walt dried.

"She said she was going to stop and see her sister one more time, but I think she was ready. I'm rather relieved she's anxious to cross over. I've found people who fear punishment in the afterlife are often reluctant to move on, worried about what awaits them."

"So what do you think Marie is hiding from?" Walt teased.

With a grin Danielle playfully bumped Walt with her hip and handed him a plate to dry. "I'll let you ask her."

Walt grinned at Danielle and dried the dish. After a few moments of silence, he said, "I suppose we should get back to the Thorpes and how we're going to handle them." Walt tossed the dish towel on the counter.

"It would have been nice had we found the papers in their room," Danielle grumbled. "But at least we know what we're up against."

Walt followed Danielle out of the kitchen. "I still can't believe you let me search their room."

"Sometimes we have to bend the rules. I'd happily kick them out, but—"

"Not until we get our hands on the incriminating evidence against Clint," Walt finished for her.

"This really puts the poor chief in a pickle. Not only can't he tell any of his people how he knows what he knows, if any of them get ahold of what Dirk has on Clint, it's going to create a major headache for us."

When searching the Thorpes' room earlier, Marie had returned. She assisted in the search and then agreed to return the next morning. Considering what they had learned from Claudia, they didn't feel Marie needed to stick around.

"We need to get our hands on it before Joe or Brian. I have a feeling Joe would take special delight in seeing me sent to prison."

Danielle cringed. "Please, I don't even want to consider the possibility."

They were about to step into the living room when the Russoms came walking in the front door.

"You're back?" Danielle said in surprise.

"Something came up with my cousin, so we had to cancel the trip to Astoria. While they're dealing with their thing, thought we'd just come back here," Mr. Russom said.

Danielle invited them to join her and Walt in the living room for cocktails. Thirty minutes later as the four were sitting in the living room, enjoying their second round of drinks, the Thorpes returned. Walt made introductions and prepared Dirk and Tanya a cocktail.

"Are you saying she was staying here?" Mr. Russom asked when Tanya brought up the subject of Claudia's death.

"Yes, she and her sister, but her sister checked out," Danielle explained. She didn't mention Rachel had gone to the Seahorse Motel for fear the killer might be staying under Marlow House's roof.

"I heard it might be suicide," Mrs. Russom said.

"Suicide, where did you hear that?" Danielle asked.

"When we came back from Astoria, we stopped into the Pier Café for a bite to eat," Mrs. Russom explained. "The waitress there said the woman had been shot with a .38, and that was the type of gun she owned, and it was missing. She said the woman probably committed suicide by shooting herself on the end of the pier and then falling in the ocean."

"Carla," Danielle mumbled under her breath.

"Such a shame," Mrs. Russom said.

"If you'll excuse me, I think I'll head upstairs and get ready for bed. I'm exhausted," Tanya said.

Danielle stood. "I'm going to go up too. I need to take a shower." Danielle paused a moment and looked at Tanya. "Unless you want to take one first. In these old houses, sometimes it's best not to take showers at the same time."

"No, that's fine. I took mine earlier."

As Danielle started for the door, Walt said, "I think I might head up and get a little work done."

"Oh, you're always on that computer," Dirk said. "Stay down and have another drink with us. I've been wanting to ask you some questions about that book of yours."

Danielle paused at the doorway and glanced back at Walt; their eyes met. They both wondered if, once Dirk had him alone, he would make his demand.

"Goodnight, everyone," Danielle said as she stepped into the hallway.

A few moments later as she made her way up the stairs behind Tanya, her hand on the rail, she heard the distant sound of the pet door swinging in the kitchen. Almost to the second-floor landing, she glanced down and spied Max strolling panther-like down the hallway, from the kitchen to the living room, where she had left Walt. She smiled, relieved to know the cat was back in the house safe and sound.

"Goodnight, see you in the morning," Danielle told Tanya as she passed her in the hallway.

Tanya lingered by the closed door into the room Danielle had given her and Dirk. "Night, Danielle."

When Danielle arrived at her bedroom door, she paused a moment and looked back down the hallway and found Tanya still standing by her door. The woman flashed her a smile and started to go into her room, her eyes still on Danielle.

"Goodnight," Danielle said one more time as she walked into her bedroom.

Once in the room Danielle closed and locked her door. She immediately went to the dresser and removed the baby monitor, setting it up so she would hear anyone knocking on the door when up in the room with Walt. Since she hadn't moved her clothes upstairs yet, she grabbed what she needed for the next morning before heading upstairs to take a shower.

A few minutes later she was inside her bedroom closet. She

opened the hidden door and turned on the light. The bulb flickered on and then went out.

"Not another lightbulb," Danielle groaned. "Walt can change this one."

Holding onto the handrail with one hand and her clothes in the other, Danielle slowly made her way up the dark hidden stairwell. When she reached the attic landing, she placed her now free hand on the wall and began pushing the panel to one side. It slid only an inch when a flash of light hit her in the eye and then zigzagged to another part of the attic apartment. She froze.

Peeking through the small opening, she looked into the dark room. The light in the attic apartment was not on, but someone was in there with a flashlight. She watched as the flashlight moved around the room. She heard drawers opening and closing.

Who is in there? she wondered. *And what are they looking for?*

Danielle stood frozen and listened, watching through the small opening. After a few minutes the door to the attic opened and light flooded in from the hallway. She could now clearly see the intruder. It was Tanya. Danielle watched as the woman turned off the flashlight and then left the room, closing and locking the door behind her.

Danielle remained in the stairwell, deciding what to do next. She wondered what Tanya was looking for, and how did she get in the attic apartment? They always locked their rooms. She debated returning to her own room on the second floor in case Tanya made another visit to the attic. The last thing Danielle wanted at this time was to reveal the existence of the hidden staircase, especially considering what Claudia had told them about Dirk.

The minutes ticked away, and Danielle was about to return to her room on the second floor when the light went on in the attic room. Peeking through the small opening, she spied Walt, who had just stepped into the room, closing the door behind him.

With a sigh of relief, Danielle slid the panel open and stepped into the room.

"I thought you would be in the shower already," Walt told her.

"I had a little visitor." Danielle slid the panel closed behind her.

"What visitor?"

"Tanya broke into your room." Danielle then went on to tell Walt what had happened.

"Interesting. I was able to come up—spared being quizzed

about my book by someone I know has other motives—when Tanya returned to the living room and told Dirk she decided she wasn't tired. They're playing a board game with the Russoms."

"Lucky Russoms," Danielle muttered. "Obviously it was her way of telling Dirk the job was done. What do you think she was looking for?"

"I can't imagine. But I suppose one way to find out is to see what's missing."

Danielle groaned and then glanced around the room. "Maybe we start where I saw her snooping with the flashlight."

For the next five minutes they searched the room, opening drawers, looking under the bed. Nothing seemed to be missing. They were about to give up when Danielle noticed one of the decorative boxes she had placed on the shelf had been moved. It was empty, so she hadn't felt it necessary to look inside when they started searching.

Walt watched as Danielle picked the box up off the shelf. "Something is in here," Danielle said, jiggling it gently in her hands, feeling the extra weight. Removing the lid, she looked inside and then let out a gasp. Wide eyed, she looked at Walt while tilting the box so he could see inside.

"A gun?" Walt looked down at the small .38.

"I'm pretty sure it's Claudia's gun, the one Dirk wrestled out of her hands when she was going to shoot him."

"I guess this answers our question. Did he keep the gun or toss it in the ocean when he pushed her body off the pier?" Walt took the box from Danielle and asked, "You know what this means, don't you?"

"Yes, that they intend to frame you for her murder."

"The good news, maybe they don't intend to blackmail me?" Walt grinned.

"Gee, nice. Framed for murder is better than blackmail?"

Walt shrugged.

"I'd better call the chief." Danielle told him.

THIRTY-EIGHT

Awake, Danielle stared up at the ceiling, thinking of the previous day's events. By her side Walt stirred, rustling the sheets. The next moment his hand touched her.

"Good morning," she whispered. She reached out and touched the hand touching hers.

"What time is it?" he groaned.

She glanced at the clock. "Time to get up. I imagine Joanne is already downstairs making breakfast."

Walt sat up and looked across Danielle to the alarm clock. He frowned. "We overslept."

"Considering yesterday might have been one of the longest days in my life, I don't think we slept long enough."

"It did seem it would never end," Walt agreed.

Together they sat up and exchanged a quick good-morning kiss before getting out of bed and dressing for the day.

Downstairs they found Joanne preparing breakfast and the Russoms in the dining room with the Thorpes, chatting and having coffee. It was the first time the Russoms had shared breakfast with them. The conversation was superficial, and when everyone was done eating, the Russoms said their goodbyes and left for another day's outing.

"I was wondering if I could talk to you and Danielle, alone, in the parlor?" Dirk asked Walt as Danielle helped Joanne clear the table. "Tanya and I have decided we should cut our trip short. While Claudia wasn't exactly a friend, we'd rather get back home and put this tragedy behind us."

"Let me take these dishes in the kitchen, and I'll meet you both in the parlor," Danielle said, flashing a questioning glance to Walt.

Ten minutes later Danielle and Walt were alone in the parlor with Dirk, who sat on a chair facing them, holding a manila folder in his hand.

"If you would like a refund for leaving early," Danielle offered, "I will be happy to give it to you, considering the tragic turn of events." *Which you caused*, she thought.

"That's not why I wanted to speak to you alone." Dirk smiled. "But I think it best if that's the reason you give Joanne if she asks why I wanted to talk to you both alone. You might also tell her I wanted to privately wish you congratulations on your upcoming nuptials."

"Umm…well, thank you," Danielle muttered.

Dirk flashed her a smirk-like smile and tossed the manila envelope on the coffee table between them. "But that's not why I wanted to talk to you."

Walt stared down at the envelope. "What's that?"

"Open it," Dirk dared.

Reluctantly Walt reached down and picked up the envelope. Danielle watched as he opened it and slid out a stack of papers.

"Those are just copies. You're welcome to keep them. But I would suggest burning them. And if you want the originals, I'll be happy to arrange something." Dirk grinned.

Walt flipped through the papers. He knew what they were, only because Claudia had told him, but Dirk didn't know that. "What are they?"

"I was hoping your memory would come back; it would save me having to explain it all to you. And now with Claudia's untimely death, I realize I need to alter my original plan. In the beginning I intended to spare your fiancée any of the unpleasantness, but now I realize including her will make everything much easier."

"What are you talking about?" Danielle asked.

Dirk looked at Danielle and smiled. "It's obvious to me how fond you are of Clint. And I'm sure you want to keep him safe."

"Safe from what?" she asked.

"From his past, of course. While Walt here doesn't remember

his life as Clint, I don't imagine the IRS will really care. In fact, they might believe it's all an act in order to avoid his blatant attempt at tax fraud."

He looked from Danielle to Walt. "You were cleaning out your desk and file cabinets, moving out of the office before leaving town for your European adventure. All those boxes piled on the desk, ready to be shredded. I didn't think you would even notice if I helped myself to some of your client files. Why let all those leads go to waste? Imagine my surprise at one of those files I grabbed. I was shocked you would keep something like that in an office you shared with a couple of dozen other agents, even in a locked file cabinet." He laughed.

Thumbing through the papers, Walt looked up to Dirk and said, "I take this to mean this is something incriminating?"

Dirk grinned. "That is the understatement of the year. I knew you and Claudia were working together, playing fast and loose with dual agency laws, but I had no idea how deep it went, or to what extent. And to think you kept such meticulous records, and in your own handwriting!"

Walt skimmed through the documents. He didn't recognize the handwriting. The reason, it was Clint's handwriting, not his. But he didn't say anything.

"Did you use these to blackmail Claudia?" Danielle asked.

"If I would have looked at the documents sooner, everything would be playing out differently. By the time I realized what I had, Clint was here, reportedly with amnesia and virtually destitute. What do they say about blood and a turnip? But Claudia had her condo and lots of equity. Imagine my surprise at finding Clint here had finally come into the chips?"

"If you know I have money now, I don't understand why Danielle has to be here?"

"Because after recent events, I have decided to simplify things. It's come to my attention your fiancée here keeps a valuable necklace and gold coins in her safe deposit box at the local bank. From what I understand, she's not especially attached to the necklace or coins, but she is to you. So in exchange for those, she will keep you out of prison. Because if I send the original documents to the proper authorities, you are going away for a long time."

Walt and Danielle exchanged quick glances and then looked back to Dirk.

"Go on," Walt said.

Dirk looked at Danielle and said, "You will find a cardboard container I have already placed by the back door of the garage. Take that with you to the bank. After you remove the necklace and gold coins from your safe deposit box, you will put them in the cardboard container. You will take it to Fisherman Park, which is located about thirty-five minutes from here. There you will find a bank of lockers behind the public restrooms. Locate locker thirty-six, open it with the combination I will give you, and lock the box inside. After you do that, return to Marlow House. Once we are safely out of Oregon with the necklace and coins, we will contact you with the number of another locker at that same location, and the locker combination. There you will find the original documents."

WALT DROVE the Packard to the bank, with Danielle sitting in the passenger seat. She looked down at the box in her lap.

"Do you think the gold coins and necklace will fit in this?" Danielle asked.

Walt looked over to Danielle. "I guess they'll have to. According to Dirk, that's the largest container that'll fit in the locker."

A few minutes later Walt pulled up to the bank and parked. He stayed in the car and waited for Danielle, who took the box with her. Inside the bank, she was taken to the safe deposit area, where she accessed both of her safety deposit boxes.

In the Packard, Walt glanced out the rearview mirror and spied Dirk sitting in a parked car alone, across the street, watching him. When Danielle came out of the bank, she was still carrying the box, but by the way she held it, it seemed heavier than it had been before she had entered. Walt quickly got out of the car and helped her with the box, placing it in the back seat while Danielle climbed into the passenger seat.

It took them forty minutes to reach their destination. It was alongside one of the public beaches, with a large parking lot and public restroom. The bank of lockers butted up against the rear of the public restroom.

Danielle reached in her purse and pulled out a slip of paper and handed it to Walt. "This is the locker number and combination."

Taking the paper from Danielle, he reached over and gave her a quick kiss. "I'll be right back."

Danielle sat in the car and watched as Walt removed the box from the back seat and made his way to the locker. Glancing in the side mirror, she spied Dirk parked some distance away, watching her. A few minutes later Walt returned without the box and jumped in the car.

"Let's get out of here. He said he won't contact us until we're back at Marlow House and they're out of Oregon," Walt said.

As they pulled out of the parking lot, Danielle looked out the back window and spied Dirk following them in his car.

"He's behind us," Danielle told Walt.

"I noticed that," Walt said as he continued to drive, Dirk trailing behind them.

TANYA GOT out of the rental car and slammed the door shut. Dirk had just sent her a text saying they were almost back at Marlow House. Glancing around, she noticed the various people coming and going—people taking pictures with their cellphones, some walking to and from the restrooms, others walking their dogs.

She made her way quickly to the lockers, her heart pounding. A few moments later she stood before one they had rented and punched in the combination. She opened the door and her heart started beating even faster. Once she pulled the cardboard box from the locker, she noticed it was relatively lightweight. With a frown she hastily removed its lid and looked inside.

With a gasp she spied the .38 sitting alone inside the box. Without thought, she reached inside and took hold of the gun by its handle, staring dumbly at it a moment. Suddenly realizing what she was holding, she dropped the gun back in the box and looked around. No one seemed to be watching her. Returning the lid, she shut the locker and quickly moved to the other locker they had rented, still holding the box with the .38.

Standing before the second locker, she quickly punched in the combination and opened the door. To her relief the papers were still there. For a brief moment she imagined they wouldn't be. Just as she reached in to remove them, she heard a voice say, "Please set the box on the ground, and put your hands up, and move very slowly."

Wide eyed, Tanya looked toward the voice and found two police officers pointing revolvers in her direction. She immediately complied, first setting the box on the ground and then nervously raising her hands.

As one officer began reading Tanya her rights and handcuffing her, a second officer reached into the locker to pick up the papers. Yet, just as he removed them from the locker, what appeared to be a gust of wind ripped them from his hand, sending them swirling into the air.

To the astonishment of all three watching, the papers burst into flames and, before their eyes, turned to ash.

THIRTY-NINE

Walt parked his Packard in front of room six at the Seahorse Motel. A few minutes later he stood at the door knocking. Someone in the room pushed the curtain open a few inches and looked outside. Several moments later the door opened.

"Walt?" Rachel said in surprise.

"I wanted to stop and say goodbye. The chief told us you would be leaving in the morning. And I wanted to tell you again how sorry I am about your sister."

Rachel opened the door wider. "Thank you, Walt. I know you don't remember her from your life in California. But there was a time you two were close. I'm sorry about what she tried to do. I should have figured out a way to stop her. If I had...maybe she would be alive today."

"I wish there was something I could have done differently to change the outcome. I am truly sorry for any hurt I caused your sister when I knew her."

"Thank you, Walt. You know, you really seem changed."

"I think I have." Walt gave her a smile and then a quick hug. "Drive carefully."

After Rachel said her final goodbyes and shut the door, Walt walked to room seven's door and knocked. After a few moments it opened.

"Clint Marlow?" the man asked in surprise.

"Are you Albert Hanson?" Walt asked.

Albert nodded. "You really don't remember me?"

"I'm sorry. I don't remember anything from before my car accident."

"The police chief stopped by earlier. I guess they caught the person who killed Claudia Dane. Is that why you're here?"

Walt pulled an envelope from his pocket and handed it to Albert. "No. I stopped by to give you this."

With a frown, Albert took the envelope and looked at it. He opened it and pulled out a check. Confused, he looked from the check to Walt. "I don't understand. Is this some sort of joke?"

"No. No joke. Chief MacDonald told me about the conversation you had with one of his officers and about the money you lost because of me. While I don't remember it, I am truly sorry for my actions back then. I hope this helps make up for it."

"Make up for it? It's the same amount as the inheritance from my parents! Is this check real?"

With a smile, Walt nodded. "Yes, it is. I'm not sure about the tax implications, you might want to check with your accountant—one you trust—to see the best way to handle it."

AN ASSORTMENT of open pizza boxes filled the dining room table. Along the edge of the table was a stack of paper plates and napkins, making it easier for people to help themselves. After the exhausting last few days, Marlow House was hosting an impromptu dinner party. Danielle had invited the chief first, including his two boys. She then invited Brian and Joe; after all, they had been the ones who had arrested Tanya.

With Joe coming, it meant Kelly would be there, and Danielle would naturally invite Lily and Ian, they were practically family. She would have invited Chris even if he hadn't done some sleuthing for them. Also in attendance was Heather, who had been the one to find the body. Two of the other guests—Eva and Marie—weren't there for pizza, but that was just because ghosts didn't eat pizza.

"Where's Walt?" Lily asked as she picked up a slice of pepperoni pizza and set it on a paper plate.

"He had an errand to run, but he should be home soon," Danielle explained.

"You said the wife flipped?" Danielle heard Chris ask. She glanced to where her guests gathered nearby, around the police chief, waiting for him to answer Chris's question.

"When she realized she was holding the murder weapon and her fingerprints were all over it, yes. Claimed she had no idea it was the weapon that had killed Claudia and that her husband asked her to hide it in Walt's room."

"Yeah, right, like that's a normal thing for your husband to ask," Lily said with a snort. "Where did she think the gun came from?"

"I want to know; how did she get in Walt's room?" Heather asked. "You always keep your bedrooms locked."

"I'm thinking she managed to lift an extra set of keys," Danielle suggested. "There's a set missing. If I don't find it, I'm going to have to rekey the doors again."

"What's the husband saying?" Ian asked.

"Not much of anything. Insists he doesn't know anything about the gun or Walt's claim he tried to blackmail Walt and Danielle."

"What was he blackmailing Walt over?" Kelly asked Danielle.

"The thing about blackmail, it's usually something you want to keep to yourself," Brian interjected.

Giving a quick sideways glance to Brian, Danielle turned her attention to Kelly. "It has to do with some real estate deals that may or may not have been illegal but happened so long ago that even if they were illegal, the statute of limitations would have long run out. But considering Walt's current situation, Dirk felt it would embarrass Walt and cause his publishers to pull away from him," Danielle lied.

"I'm still trying to figure out what in the blazes happened to those papers," Joe said.

"Nice play on words," Brian snorted.

Joe chuckled. "That wind just came out of nowhere—but the fire, I have never seen anything like it."

"Those papers had to have been contaminated with some sort of pyrophoric substance—maybe left there by the previous user of the locker—and when that gust of air caught hold of the papers, they ignited," the chief suggested, knowing that wasn't what happened.

Marie piped up cheerfully, "Or it could be the matches I had with me. Funny how no one noticed the matches floating nearby, since everyone was looking at the papers I'd grabbed. Getting that match to light was a little tricky, but once it did, those papers went up like kindling!"

The chief glanced down at his youngest son, Evan, who looked like he was about to laugh. "What's so funny, Evan?"

The boy looked up to his father and smiled. "Umm...I'll tell you later."

The chief heard Heather chuckle. He glanced to her and then noticed Chris standing next to her, smiling. It was then he understood. There was obviously a ghost in the room, and he was fairly certain it was Marie or Eva. Probably Marie, considering Danielle had told him she had been the one to grab and destroy the incriminating documents.

"What I find chilling, that Dirk character wasn't just going to blackmail Walt and Danielle, he was attempting to frame Walt for that woman's murder," Heather said in disgust.

"At the moment he's refusing to talk until his attorney gets here," the chief said.

"I suspect when they look into his bank account, they're going to find the money Claudia gave him when he blackmailed her," Danielle said. "He basically admitted it all to us."

Ten minutes later Danielle went to the kitchen, where she had set up a makeshift bar on the counter. She wasn't in the room alone long. Just as she poured herself a glass of wine, Kelly and Joe walked in.

"Can I get a glass of water?" Kelly asked.

"Sure, help yourself." Danielle looked at Joe and said, "Want another beer? There's some in the fridge."

"Thanks," Joe said as he opened the refrigerator.

About to fill a glass with water, Kelly glanced to Danielle, who was just putting the glass of wine to her lips.

"Danielle!" Kelly called out sharply.

Danielle stopped and looked at Kelly. "What?"

"You can't drink that wine!"

Danielle frowned. "Why not? Did someone poison it?"

"Because...because...well, your condition."

In all that had happened in the last few days, Danielle had forgotten what Marie had told her she'd overheard at the police station—until now. Deliberately, she set the glass on the counter and looked from Kelly to Joe. Kelly looked rather pleased with herself while Joe looked embarrassed.

"I understand you've been drinking coffee too. That's probably not a good idea either. But you might want to check with your doctor," Kelly whispered.

"I am not pregnant. And please tell me where you got that lame idea."

"You're not pregnant?" Kelly squeaked. "I…I saw you buying a pregnancy test."

Danielle thought back to that time in the pharmacy when she had picked up the pregnancy test for Lily. Kelly had been there. "You know, Kelly, things are not always as they seem. And someday, when Walt and I decide to have a baby, I promise, I won't be drinking wine or coffee." She picked up her glass of wine and took a gulp.

"I'm sorry," Kelly stammered, looking sincerely confused.

"Now I would like to talk to Joe a moment in private," Danielle said.

"Umm…okay…" Kelly took her glass of water and fled the room, leaving her boyfriend alone with Danielle.

When Kelly was out of earshot, Danielle asked, "I know you know about Walt's and my marriage. Have you told Kelly? Have you told anyone?"

Joe shook his head. "No. It was part of the investigation, and I didn't feel it was proper to tell her, or anyone."

"I plan to have this talk with Brian too. I know he was there when you discussed it."

"You talked to the chief?" he asked.

"Yes." *But Marie told me first,* she thought. "I know you don't understand or necessarily approve of Walt's and my relationship. And I imagine you don't understand how we married months ago, such a short time after his accident. But you don't have to understand, and it really is my business. And I am asking you not to share this information, because frankly, most people won't understand. I love Walt, and he loves me. That's all that's important."

"I just want you to be happy."

"I know you do, Joe. I appreciate that. And I am happy. I'm married to my soulmate."

ON THE WAY home from Marlow House, Brian stopped at the

mini-mart to pick up a six-pack of beer. He would have had a couple more beers with his pizza, but if he was going to tie one on, he would rather do it at home, where he didn't have to drive anywhere. And after a day like today, he needed to throw back a couple more beers.

Just as he stepped into the mini-mart, he came face-to-face with Albert Hanson.

"Officer Henderson!" Albert greeted him exuberantly.

"You look happy. I understand the chief told you we've arrested someone for Claudia Dane's murder."

"Yes, so tragic, poor woman. But I'm so glad to run into you before I leave town. I wanted to thank you. If it hadn't been for you, I wouldn't have my life back."

Brian frowned. "Umm…I don't understand?"

"Clint Marlow, he came by the motel this afternoon. He apologized for what he had done. He said he didn't remember any of it, but he wanted to make it right. He gave me a check for the money I lost."

"He gave you a check?"

Albert nodded. "You don't know what this means to me. I was barely scraping by. I came up here to shame him, yet I didn't even have the courage to see him. But he came to me after you told your boss about what he had done, and then your boss told him. So thank you, Officer Henderson!"

FORTY

There were no guests scheduled to arrive at Marlow House in February, because wedding plans were underway. In less than two weeks Walt and Danielle would be surrounded by friends while exchanging their vows for the second time. Danielle and Lily were on their way to Astoria to pick up the wedding dress from the seamstress who had made the alterations.

The wedding cake had already been ordered from Old Salts Bakery, which proved to be a story in itself. Danielle wanted to bake her double fudge chocolate cake, Walt's favorite and a recipe that had been passed down in her family. While she loved many of the treats from Old Salts Bakery, she didn't feel bakery cakes matched homemade. Walt didn't want her baking her own wedding cake, believing this was a time she should be pampered, not cooking for others.

A compromise was made when Old Salts Bakery agreed to use Danielle's recipe. After all, Marlow House was a regular and faithful customer. They baked a practice cake and so loved the results that it was agreed the bakery would add *Marlow House Double Fudge Chocolate Cake* to their menu. While another person might have refused to share a family recipe with someone else—especially a bakery—Danielle loved the idea.

She selected antique roses—cream and red—for her bouquets and arrangements. To keep in theme with Valentine's Day, she chose red dresses for her bridesmaids, and instead of having them pay for their dresses, as was normally the custom, she purchased them. Walt chose a black and gray three-piece suit for the men, as opposed to a traditional tuxedo. Music would be provided by a guitarist they had found in Astoria. Food was being catered, with Joanne supervising the overall event on the wedding day.

They were able to move past the recent unpleasant events and focus on the wedding since Dirk Thorpe had made a plea deal. They didn't have to worry about rescheduling their calendar to accommodate a court trial. After consulting with his attorney, Dirk told the authorities his version of the story, which resulted in lesser charges.

According to Dirk, he had run into Claudia at the pier, and she had pulled her gun on him, threatening to shoot him for blackmailing her. In wrestling the pistol from her hands, it went off, sending the bullet through her heart. Dirk insisted she was already dead when he pushed her off the pier, a version the coroner agreed with. Comparing his and Claudia's bank statements substantiated his confession that he had blackmailed her—and as his wife had once noted, it proved Claudia had a motive to murder him, not that he had a motive to murder her. But as he had reminded his wife at the time, blackmail was still illegal—so was unlawfully disposing of a body.

THE SEAMSTRESS HELPED Danielle into the vintage dress as Lily adjusted its hem. A moment later they stood before the floor-to-ceiling mirror in the dressing room while Lily patiently buttoned up the back of the ecru silk and lace dress, gently tucking each of the countless tiny covered buttons into a lacy loop. When she was done, Lily readjusted the train as she stepped back to get a better look.

"Oh my, you look utterly gorgeous in that!" Lily gushed.

Smiling, Danielle looked down and ran her hands gently over the fabric and lace. "It is a beautiful dress."

"Dani, it's not just the dress, it's the dress on you! I can't believe how well it fits you!"

"It does look like the dress was made for her," the seamstress agreed.

FORTY MINUTES later Danielle and Lily were on the road, heading back to Frederickport with Danielle's wedding dress.

"I still can't believe you found the perfect dress at the first shop we looked at. I swear, Dani, I liked it even better today," Lily told her. "Walt is going to see you in that dress and fall in love with you all over again."

Danielle grinned as she steered the car down the highway. "I know he's going to like it. Walt's a bit of a sucker for feminine dresses."

"Dani, this wedding is going to be perfect, I just know it."

Danielle let out a sigh and said, "Almost…"

Lily glanced at Danielle and frowned. "Almost?"

Danielle shrugged and smiled sadly, still looking ahead as she drove down the highway. "I wish my parents were here. I wish my dad was walking me down the aisle."

Turning in the seat to get a better look at Danielle, Lily said, "I imagine you felt this way when you married Lucas."

"Yeah. But this is different somehow," Danielle said.

"Different how?"

"I loved Lucas, I really did. It's true he hurt me, but I did forgive him. Yet, even if he hadn't cheated on me, I feel this marriage is different."

"Different how?" Lily asked.

"I don't know…I just wish my parents could be there—to meet Walt—to get to know him and know how right he is for me. I wish Dad could walk me down the aisle. I've never trusted a man like I do Walt. And he's not just the man I love, he's my soulmate, my best friend…"

"Hey! I thought I was your best friend?" Lily teased.

Danielle flashed Lily a quick grin. "You know what I mean."

Lily nodded solemnly. "Yes, I do."

They drove in silence for a few minutes. Finally, Danielle asked, "So tell me, best—girlfriend—how are you feeling?"

"Pregnant." Lily laughed. "Fortunately, my morning sickness went away. I was worried it wouldn't, considering Mom had it so long with Cory. The doctor says everything looks great, and after you and Walt come home from your honeymoon, I'll announce my pregnancy."

"Why are you waiting that long?"

Lily rolled her eyes as if it was a foolish question. "This is your moment, Dani. I don't want to steal your spotlight."

"Don't be silly. Anyway, you need to at least tell Kelly. For one thing, she keeps looking at me funny because of that pregnancy test she saw me buy. But, the main reason, she's your sister now. You should tell her before you announce the news. I know she can be annoying sometimes, but she loves her brother dearly, and, Lily, family is so very important. You never fully realize it until they're gone."

Lily considered Danielle's words a minute and then let out a sigh. "Kelly's definitely not as annoying as Cheryl was, and considering you were able to overlook Cheryl's quirks and miss her like you do, then I suppose I should start making more of an effort with Kelly. You're right. Okay, I'll tell her tonight."

THAT NIGHT LILY told Kelly she was going to be an aunt. The news put the world in a different perspective for Kelly, who was now able to look at Walt more favorably after realizing the conversation she had overheard outside the back door of Marlow House had truly been misunderstood. She was also tickled to know that while the pregnancy was a secret—until Danielle and Walt returned from their honeymoon—it was a secret she had not been excluded from.

Time flew by as Walt and Danielle's second wedding date approached. Days before the wedding, Lily hosted a bridal shower for Danielle, while Chris threw Walt a bachelor party. The night before the wedding, Walt hosted a rehearsal dinner for the wedding party.

Danielle's two bridesmaids were Heather and Melony, with Lily as the matron of honor. With Chris as Walt's best man, and Ian officiating, Walt asked his agent to be one of his groomsmen. The two had grown close since first working together on *Moon Runners*. His choice for his second groomsman was Adam Nichols, which surprised no one more than Adam himself.

Adam assumed the only reason Walt had asked him was because Melony was in the wedding and he had come to be close friends with Danielle. While he still had reservations about Walt, he couldn't bring himself to decline, and he accepted Walt's request.

THE GHOST WHO WAS SAYS I DO

What Adam didn't know, the primary reason Walt had asked him to be in the wedding was Adam's grandmother. Walt knew how happy it would make Marie to see her grandson included in the wedding party.

During the rehearsal, Evan MacDonald practiced his role as ring bearer while Sadie trotted down the staircase, the handle of the flower basket in her mouth, as she played the role of untraditional flower girl. Several attending the rehearsal dinner were amazed at how well Sadie performed, yet questioned if she could repeat the act during the actual wedding ceremony. Walt had no doubt she could.

After everyone went home after the rehearsal dinner, Walt and Danielle decided not to sleep in the same room that night. While they were already man and wife, they felt sentimental about the quaint custom of the bride and groom not seeing each other on the day of the wedding until the bride walked down the aisle.

Tucked into her cold bed on the second floor, Danielle decided sleeping apart was a stupid idea. Since she was utterly exhausted, she told herself she might as well tough it out. With a yawn, she rolled to one side, hugged a pillow to her chest, and fell fast asleep.

"HOLD STILL, there's just a couple more," Danielle's mother said as she buttoned up the back of the wedding dress. "I know you're anxious to walk down those stairs to get to Walt, but just hold on. You two have your entire life ahead of you."

Standing before a large mirror in her bedroom on the second floor of Marlow House, Danielle looked at her reflection as she wore her wedding dress. Behind her was her mother, smiling lovingly.

"You look beautiful, dear," her mother whispered.

"I'm so happy, Mom. I love Walt so much." Grinning broadly, she turned to her mother.

"And he loves you, dear. I see the way he looks at you. I'm so happy for you both."

A knock came at the door.

"Can I come in now?" came a male voice.

Her mother grinned. "Your father, I swear. He can be so impatient sometimes!"

"Come in, Dad!" Danielle called out.

The next moment her bedroom door opened, and in walked Danielle's father dressed in one of the three-piece black and gray suits Walt had picked out.

"Oh, my baby girl, you look beautiful!" her father said, tears in his eyes. "Of course, you always look beautiful."

Danielle grinned at her father and gladly accepted his hug. Leaning closer, she rested her head on his shoulder, cherishing the embrace.

"I love you, Danielle," he whispered into her ear.

"I love you too, Dad."

"Enough, you two! If you make Danielle cry and ruin her make-up..." Danielle's mother scolded.

With a chuckle, Danielle's father released her from the hug, a wide grin on his face.

"Before we go downstairs, there's something I want to give you," her father said, dipping his hand in his coat pocket. From his pocket he pulled out a gold heart locket, its delicate gold chain dangling from his hand. "This is for you, sweetheart."

"Oh, Dad!" Danielle took the locket in her hands and looked at it, turning it from side to side. "It's beautiful."

"There's nothing in the locket now, but later I thought you could put a wedding picture of you and Walt inside. I had the back engraved."

Turning the heart locket over in her hand to inspect the back, Danielle ran one finger over the single engraved letter: *M*. "It's beautiful," she whispered.

"When you look at this locket, I want you to remember how happy I am for you today—how much your mother and I love you. You and Walt are good together. I've always wanted you to have what your mother and I do. I think you'll have that with Walt."

THE ALARM CLOCK WOKE HER. Danielle opened her eyes and looked up at the ceiling. She was alone in her bed. The dream had felt so real, but it didn't feel like a dream hop. In a hop she always knew it was a dream, while the one last night had felt too real. It left her both happy and sad. But today was her wedding day, so she refused to be sad. She also felt a little closer to her parents, as if they had actually visited her. Had it been a dream hop, that would have been the case. Perhaps it had been nothing but a regular dream, but she refused to allow that to diminish the joy it had given her.

After a quick trip to the bathroom, Danielle returned to bed and went over in her mind all that needed to be done today. She suspected Walt had already left. He was spending the morning with Ian and his agent.

When she and Walt had said goodnight the previous evening, Walt had told her he wouldn't see her again until she walked down the aisle—or more accurately, the staircase. He had moved his wedding clothes to the downstairs bedroom, where he intended to dress to avoid running into Danielle before the three-o'clock ceremony.

A knock came at the door. "Danielle? Are you awake?"

"Come in, Joanne," Danielle called. She hadn't bothered locking her bedroom door the previous night since there had been no guests in the house.

The door opened and in walked Joanne carrying a tray of food.

"What's that?" Danielle asked brightly, sitting up in bed.

"It's your wedding day. Breakfast in bed!"

"Oh, you shouldn't have," Danielle said not too convincingly as she eyed the eggs Benedict coming her way.

Joanne laughed. "Actually, I didn't. Walt made it."

"Walt?" Danielle said in surprise as she watched Joanne arrange the tray on her lap. Next to the plate on the tray was a freshly cut camellia.

"He insisted his bride have breakfast in bed. I offered to make it, but he wanted to do it himself. I will say I'm rather impressed. He makes a mean hollandaise sauce."

Danielle picked up the camellia. "Where did he get the flower?"

"I'm pretty sure he snagged it from your neighbor. The new neighbor." Joanne chuckled. "He wanted a rose, but they aren't blooming yet, and the florist won't be delivering the flowers until noon."

Danielle set the flower back on the tray. "This one is lovely. Even if it is stolen."

LILY SHOWED up an hour later with Heather and Melony. They brought fresh cinnamon rolls with them. Despite her delicious breakfast, Danielle didn't have any problem finishing off her share of the sticky sweet rolls.

While Joanne coordinated the placement of chairs downstairs with the men from the wedding party, Eva and Marie joined the ladies upstairs and watched as they gave each other manicures, fixed each other's hair, shared stories, laughed, and sipped mimosas.

The morning quickly melted into the afternoon, and before she knew it, Danielle was once again standing before the mirror while Lily buttoned up her wedding dress. Just as Lily finished buttoning her dress, a knock came at the bedroom door.

For a brief moment, Danielle thought of her dream the night before, and she had the whimsical notion it was her father knocking, as he had in the dream.

"It's Edward? Can I come in?" came the voice beyond the door.

"Come in, Chief," Danielle called out.

The next moment Chief MacDonald walked into the room, wearing the same suit her father had worn in her dream. He would be standing in for her father today and would be walking her down the aisle.

"You look gorgeous, Danielle. Walt is a lucky guy," the chief said.

"Thanks. I'm the lucky one."

"You look pretty sharp yourself, Chief," Lily told him.

MacDonald looked to Lily and smiled. "Maybe I'm the lucky one, upstairs with two gorgeous women. That dress looks outstanding on you, Lily."

Lily grinned. "Thanks, Chief."

MacDonald turned to Danielle and reached into his coat pocket. "Danielle, I have something for you." He pulled out a gold heart locket; its chain dangled down from his fingers.

Danielle's eyes widened as she stared at the delicate piece of jewelry.

"I don't know if this is your style or not," the chief explained. "But I saw this the other day in an antique shop, and I thought of you. After all, you're getting married on Valentine's Day, and it looks like something that would go with a vintage dress, like I heard you were wearing." As he handed it to her, he turned it over, revealing the engraving on its back. "It was already engraved with an *M*, like it was made for you. I had to buy it. But if you don't feel it goes with your dress, I won't feel bad if you don't want to wear it."

"Oh my…" Danielle muttered, reverently taking the locket in one hand. With her right thumb she gently stroked the gold metal. It looked exactly like the heart locket from her dream. "This is perfect."

"Danielle, don't cry!" Lily scolded. "You're going to ruin your makeup! Chief, you made her cry!"

"That's okay, Lily." Tears slid down Danielle's face. "I can redo my makeup."

THE WEDDING STARTED EXACTLY at three. The chairs had been arranged as they had been for Lily and Ian's wedding. All the guests were seated as the guitarist began playing. Sadie came down the staircase first, the basket of flowers dangling from her mouth as her tail wagged.

As Walt had predicted, Sadie repeated the performance from the night before, but what he had not anticipated was Max, who joined Sadie midway down the staircase, the pair walking side by side to the first-floor landing. When they arrived at Ian and Walt, the cat and dog sat at attention, as if the entire thing had been perfectly choreographed. The fact the cat and dog sat at attention for the entire ceremony would be a story told and retold for years to come in Frederickport.

Walt didn't think too much about Max joining Sadie; his full attention was on the bride coming down the staircase. His heart swelled at the sight of her, ravishingly feminine while at the same time bold, stubborn, and fiercely loyal. He remembered being attracted to her the first time they had met, in spite of the fact he believed her to be a burglar. Even when he had insisted she leave that day, he had wanted her to stay. She had been the woman who threw open the parlor windows and let him smell the ocean breeze again. Without her he would never have had the courage—or desire—to take his second chance. She was truly his life.

For Danielle it was all a blur—a magical wonderful blur.

"You may kiss the bride," Danielle finally heard Ian say.

Before all their friends, Walt took Danielle in his arms and kissed her. When the kiss ended, but the embrace did not, Danielle whispered in Walt's ear, "Lily was right. This was the perfect wedding."

THE GHOST AND THE BABY

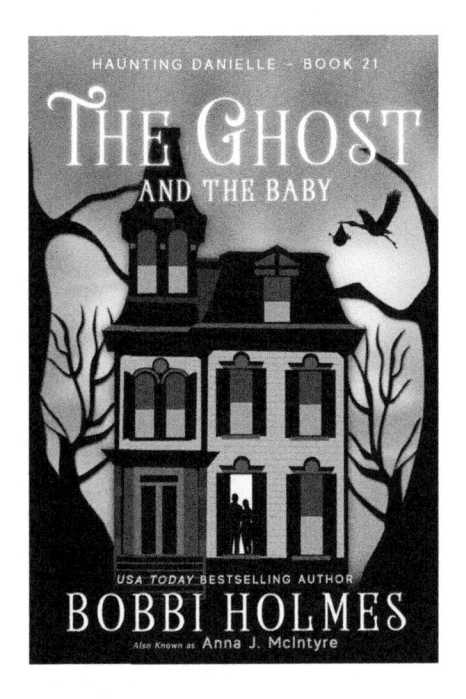

Return to Marlow Houses in

The Ghost and the Baby

Haunting Danielle, Book 21

While the residents on Beach Drive prepare for the welcomed arrival of a new baby, they are blindsided by the newest resident's plans to close down Marlow House.

No one is prepared for the deadly secrets the new neighbor unwittingly conceals.

Walt knows more than he realizes. If he can just remember.

NON-FICTION BY

BOBBI ANN JOHNSON HOLMES

Havasu Palms, A Hostile Takeover
Where the Road Ends, Recipes & Remembrances
Motherhood, a book of poetry
The Story of the Christmas Village

BOOKS BY ANNA J. MCINTYRE

COULSON FAMILY SAGA

Coulson's Wife
Coulson's Crucible
Coulson's Lessons
Coulson's Secret
Coulson's Reckoning

UNLOCKED HEARTS

Sundered Hearts
After Sundown
While Snowbound
Sugar Rush

Printed in Great Britain
by Amazon